NEW CASTLE COUNTY

HARD
GUY

HARD GUY

BY

THORNTON ELLIOTT

DONALD I. FINE, INC.

New York

Library of Congress Cataloging-in-Publication
Elliott, Thornton.
    Hard guy / by Thornton Elliott.
        p.   cm.
    ISBN 1-55611-306-4
    I. Title.
    PS3555.L5932H3   1992
    813'.54—dc20   91-55179
                                                                         CIP

Manufactured in the United States of America

10   9   8   7   6   5   4   3   2   1

Designed by Irving Perkins Associates

For the real Tina, St. Petersburg, late summer of '73. They'd run me to the ground, and she gave me refuge. And when they came to get me they didn't give me time to tell her good-bye.

ACKNOWLEDGMENTS

There are always several people who need to be recognized with a first novel. No doubt I've failed to name some of those people here. I apologize to them.

I owe many thanks to Steve Womack, for pointing out what I was doing wrong. The timing of his appearance was enough to make me wonder about such things as fate and destiny.

There is Captain Harvil McCrary, with whom mutual respect developed into friendship. It was he who first realized I stood on the border between right and wrong. He offered the hand that guided me across.

Thanks to J.B. Bounds, Woody Eargle and Ken Arvin, for being there to listen. Like me, they are a captive audience. Still, they didn't have to listen.

Most of all I thank Knox Burger. None of this could have happened without his advice, patience and friendship. I have sorely tested all three qualities and found them all to be rock solid.

HARD
GUY

PROLOGUE

THERE WERE only four people in the jewelry store, three clerks and a single customer, when the two robbers burst in. Both wore gloves, heavy field jackets and carried .45 automatics. Ski masks made them appear even more sinister.

The one in the black mask stood close to the door, his back against the wall. He held his pistol in a two-handed grip, moving it back and forth to cover the people. His companion in the blue mask carried a dark green gym bag. He stepped behind the counter with quick strides.

"Everyone on the floor," said black mask. "Just lay quiet and nobody gets hurt."

His partner walked up to the display case containing the most expensive diamond jewelry and used his pistol butt to shatter the top. He lifted a tray out and emptied it in the bag. In seconds the case was empty.

He took two steps to a clerk, a short chubby man in his late forties. Fear, along with thick glasses, magnified the size of his eyes. The gunman stuck the .45 in the center of the clerk's forehead.

"You own this place or just work here?"

The clerk's eyes rolled up, blinking so rapidly his eyelashes resembled hummingbird wings. He swallowed, then opened his mouth, only to make croaking sounds. He swallowed once again.

"I work here," he managed to whisper.

The gunman thumbed the hammer back slowly, the double click seeming to echo in the silence. "They pay you good enough to die for what's in the safe?"

The clerk shook his head no, at the same time turning to the safe. He spun the dials rapidly, but his fingers trembled too much. When the door failed to open he flinched and slumped to the floor, expecting to be shot.

The gunman kneeled beside him and spoke in a calm voice. "Take it easy. Me and you want the same thing—for you not to get hurt and for us to get out of here. Right?"

The clerk nodded, took a deep breath.

"Good, but I can't go until you open the safe. Now try again, a little slower."

The man tried again and this time the door swung open. The gunman began lifting trays from the center compartment, not bothering with the others. He emptied four of them, zipped up the bag, then stood. With a nod to the man against the wall they left, three and a half minutes after entering.

Slivers of glass reflected the light, sparkling in lieu of the rubies, diamonds and emeralds taken by the robbers. The men were out of the parking lot before one of the clerks summoned the courage to push an alarm button.

Later she would tell police the men seemed to know where each alarm button was located.

The thieves, in a black Chrysler LeBaron stolen from a shopping mall ten minutes before the robbery, turned right at the first side street. They turned right again at the next corner and headed back in the same direction. A mile later they parked behind a laundromat. They left their coats and masks in the getaway car and walked calmly to the front of the building.

The one who'd worn the black mask unlocked the trunk

of a gunmetal gray Cougar and placed the gym bag inside. The other man got in a Mazda RX7, pulled beside the Cougar and rolled the window down.

"I'll meet you at your house, Glenn. Be careful."

Glenn nodded as he opened his car door and got in. He pulled the .45 from his waistband and stuck it under a brown sport coat lying on the passenger seat.

"No problem. Speed limit all the way to Memphis." He flashed a lopsided grin. "The hard part's over, and that was a piece of cake."

The Mazda pulled away and Glenn followed a minute later. He was forced to wait for two Chattanooga patrol cars to go by, lights flashing and sirens screaming, responding to the robbery squeal.

"Go get 'em, boys," he said. He chuckled as he turned in the opposite direction.

He turned onto Bonny Oaks Drive, the tension from the robbery gradually leaving him. The interstate came in sight and he eased over into the left lane in preparation for getting on it. He allowed himself a smile, thinking of all that jewelry in the trunk.

Beautiful, he thought. In and out, even faster than we figured. Sweet Jesus, have we made a lick.

He was so busy congratulating himself he failed to see the '70 Nova, ass end jacked up, coming up on his right. Glenn looked over when it drew alongside him. Four teenagers rocking to the music and passing joints around. The music was loud enough that he could hear it through his rolled-up windows. He watched the driver reach for the joint, and saw the car suddenly start to drift into his lane.

He honked his horn, too late. The kid didn't see him until the two cars smacked together with a protesting screech of metal. The impact was hard enough to push him over the center line into oncoming traffic.

With a muttered curse he turned the wheel, trying to pull the Cougar back into his lane. He would have made it if the teenager hadn't panicked. The kid just kept coming instead of getting the hell over so Glenn could make it back to safety.

He yanked the wheel and slammed into the car again but could not force it over. The blare of a horn brought his attention back to the road. A Cadillac came straight at him, hemmed in by traffic and unable to swerve away, or stop in time.

Great, he thought in the instant before impact. Everybody wants to get in the act. Why not a fucking truck?

The heavy car collided with the Cougar, hard enough to make the stopping sudden and complete. Glenn felt his left leg snap above the knee as the impact drove the fire wall inward. The steering wheel smashed into his chest, breaking his left wrist on the way.

He shook his head to clear it, at the same time grabbing the door handle with his left hand. Pain shot through him and he released it with a grimace. The movement grated the bones in his wrist together, churning up waves of nausea in his stomach. He used his other hand, to no avail. The door might as well have been welded shut.

He was trapped, no two ways about it. The steering wheel pushed into his chest and the dashboard he'd once thought had such elegant curves now curved around him.

His eyes flew to the passenger seat, empty of both coat and pistol. The dashboard hung down, keeping him from seeing the floorboard. All he could see was one sleeve of the coat stretched across the console.

He tried to get his right leg up to push the dashboard back. He could still come out of this smelling like a rose as long as the pistol wasn't found. He strained, ignoring the pain, but it was useless. The steering wheel was in the way.

Maybe it's still under the coat, he told himself. Don't panic. Just because you can't see it doesn't mean it's visible.

That's what part of his mind said, and wanted to believe. But another part disagreed.

You fucked up big time, and you know it, it told him. You fucking dreamer. You know that gun didn't stay under the coat. They're going to see it and then they'll open the trunk.

An old couple approached and the man leaned down to peer in at Glenn. Folds of skin hung from a skinny neck, its back covered in a diamond pattern etched by the passage of time.

"How bad you hurt, son?" The question was asked in a thick mountain twang.

"Pretty bad. I know I got an arm and a leg broke." He touched his right side and winced. "Maybe a couple of ribs too."

Glenn looked at the Cadillac. "How about the other fellow?"

The old man waved a hand in dismissal. "He's okay. Got a busted nose. He's standin' over yonder, tryin' to get it to stop bleeding."

All hope was suddenly washed away. The old man's wife made an *O* of her mouth and jerked on his arm. She pointed, then started backing away.

"That wouldn't be a pistol she saw, would it?" said Glenn.

The old man leaned a little closer, nodding his head slowly. "I'm sorry, mister. If she warn't with me I'd take the damn thing outta there for you. I carry one in the pickup myself. But it wouldn't do any good. She'll have all them onlookers told in less'n two minutes."

"I know you would, old-timer, and I appreciate it."

Glenn watched him walk away, then closed his eyes and rested his head on the back of the seat. Now's a good time to panic, he thought. Jesus, I'm caught. If it was raining pussies I'd get hit with a dick.

The cops arrived before the ambulance, and he watched the old woman hurry over to speak to one. The finger she pointed at him gave Glenn the distinct feeling it was him she was talking about.

The cop held a whispered conversation with his partner, whose eyes narrowed as he looked at Glenn. Both of them unfastened the safety straps of their holsters and started toward him.

They were nervous, showing it, and it scared Glenn. Come on, guys, he thought. Be cool. No need to be scared. I can't fucking move. If you think you've got something now just wait 'til you open the trunk. You dipshits. You have no idea you just stumbled onto the best fucking bust either one of you'll ever make.

He thought of Eddie, on his way to Memphis, mentally counting the money the jewelry would bring. Dream on, Eddie, while you can. You're not gonna believe this shit. I don't, and I'm in the middle of it.

"GLENN ODOM, rise and face the Court."

Glenn glanced briefly at his attorney, then stood and faced the judge. The black-robed figure shuffled papers, then peered at Glenn over half-rim glasses.

"Mr. Odom, you seem to be a man of intelligence. I see it is the first time you've come this far in the judicial system. You have displayed courtesy each time you appeared in my court. You have an excellent military record, one most men would envy." His face was grim. "I'm sorry you've decided to go against the rules of society, Mr. Odom. I don't often see men such as you in front of me. Each one of you causes me many hours of wondering why you are what you are."

He shook his head, then cleared his throat. "Due to your plea of guilty to the charge of armed robbery I hereby sentence you to a term of thirty years. You are forthwith under the custody of the Tennessee Department of Correction."

CHAPTER ONE

THE JULY sun beat down on the four men seated around a concrete table in the recreation yard of the Tennessee State Prison. Heat waves caused the distant Nashville skyline to shimmy and waver. A fifth man stood at the end of the table, dealing cards.

Glenn Odom waited until all five cards were lying in front of him before picking them up. He slowly fanned them apart to see four clubs and a diamond.

The man to his left threw two white chips in the center of the blanket-covered table. "I'll open for two bucks."

Nobody dropped out. When it got to Glenn he hesitated, then threw five chips on the table. It was a good hand to draw to.

"Raise the open to five."

The PA speaker crackled, then came to life. "Odom, nine-five-nine-eight-seven. Report to the Counseling Center."

Only one man dropped out when he raised the open, a black guy directly across from him. Two of the remaining players he could figure for good hands. The third man was nobody to worry about. The kind who stayed in on hope.

"Ain't that you?" asked the dealer, Jimmy.

Jimmy was in his late thirties, with a smooth baby face.

7

But his hair had been iron gray fifteen years. It started turning two years after getting locked up for killing a cop.

Glenn flipped a card at the discard pile. "Yeah. Let me have one."

The man on his left studied his cards longer than necessary. He tightened his face, bringing the nose, twisted to one side from some long-ago break, into greater prominence. He started to discard two cards, changed his mind and threw one away. Glenn figured him for trips, holding an ace kicker.

"Well, ain't you gonna go see what they want?" the man asked.

Glenn placed his card on the bottom and separated them one at a time. A heart.

"Why?" he asked. "You think I need some counseling, Mike? What the hell can they do for me? The parole board told me six months ago to bring 'em the rest of this thirty years. Check."

"Checks come on Friday, and this is only Tuesday," said Mike. He bet ten dollars. "Yeah, you need counseling, on how to play poker. They might be wanting to put you in the outside dorm. How much you got left to do, a year?"

"About that." The bet reached Glenn and he threw his cards in. "I fold. They're not wanting to make a trustee out of me, Mike."

"You cain't never tell," spoke up one of the other players, a short, wiry man. "You ain't got no escapes on you, do you?"

"No. But you know I'm not trustee material, Sammy."

"Would you run if they did put you out there?"

"No. I'm too short. But talking about it's a waste of time, because that ain't what it's about."

"I bet that's what it is," said Mike. He raked in the pot, winning with a full house.

Glenn grinned. "I ought to take you with me, greasy lucky as you are."

"I'm telling you, you oughta go see what they want," urged Sammy. "They could be wanting you to go outside."

"Then you ought to be there when they tell me. If that's what it is, a monkey'll jump out of my ass singing 'Who'da Thought It.' "

The cards came around again, and once more Glenn drew to a good hand but failed to hit. He wouldn't admit it, but Mike had put the thought in his head. Maybe they did want to make him a trustee. He tried to draw to another flush, spades this time. Another heart. He threw his cards in and stood up.

"Fuck it, I couldn't catch a hand with a net. I might as well go see what they want. How much do I owe, Jimmy?"

Jimmy did some figuring, one eye closed and squinting the other one against the glare reflecting from the paper.

"Forty-one dollars."

"Okay. I'll bring the money after supper." He looked at his watch. "I won't be able to get in my stash and back up here before count anyway."

"No problem. I ain't goin' anywhere."

He walked down the hill, one hand in his pocket, swinging the other one loosely. Each time his weight came down on his right leg he limped almost imperceptibly. As he walked he looked beyond the wall at the city.

Just a few more months, he told himself. Then I'll be looking back at this place. He pushed the thought aside quickly. Thinking about the outside just made the days pass that much slower.

He went inside the cinder block building that housed the Counseling Center and gave his name to the inmate clerk sitting behind a desk. The bearded man looked up at him, irritated.

"Where the hell you been, Odom?" He got up, opened a file cabinet and looked through it.

Glenn frowned at the clerk's use of his last name. "I was playing poker."

"You guys wear me out. Always fucking off, like I don't have anything better to do than wait on you to show up."

Glenn held a hand up and shook it back and forth. "Whoa, hold up, dude. Are you the one who wants to see me?"

"Your counselor wants to see you, not me. I've got better things to do."

"Then why don't you quit bitching and get on with 'em? You act like you had to come to the penitentiary to get a job."

He walked down the narrow hall to the third office, giving no more thought to the clerk. He rapped lightly once, at the same time turning the knob and walking in.

"I'm Odom," he said to the small, nattily dressed black man behind a cluttered desk. "What's up?"

His tone was civil but guarded. He took the only other seat in the tiny, cramped office, a straight-back chair, and crossed his legs.

The man grinned, showing a gold-capped incisor. "I've been looking for you the better part of an hour, Odom. You'd make a man think you like it here."

"It really ain't that bad a place, once you get used to it." He ignored the PLEASE DO NOT SMOKE sign and pulled a pack of Marlboros from his shirt pocket.

Fuck him, he thought as he lit it. They've took damned near every other vice from me. So far they still sell cigarettes in the store.

The counselor looked at him, debating whether to object or not. He decided not to and brought the smile back.

"The powers that be have decided they don't want you here anymore, Odom."

Glenn looked surprised. "Does that mean I'm going to the outside dorm?"

"Better than that. The prison overcrowding's got so bad they've worked their way down to bad guys like you."

Glenn sat up straight and stubbed the cigarette out on the heel of his shoe. Maybe it wouldn't hurt to bend a little.

"You mean I'm getting out early?"

The counselor nodded.

"How early?"

The counselor looked at his watch. "If you'd waited another fifteen minutes, not until tomorrow. But since you made it in before three-thirty you leave today."

"Hell, let's get started then. What all do I need to do to get out of here?"

"Not that much. I've got some papers you'll need to sign. While I'm getting them ready you need to get what personal property you want to take with you."

Glenn was back in half an hour, carrying nothing but photographs in a manila envelope. His radio and television he'd given away. He signed the papers the counselor put in front of him, glancing at them only long enough to make sure there was no parole. Another thirty minutes and he was in free world clothes, headed for the Administration Building—and beyond.

The guard escorting him motioned toward some stairs after they were through the trap gate. "We'll have to go up to Accounting so you can get your money, Odom."

Halfway up, the guard asked, "How long were you locked up?"

"Sixty-two months. Five years and two long fucking months."

"That's a pretty good stretch, but think about all them back there who've been locked up three times that long and still can't see an out date."

"Yeah, you got a bunch of 'em. About half your system. But you folks better be thinking about them. You can bet your ass the guys who've got those thirty-year parole dates are thinking about it. You're sure as hell going to have serious trouble out of 'em one of these days."

Twenty minutes later he stood in the parking lot waiting

for a taxi. He'd had a little over two thousand in his account. The woman tried to talk him into only taking a hundred in cash and a check for the rest, but he'd insisted on five hundred. Now it made a comfortable bulge in his left front pocket.

He turned around and looked back at the prison. An hour ago he still had ten months to do on his sentence. Now, here he stood, on this side of the wall. True, he was standing here in a white shirt two sizes too big and a pair of off blue pants that stopped a good two inches above his Nikes. But the important thing, by God, he was standing *here*.

He saw the taxi coming down the long, curving drive and walked a few steps into the parking lot, eager to meet it. It stopped and he opened the rear door, then hesitated a few seconds to look back one final time.

He recalled thinking it looked like a castle the day he saw the prison the first time. Today made the second time Glenn had seen it from this side, and he vowed never to see the other side again.

Cell blocks stretched on each side of the Administration Building, with opaque windows rising up thirty feet, heavily barred. Gun turrets were built in at each end, no longer used, replaced with gun towers several yards from the building itself. The gun turrets were what made the prison look like a castle.

It still looks like one, he decided. Only thing is, there ain't no golden-haired princess waiting on the other side, just the fucking dungeons.

CHAPTER TWO

GLENN CLOSED the door of the cab and said "Airport" before the driver could ask. He turned his head left and right, trying to look at everything. Now that he was off the prison grounds he was willing to believe it—he really was out. It was too late for someone to tap him on the shoulder and say come on back, we made a mistake.

He met the cabbie's eyes in the rearview mirror.

"Just get out?" It was asked in a neutral tone.

Not an unreasonable question, nor an unexpected one. Still, he resented it.

"Yeah." He broke eye contact and went back to looking out the window.

"What'd you do?"

He could feel the driver looking at him in the mirror but said nothing. After a second the driver looked back at the road and said no more.

He saw a branch post office and told the cabbie to pull in. He bought a fifty dollar money order and addressed it to Jimmy, smiling as he wrote in a loose scrawl. By now Jimmy would know he was out and be thinking he'd never see the money.

That'll surprise his ass, thought Glenn as he got back in the cab. He owed the money; getting out didn't change it.

13

But he knew Jimmy, from experience, had already written it off.

Delta was the first flight out and he took it, getting less than two bucks' change from a hundred. He winced at the price, then shrugged. Being able to go two hundred miles in thirty-five minutes was worth it.

He wanted a drink. He could see a glass in his mind, frosted, with beads of water running down it. But the plane boarded in five minutes so he passed it up. No hurry. He was out.

He took a seat in the passengers' area, drinking in the mass of colors. After five years of seeing only two-tone denim, the many hues were dazzling. Different smells too. They assaulted his nose and it was wonderful.

He sat there, smoking, outwardly calm. He was medium height, slim and looked younger than his forty years. His hair was brown, brushed back, and in the last year had started showing traces of gray. The short, neatly trimmed beard he wore was more gray than brown.

Glenn became conscious of his clothes and a smile played briefly at the corner of his mouth. For a moment he felt like everyone could tell he was fresh out of the joint. The smile grew larger as he shrugged away the feeling.

They can't tell, and if they can, so what? To hell with 'em. I'd be happy here sitting in nothing but my boxer shorts. The smile grew, then flashed off. Yeah, I would, by God. Doing just what I'm doing now, grinning like an idiot.

HE WALKED out of the Memphis airport an hour later and into another taxi. He told the driver to take him to the Dixon Motel on Summer Avenue and settled back, looking out the window at home. Home. It felt good to be out, and back, but being back didn't make it home. He supposed Darleen had something to do with the feeling.

It was rush hour and it took the cab as long to get to the

motel as it did to fly from Nashville to Memphis. He paid the fare and got out.

He looked the place over as he moved toward the office. The Dixon Motel, built in the late sixties, had never been what could be called a classy place. Duplex cabins formed a half circle behind the office, all painted the same color, white, with a mustard brown trim. It looked even seedier than when he'd seen it last. He shrugged and opened the door of the office. It would do for a night or two. He wasn't going to make it his home.

The tiny office was empty, but canned laughter could be heard coming from the room behind the counter. A flower-patterned plastic curtain hung across the doorway leading into it. He tapped the bell once, lightly. The curtain parted and a man emerged, wearing a stained undershirt and scratching in his armpit.

"Ray around?" Glenn asked as he signed the register.

The desk clerk turned the register around and read it. "Old man Dixon died three years ago. How long you planning on staying?"

Glenn briefly considered saying he wouldn't be staying after all. Seeing Ray was the reason he'd decided on this motel. He had run a poker game in one of the rooms for several months, with Ray getting a cut. Ray's death surprised him. He had been one of those men who seemed too contrary to die.

"A couple of days." Dixon dying didn't stop the need for a room.

He took the key and walked around the side of the office toward his room, located almost directly in the center. Most of the roofs had shingles missing and the paint was peeling from all the cabins. Halfway there he turned and went back to the street.

He walked a few blocks to a shopping center, passing a bread bakery on the way. Lots of things might have changed, but not the smell of the bakery. It still smelled as delicious as when he was a kid.

Glenn bought himself a pair of gray slacks and a pale yellow shirt. Next stop was a shoe store where he picked out a black pair of Florsheim loafers. He wore the shoes back to the motel. They felt light, the soles thin, after having worn bulky running shoes all the time he was in prison.

The room had furniture that looked like it had been there since the place was built. A dresser with a yellowed mirror that also served as a desk, and a single straight-back chair. The bed had a thin blue spread covering it that failed to hide the sag in the middle.

What stood out the most was the strong odor of cheap industrial disinfectant. For a moment the smell reminded him of prison, and the room wasn't a hell of a lot bigger than his cell had been. But there was a major difference. He could open the door and walk out any time he chose.

He changed into his new clothes and had a hamburger and fries at the diner next to the motel. By then it was dark. He called a cab, waiting for it at the motel office. He told the driver to take him to the Willow Inn on Poplar Avenue. The cabbie didn't know where it was so Glenn said just drive down Poplar and he'd tell him when they got there.

The Willow Inn was now called the Stalactite. He paid the fare and got out, hesitating before going inside. When he had frequented it the place featured a Forties jukebox and music to go with it. He doubted he'd hear such music tonight, not with a name like the Stalactite.

He was right, and started to leave but changed his mind. No doubt he'd only run into more changes, and what the hell, it wasn't crowded. He took a seat at the bar and ordered George Dickel and water. He had to raise his voice to be heard over the hard rock pounding from a new state-of-the-art jukebox.

He stirred his drink and took a swallow. It went down smooth. The whiskey exploded in his stomach before he could savor the taste, sending warmth through him. He took another sip, enjoying it, because he knew by tomorrow it would taste like it always had. He turned to look the place over and immediately spotted a young woman playing shuffleboard.

She looked about twenty-two, with long summer-blond hair falling halfway down her back. Legs like the hair, long and tanned, stretched up to an ass that threatened to spill out of the cut-off Levi's.

She leaned over the board and let the puck go, using body English, throwing her hips to one side. The sight of those tight cheeks jiggling caused a tingling ache in Glenn's groin.

Jesus, he thought, old Levi Strauss never had any idea his jeans would ever look like that.

He felt her date's eyes on him. He looked from her to him and nodded an apology to the younger man. The guy glared another moment, then looked away, satisfied he'd defended his territory.

Glenn turned to face the mirror behind the bar and liquor bottles that shone softly in the dim light. He smiled at the kid's posturing, not blaming him. He had been staring, but it was worth staring at. The kid had a right to be proud of being with her. He took another drink, the smile lingering, thinking of himself at that age.

There were only three other people sitting at the bar, which suited Glenn. It meant not being dragged into a conversation with someone he didn't know. He looked around again as he nursed his drink. The tingling in his groin became worse.

There were six other women in the bar girls to him, all of them dressed in jeans of one kind or another. Not one was over twenty-five and not one was less than beautiful to his starved eye.

Being close to women drove home how long it'd been since he'd been with one. He watched a brunette, sitting alone, get up and walk to the jukebox. She was pretty, and God, she had such firm, pert little titties. She was equipped with everything he'd dreamed about so damned many long nights.

Glenn watched her walk back to her table but made no move to go talk to her. He knew he wouldn't go over later either. He hadn't tried to pick up a girl in ten years. First marriage, then prison took him out of circulation long enough to make him scared to make the move.

A deeper fear was also there. He had heard a couple of guys say they'd been unable to get it up the first time after getting out. Just the fear it might happen was enough to kill any confidence he might have had.

Well, so much for getting laid tonight, he told himself. Since he'd owned up to the truth he downed the last of his drink and went in search of a bar with a sound level more to his liking. Leave this place to the kids.

He walked a few blocks further down Poplar. The night was typical of the southern bottomlands, sultry and muggy. He could feel a trickle of sweat roll down the small of his back, but the heat felt good. So did being able to walk in a straight line without a wall stopping him.

He ended up in a neighborhood bar on Madison, where he made the fourth customer. He sat there in the quiet, wondering why he was making such a subdued celebration of getting out.

Three drinks later he was moderately drunk, a nice feeling. He snickered to himself as he watched two old geezers at the other end of the bar. It was evident they'd known each other for years. The one talking looked around as he spoke while his companion watched the television on the wall. He never took his eyes from the TV, just nodded at a steady, rhythmic beat.

Dip. Pause. Dip, dip. Pause. Dip. Pause. Dip, dip. He had the timing down so pat Glenn figured he hadn't heard anything his buddy had said in years.

He wiped his mouth with the back of his hand. His lips tingled and were starting to grow a little numb. Time to go. He told the bartender to call a cab, giving the man a five. Ten minutes later he heard a horn honking outside. He got off the stool, and using care managed to walk fairly straight as he left.

He was in bed a little after midnight, which was two hours later than he'd been up in a long time. He lay there in the dark, thinking about Darleen. He had to go see her tomorrow. Riding around in cabs just didn't get it.

CHAPTER THREE

GLENN WOKE up at ten o'clock, showered and put on the clothes he'd worn the night before. They were all he had; he'd thrown what he wore out of prison into the trash.

It was a little after noon by the time he finished breakfast at the diner. He called another cab, giving the driver Darleen's address.

The cab turned onto a small street off Cooper and stopped in front of a brick ranch-style three-bedroom house. He got out and stood there, staring at the house. The blue Camaro Darleen had bought two years ago sat in the driveway, along with a black Ford pickup he was unfamiliar with. But he knew who it belonged to.

He lit a cigarette and started to walk down the street, not ready yet to knock on the door. As he walked, his thoughts went back to the last time he'd seen Darleen.

They'd visited on the picnic grounds, a fenced-in area outside the walls, a privilege reserved for those with medium custody or lower. It was a warm, beautiful Sunday, the day his world caved in on him.

She was distant that day, as she'd been the last three or four visits. Glenn recognized the signals almost immediately, but waited those two months before speaking of it.

He knew she was falling for somebody, attracted to someone for more than just a roll in the sheets.

"You're getting serious about somebody, aren't you, Darleen?" He was cooking hamburgers, and he gave them his full attention. He knew it would be easier for her if he wasn't looking at her.

She hesitated, and he helped her with it.

"The signs are there, sugar. They've been there a while. You're starting to fall for him, aren't you?"

She gave a strangled sob and threw her arms around his neck. "It's worse than that."

He held her tightly, rubbing the small of her back. "How much worse? You pregnant too?"

She drew away and went to sit at the picnic table. She tried to look him in the eyes but failed.

"I mean I can't get him out of my system, Glenn. And I don't really want to. I find myself wanting to be with him more and more."

Her words hit him like bullets. He felt his breath leave him and worked to get it back. He walked over to sit across from her, struggling to keep his face expressionless.

"Who is he?"

She shrugged and waved a hand. "Like you. A thief, but you don't know him. Who else would I meet?"

He smiled, remembering their meeting. Darleen had come into the bar he owned and tried to sell him some phony stock. He played along until time to let go of the money. The game was worn-out when she was a baby and he told her so. Then he asked her out.

He supposed he became her mentor because there sure as hell was as much larceny in her heart as his, if not more. Inspired by her enthusiasm, he began to teach her the finer points of pulling a con. She soaked up knowledge like a sponge, rarely needing to be told something twice. It wasn't long before she could estimate the value of jewelry better than most guys who'd been doing it for years.

Sure, he and Eddie knew where all the alarm buttons were in the jewelry store. Darleen got a job there, worked a month. Just long enough to get the security system down.

Whatever he became to her, she became the one thing he loved. The last five years before he was arrested he'd built his life around her.

Now this. Oh, God, a god I don't even believe in, please, not this.

"So, are you leaving me?"

She said nothing. She sat there, staring at the prison and brushing tears away. Glenn wanted to take her in his arms but this was not the time.

"I don't know what I want. Not really. I know I love you, but I love Larry too."

Glenn kept quiet. What could he say?

"Please understand, Glenn. I can't handle the guilt of loving two men at the same time. You're in here, and he's out there. I'm too weak to cut it off with him because he makes me feel good."

"So you want a divorce."

"I won't file because I'm not sure yet. This is the only thing I see to do. You've got another eighteen months or so. I want to stay away for a while, get things sorted out about how I feel. If it's you, I'll be back. If it's him, then we'll get a divorce."

He looked at her, lips pursed, finally chuckled and looked away. "Let me get this straight, Darleen. You love me, and you love him too. You're mixed up, so you want to stay away a while, sort things out. But during all this sorting out you aren't going to stop seeing him. But you want me to go back in there and just wait for you to make up your mind. Have I got it right?"

She chewed on her bottom lip, fresh tears glistening in her eyes. After a moment she nodded.

"I think you're being a little cold, but yes, I guess that's what I want. Will you go along with it?"

"Darleen, we've been down a lot of roads together. And like anybody that drives too fast we ended up in the ditch a couple of times. But if that's the best deal I can get, I think I'll just get out right here."

"Glenn, I need some time to decide."

He stood and looked down at her. "You've already decided and we both know it. Now one of us has to make the move. I'll file for the divorce."

She reached for him but he stepped back. "No, it's over."

He took her hand, pulled it up and kissed her fingers. "I'm not mad, not yet. Right now I'm just sorry, because I love you. But I'm too good to play second string on anybody's team."

He turned and started for the gate leading back inside the prison. Darleen called his name, his step faltered, then continued. It was the last time he saw her. . . .

He came back in front of the house but still didn't go up the sidewalk. He lit another cigarette and decided to make another circle around the block. He thought of Rick, the only real friend he'd made in prison. Right about now he'd be locked in his cell for afternoon count, lighting a joint the moment the guard passed his door.

The breakup had torn Glenn apart, and it was Rick who helped the most—by doing nothing.

For a week he went to his job; other than that, he lay in his cell, light out, staring at the dark. Morning and evening Rick stopped and checked on him. Each time he threw a joint through the bars and went on.

Rick never asked why she left—in prison the reason is always the same. He just made sure Glenn had weed to ease the pain a little, put his thoughts on a softer level. The following Sunday night he came out, and Rick silently made room for him to lean against the wall like before.

He came around once again. Time to go in, get it over with. He wasn't going to be free until this was out of the way.

He rang the bell and waited. Part of him wanted the door to open just so he could see her again. Just as much of him dreaded it, it would be slicing through a lot of raw emotional tissue.

The door opened but Larry stood there instead of Darleen. He was young, something Glenn hadn't expected. Blond hair, hazel eyes. A scar sliced from the top of his forehead through the center of his right eyebrow. In a few years, when he was older, it would make him look sinister.

Larry said nothing, not recognizing him. He stood in the doorway and waited for him to state his business.

"I suppose you're Larry." He waited for Larry to acknowledge him before continuing. Larry nodded, wary.

"I'm Glenn, I've come to see Darleen."

"Glenn?" came a voice from in the house. "Is Glenn out there?"

Before he could answer she was there, looking around the door. She stepped into full view, her mouth in an O, both hands rising to cover it. She lowered them slowly, a smile replacing the surprised look.

Glenn said nothing, just looked. Looked in her eyes and ached. That's all it took to bring it all rushing back. Strange eyes, he'd always called them, because of their light shade of gray. He'd lost himself countless times gazing into them.

She pulled Larry back a step, out of the door. "Come in, Glenn. Don't stand out there. I certainly didn't expect to see you. You look good. How, when did you get out? Have you been to Eddie's?"

She laughed as lightly as wind chimes to his ears. "Listen to me run on. Let me get you in a chair."

She took his arm and guided him to the living room. It was the same, yet different, not his any longer. A new stereo system, a new recliner chair in the corner. And pictures of Larry where his used to be.

He sat in the recliner. "Let's see if I remember them in order. Thank you. Yesterday. Early release, overcrowding. I haven't seen Eddie yet. I'm staying in a motel. You look good yourself."

She sat on the couch, one leg tucked beneath her. It was true, she did look good. Thirty-six, flat stomach, small high breasts. And the legs, still catching his eye like the first time he'd seen her.

Larry was still standing, and now he walked over to offer his hand to Glenn.

"I'm Larry. I wish it could've been under different circumstances but I'm glad to meet you."

Glenn reached out and accepted the handshake. "Hello."

"Darleen's told me a lot about you," he said.

Glenn studied him, trying to gauge how old he was, surprised. She hadn't mentioned he was a kid, lucky to be twenty-five.

He cut his eyes at Darleen. "Well, take most of it with a grain of salt. She probably shaded some of those stories to make 'em more interesting."

"I've talked to others. We know some of the same people and none of 'em had anything but good to say about you."

"What kind of stuff are you into, Larry?"

"Burglary, for the most part. Nothing as heavy as you. I don't like guns, and armed robbery scares me to death."

"It's a good way to think. The day they hit me in the ass with thirty years I got terrified of them myself."

"I'm glad you got out early," said Darleen. "Why didn't you let someone know?"

"I didn't know it myself. They just came and got me, said sign this and you're out."

He could see both of them were uncomfortable with his being there. He'd known they would be, such thoughts used to give him comfort in the dark hours of the night. But now he discovered he found no pleasure in the feeling.

"I came to get my clothes."

"They're in the first bedroom, Glenn. I've kept them clean for you."

He stood and started for the bedroom. She came into the room behind him and sat on the bed while he sorted through the clothes.

"You look like you picked up a few pounds."

"Yeah. But I don't expect it'll take too long to drop 'em now that I'm out."

Glenn filled two suitcases, leaving as many clothes as he took. Darleen asked if he didn't want them too and he said she could give them to Goodwill. He stopped in the doorway.

"There's one more thing I've got here."

"No, Glenn. I put everything of yours here in the bedroom."

"Not all of it, Darleen. Only what you knew about."

Glenn looked at Larry, standing in the hall. "Wonder if I could borrow a hammer and screwdriver?"

"Sure." Larry turned with a puzzled look and went through the kitchen into the garage.

He came back with the tools and Glenn stood up to take them from him. He turned back to Darleen, a corner of his mouth lifting up in a tiny smile, one that was always good for making her angry in another time. She called it his "Now I'll show you what you missed" smile.

He started down the hall, followed closely by Darleen. Larry held back, standing in the doorway to the living room, watching as Glenn stopped at the bathroom.

Glenn knocked the pin out of the hinge at the top of the door, then knelt and did the same at the bottom. He stood up, pulled the door away and laid it flat in the hallway.

Like most modern doors it was hollow, two sheets of plywood over a frame of two-by-fours. Glenn knelt again and used the hammer to tap the screwdriver against what looked to be solid wood at the bottom of the door. A strip of wood one-eighth inch thick popped out a little at the other end. He grasped it with his finger and thumbnail and pulled it all the way out. Darleen bent down to see where Glenn had routed two grooves for the strip to slide along.

He slid the screwdriver inside the door and wiggled it around. A gasp came from Darleen when packets of money wrapped in plastic begin to fall out.

Glenn hadn't made the hiding place with any intention of keeping quiet about it all these years. A one-man job had come along, a car dealer on his way to Vegas with twenty grand. Darleen was out of town at the time. He'd intended to bring the money out when she returned and surprise her with a cruise, something she'd always wanted to go on. But the bust came and Glenn decided to keep quiet. There might be a need for it someday. And look how things had turned out.

He pulled the last of it out and took a small paper sack from his back pocket. After ripping the plastic off the money he dropped it in the sack.

"When did you get that, Glenn?" Darleen asked.

He shrugged, his fingers working swiftly. "A month or so before I got busted.

"I really didn't put it here trying to hold out on you. Then I went to jail, and what with one thing and another, I just decided not to say anything about it."

"What if I'd moved?"

He glanced up. "Then the new owners would've come home one night and wondered why in the hell somebody would want to steal their bathroom door."

"Well, the house belongs to Darleen," said Larry, stepping into the hall.

That was true. But only because Glenn voluntarily signed it over to her as part of the divorce.

"I think she should have half of what's there."

After folding the sack over he stuck it in his waistband and let his shirt hang over it. He first looked at Darleen, then down the hall at Larry.

"I don't give a shit what you think, Larry. The money's mine. I either leave here with all of it or none of it."

"Don't, Glenn," said Darleen. She turned to face Larry.

"It's his, Larry. And you can't take it, so go on back in there and sit down." She turned back to Glenn.

"Let's go have a drink, I need to talk to you anyway."

Larry had gone into the living room. He heard Darleen and came back to stand in the door.

"I don't like the idea of you leaving here with him." The words came belligerently but the tone lacked authority.

An exasperated look crossed Darleen's face, so quickly Glenn almost missed it. But he saw Larry didn't; the fire in his eyes died.

Glenn was a great believer in eyes, thought they told a lot about a man. It started in Vietnam, with the new guys. When they talked about their eagerness for a firefight he looked in their eyes, way down deep. By the middle of his second tour Glenn believed fanatically it was keeping him alive.

No problem if there was a little fear showing. Fear was natural, just as natural to want to hide it. But in some the fear shone like quicksilver, and Glenn stayed away from those men. And there were those whose eyes displayed no fear, not even where there was plenty of reason. Glenn also stayed away from that kind, far away. They'd get you killed the quickest.

Now he looked in Larry's eyes, and what he saw amused him. They showed Larry for what he was, a kid in over his head. Head over heels in love with what to him was an older woman, and scared to death he might lose her.

Darleen walked the few steps to Larry and kissed him on the cheek. She spoke in a soft voice.

"I'm just going for a drink, Larry. We've talked about this part several times. It just came earlier than we thought. I'll be back in a little while."

She opened the front door and looked back at Glenn, still

standing at the bathroom. He looked at the door leaning against the wall, then shrugged. He handed Larry the screwdriver and hammer, then picked up the two suitcases. At the front door he stopped and looked over his shoulder.

"That's a pretty good hiding place, Larry. Served me well. Feel free to use it any time."

CHAPTER FOUR

"You didn't have to say that," Darleen said after they were in the Camaro.

The nearness of her in the close space almost made Glenn giddy. It was like she was his again. He looked over and smiled.

"I shook his hand. What do you want?"

"And you made that remark to salvage a little pride. Who's going to use a stash somebody else knows about?

"There's no need to stand on pride about this, Glenn."

It's everything when it's all you've got, thought Glenn. He changed the subject, opting for a safer course.

"You look great, Darleen."

"Thank you. So do you." She hesitated. "I'm really glad you got out early."

There was a shopping center on Glenn's side and he told her to pull into it. He got out, walked around and opened her door.

"There's a little bar in that bowling alley. I figure it'll be quiet in there this time of day."

The lounge was small and cozy, the lights dim, and it was quiet, almost deserted. Two middle-aged women sat at the bar, their shirts identifying them as being on the same bowling team. None of the few tables were occupied.

They took a table in the farthest corner and then discovered there was no waitress. Glenn went to the bar and returned with a bourbon for himself, a Vodka Collins for Darleen. She broke the awkward silence that followed.

"Glenn, I know of a burglary where there's a big score, real big. We could use you."

"What is it?"

In spite of himself he felt his interest quicken. He'd promised himself he was through with crime, yet here he was, all ears, because she had something in mind.

"It's a house. I guess you could say it belongs to a fence."

"What the hell you mean, you guess? You're thinking about pulling a job where you're guessing on something?"

"No. What I meant is this man is more than just a fence. He lives in a small county and he's the big dog there. He gets part of anything that goes on. He puts the sheriff and judge in office. That kind of person. Anyway, the house is full of money, and jewelry."

A small red bowl with a candle burning in it sat in the center of the table. Glenn turned it slowly, a thoughtful look on his face.

"Have you seen all this yourself?"

"No, but Larry has. He's taken me where the man lives. The house would be no problem to get in and out of. Catching him gone has been the only problem. Are you interested?"

Glenn shook his head. "I'm going to pass. And if you've got any sense you will too."

"Why, Glenn? It would be a good score, maybe bigger than anything you ever pulled. It's that big."

"Because I'm out of that kind of life."

Darleen's eyes sparkled in amusement. "Do you really expect me to believe that?"

"I don't care whether you do or not. But you better take

my advice and pass it up yourself. If this guy is what you say he is he'll kill you."

"He has to know who to kill first."

"That's true. Still, count me out."

"Okay. If you change your mind let me know. But don't wait too long. It's going down Friday night."

Glenn shook his head and sipped his drink. "Evidently things are working out with you and Larry."

She gave a shrug. "He isn't you, Glenn, not by a long shot. I've no doubt we'll break up sooner or later."

Glenn held his glass of water up to the light and appeared to study it. "Got one a little younger than you, huh."

Darleen fished in her purse for a cigarette and Glenn lit it. She placed a hand over his as her head bent to the flame. Her touch, light as it was, sent chills through him.

She leaned back and looked at him. "Does that bother you, his age?"

"Not really. But I've got a feeling he's got a weak streak in him."

"He does."

Her answer, said so calmly, angered Glenn. It went against everything he'd taught her. Weak people caved in when the shit hit the fan. She knew this.

"Then what the hell are you doing with him?"

He leaned forward, not trying to conceal his anger. "Goddamn, Darleen, I can understand you leaving me. But not this. Why would you want a guy that shows all the signs of being a punk?"

Darleen took a moment to answer. She took a draw on her cigarette, stubbed it out.

"I'll admit Larry isn't what I thought he was. It happened partly because he's young. It tickled me being able to attract him. Right now he's there because I can control him. Just like you used to control me, Glenn."

He shook his head. "It wasn't because I wanted to control you. You know there can't be two bosses."

"I know." She reached over and covered his hand with hers. "I don't know if I can explain where you'll understand it. When you went to prison I felt like part of me had been cut off. I missed you so damned much. I know you don't believe me, but I waited over six months before going to bed with anyone. I knew whoever I chose wouldn't compare with you."

She stopped and picked up her drink. Her eyes glistened in the dim light.

"Then a couple of years went by and I got used to not having you around. It was sort of like before I met you, but better. I had all the knowledge you gave me."

She smiled, and it lit up her face. Glenn loved that, because it came when she was proud of herself.

"A few months ago I ran the phony jewelry scam. Made the switch myself, smooth as silk. I made twelve thousand on that deal and I worked it myself from start to finish. You taught me how but I did it myself. *I* was the boss that time."

Glenn watched her closely as she talked, searching the depths of her eyes. The truth shone in them, bright enough that even he could see it.

"Then it was just a matter of time," he said softly.

Darleen hesitated, then nodded. "Probably. I knew before you went to jail it would always be you running the show. I'm the boss with Larry, and I like it that way." She took another drink and changed the subject.

"So tell me about your first night out. I'll bet the girl wondered about you when you came."

He smiled. "Yeah, I went to bed early, all right. Alone. I saw plenty of pretty ones but I was too damn scared to approach one of them."

"Are you saying you haven't been to bed with anybody yet?"

"Afraid so."

A soft expression flowed across her face. "I'll go to a motel with you if you'd like."

If he'd like. Sweet Jesus on a motorcycle. Why not get really stupid and ask him if he wanted to be alive tomorrow.

Glenn looked at her, wanting more than anything to say yes. He knew he could have her back if they spent two hours in bed. She knew it too.

"No. When we were together I never once worried that you might step out on me. I won't be the one starts you down that road. Besides, I'd be thinking it was just a sympathy fuck."

The remark angered and hurt her, and it showed. He started to apologize, bit it back.

"It wasn't offered in sympathy." Her voice was cold. She finished off her drink and looked at her watch.

"We'd better get back. We've been gone over an hour and Larry will be asking questions. Questions I don't feel like putting up with."

Glenn pushed his chair back and stood up. "But you can control him, right?"

"That's right, Glenn, I can control him," she said tightly as she brushed past him.

They were quiet until Darleen turned in at the motel. Her anger appeared to be gone.

"What're you planning on doing now that you're out?"

"I don't know yet. I haven't made any plans. Just lay back for a while, enjoy myself."

He opened the car door, then looked back at Darleen before getting out. He saw what he thought was some of the old caring.

"Take care of yourself, Glenn. If there's anything I can do I hope you'll call me. Most of all I'd like to think you don't hate me."

"I tried, girl, but I couldn't do it," he said, and closed the door. He didn't look back as he walked to his room.

DARLEEN TOOK a second to compose her face before she unlocked the door. Larry, hearing the click, stood in the center of the living room.

"You've been gone over an hour," he said. "Did you go to bed with him?"

She leaned against the wall and closed her eyes. No, she thought, we didn't go to bed. But only because of his pride. Something he has too much of, and you don't have enough of.

"No, we just talked. I told you I wouldn't go to bed with him."

She edged past him, toward the bedroom and on into the bathroom. Larry followed her, tried the knob and found it locked.

Darleen thought about taking a shower, then decided against it. It would only make Larry all the more suspicious. She put cold cream on her face and wiped it off.

Did I do right to let him go? She shrugged, it was too late for second thoughts.

When she came out, Larry put his arms around her from behind. Darleen sighed, anticipating his next move. Sure enough, his hand snaked beneath her blouse to cup a breast.

"I don't like the way he waltzed in here and took all that money out. How much was there, anyway?"

"I didn't ask him, Larry. Besides, it was his, not ours."

She was not in the mood to make love, but giving in would be easier than going through an argument. She reached behind her, unfastened her bra and removed it. Because her breasts were small, gravity had not affected them. They stood out, the nipples dark brown and pointing up.

Larry quickly undressed and waited on the bed for her. He locked his arms behind his head.

"Well, I don't want any trouble with him, but I'll give that old bastard plenty of it if he tries to mess with you."

Darleen smiled as she pushed her skirt and panties down at the same time. Her pubic hair was darker than the hair on her head, almost black, thick and lush. She stood there facing him, hands on her hips.

"Listen to me, Larry. Don't ever make the mistake of thinking Glenn is old. He was already back from a war when he was younger than you are now. And he was wounded twice, so bad that most men wouldn't have lived."

She left her clothes on the floor and crawled up on the bed on her hands and knees. She looked at him as she raised her knees and slipped beneath the covers. When she spoke, her voice was more gentle.

"Just let it alone. He won't bother us. But if he wanted to there wouldn't be much you could do to stop him."

"He don't look so mean to me."

She sighed. "He isn't mean, baby. He's dangerous. If he even thought you were a threat he'd move first. That's why you leave him alone. You wouldn't take it as far as he would, so don't start it."

Larry snuggled against her, one hand trailing across her hip and between her legs. He stroked her for just a second and then plunged a finger inside. Darleen winced, she was dry. But she lay quietly, knowing he was hunting for any sign of infidelity.

His head moved down to suck a breast. She wanted to push him away but didn't. He'd be sure to think she'd gone to bed with Glenn if she did. Better to keep things going smoothly. She would need Larry in the next couple of weeks. She put her hand to the back of his head and pulled him closer.

Larry was impatient, wanting to stake his claim to her

again. He pushed her legs farther apart and rolled on top of her, going all the way in with a sudden, hard lunge.

She gasped and bit her lip, still not fully wet. She wrapped her arms around his back, urging him on, rocking her hips back and forth. She wanted him to finish quickly.

Glenn wouldn't do this, she thought. If the tables were turned he would've waited until I came to him. If it took a month, he would've waited.

CHAPTER FIVE

THE NEXT morning Glenn called his partner on the jewelry store robbery, Eddie Cox. He had to explain that no, he hadn't escaped, just early release. When that was out of the way he asked Eddie to meet him at the diner. And one other thing, would Eddie bring him a pistol?

Half an hour later Glenn watched Eddie open the door of the diner and walk toward him. He wore a gray Stetson cowboy hat pushed back on his head that Glenn knew didn't cost less than a hundred bucks. Faded jeans covering lizard skin boots, so long the cuffs were frayed in back from dragging the ground.

Eddie was tall, almost cadaverous, in his mid-forties. His face was a contradiction, a constant mournful set to his expression, but his brown eyes always showed humor. Glenn got off the stool and shook hands, noting how the lines around those eyes had deepened.

"Man, it's good to see you, Glenn. You're looking good."

"Feel good, now that I'm out. When are you gonna put on some weight?"

Eddie took a stool, ordered a beer for himself and another one for Glenn. "Don't reckon I ever will. You know how good Lois cooks. I pack it away but don't gain nothing."

"How is Lois?"

"Like always. She ain't happy if she ain't givin' me hell about something or other."

"And you wouldn't be happy if she didn't."

Eddie drank from the bottle, wiped his mouth with the back of his hand. "What the devil are you staying out there for? And why didn't you call me to come pick you up? You know you coulda stayed with us 'til you found a place."

"You and Lois don't need me underfoot."

"Well, she told me to tell you she's insulted."

"She'll be all right. What's Bert Conley up to? He still in business?"

"So that's what you wanted a pistol for. He's going stronger than ever. Owns three titty bars now. His newest one ain't more'n ten blocks from here."

"Good. Then we don't have far to go."

Eddie shook his head in disgust. "That bastard slow-walked me six months on my money."

Glenn and Eddie had given Conley a hundred thousand dollars' worth of jewelry a month before Glenn was arrested. Conley was supposed to sell it and give them thirty thousand. No problem, except Glenn went to jail.

"Yeah. Well, he's had five years to get my money up."

"He's gonna tell you the stuff got ripped off, that he didn't make a dime on it."

"That's his problem, not mine. When it went in his hands he took responsibility for it. He owes me fifteen grand."

"You getting out now is unreal, Glenn. Two weeks ago I found a perfect little jewelry store up in Jackson. Man, you're gonna love it."

Jesus, offers were coming from everywhere. Glenn drained the last of his beer, then shook his head as he set the bottle on the counter.

"You better look for someone else."

Eddie looked at him. "Did prison really turn you around?"

"Prison didn't do it, Eddie, but yeah, I'm through with it. I'm not going back to the joint. I guess I just grew up the last couple of years. Besides, I'm not going to be staying in town."

"Where you going?"

"To see Frank. You heard from him lately?"

Eddie shook his head. "I guess it's been six, eight months since I talked to him."

"I got a letter from him a month ago. He said he reckoned he'd be seeing me pretty soon, that he'd caught himself a case."

"No shit. What'd they bust him for?"

"That's just it. I don't know. He writes like every word costs a fortune. Finish your beer. I want to talk to Conley."

When they were in the car Eddie fumbled beneath the seat and came up with a .45 automatic. "I figured you'd want one of these. You always were partial to 'em."

Glenn took the pistol and removed the magazine to see that it was fully loaded. He put it back in and worked the slide to chamber a round, then stuck it in the small of his back.

"Yeah. If I have to use it I want the bastard to know he's been hit."

They got to the bar before it was open. They hadn't much more than settled in to wait when a flashy white Cadillac parked in front of the door. The driver got out, a big bear of a man, and opened the rear door. Glenn watched Conley step out, playing the gangster role to the hilt. He stood by the door, straightening his beige suit coat while the bodyguard unlocked the bar.

Glenn opened the car door and Eddie started to get out too. Glenn shook his head.

"I appreciate it, Eddie, but just wait in the car."

"Goddammit, Glenn, you're gonna need help. You saw the size of that fuckin' bodyguard."

"I might need to get away in a hurry. You just have the engine running when you see me coming out."

The door was locked. Glenn knocked loudly. It opened a crack, just enough for the bodyguard to stick his nose through. The eyebrows above it looked like they were an inch thick.

"Come back in a few minutes, we ain't open yet."

The voice sounded like it came from the bottom of a well. Cold as well water too.

"No problem. Me and Bert are old friends. He'll be glad to see me."

Glenn pushed against the door, catching the bodyguard off balance, and stepping inside. He called out as he entered, hoping it would keep this trained bear from grabbing him.

"Hey, Bert. C'mon out here. It's Odom."

The bodyguard glared at Glenn, eyebrows making a continuous line across his forehead. "You better hope he wants to see you."

A partition separated the bar from the entrance, and Conley now stuck his head around the corner. He frowned when he recognized Glenn.

"Don't seem like you oughta to be out yet," he said.

"Well, I'm real happy to see you too, Bert." Glenn jerked a thumb at the bodyguard. "Call off your yard dog so we can talk."

Conley hesitated a moment, clearly not wanting a conversation. But he nodded at the bodyguard and waved a hand for Glenn to come into the bar. Glenn did, followed closely by the bodyguard, who took a seat across the room, out of hearing.

Conley went behind the bar, picked up a bottle of George Dickel, poured a shot for Glenn and set it in front of him. For himself he poured it over cracked ice and added a dash of soda. He came back around and leaned over the bar, resting on his elbows.

"How about that, Glenn. I even remember what you drink. How'd you get out so early?"

"It got crowded. They had to let some of us go." He knocked the shot of whiskey back in one swallow. "You got a good memory. I'm sure you remember the money I never got from you."

Bert picked up a swizzle stick, stirred his drink, gestured around the bar. The glare from the lights revealed cigarette burns and threadbare spots in the carpet. Even the stage the girls danced on looked shabby.

"You couldn't have come at a worse time, Glenn. I just sunk a mint in this dump and I ain't got a thousand I can lay my hands on. Besides, you know the merchandise got ripped off. I figure when I gave Eddie fifteen grand I paid more than I shoulda."

Glenn picked up a napkin and appeared to study the cartoons of big-breasted girls. "How do you figure that?"

"Goddammit, because it got ripped off, that's why. I didn't make a nickel, so why in hell should I pay for the shit?"

"You know why, Bert." Glenn kept his voice low and calm. The last thing he wanted right now was trouble from the bodyguard.

"You took the jewelry, Bert. It wasn't something you could insure. Me and Eddie quoted thirty grand and you said you thought it was a good deal. Now, I'm sorry you got ripped off, but that's not my problem. My problem is you agreed to thirty grand and I never got my end."

"And you ain't gonna get it. I told you, split the fifteen grand with Eddie." He poked a finger in Glenn's chest. "I ain't gonna fuck with you, Glenn. Get out now or I turn Carl loose. You bother me again, I'll do worse. I'll call the fucking parole office and get you shipped back. You want to stay out, you'd best not fuck with me. Understand?"

Glenn nodded. So Carl was the bear's name. Bruno would suit him better.

"I understand," he said, turning as if to leave.

Conley watched with a smile, one that vanished when Glenn kneed him in the nuts, hard. Glenn shot his left hand out at the same time, grabbed a handful of Conley's hair and smashed his face against the bar.

Conley's face met the edge of the polished wood with a wet smack. Blood sprayed from both sides of his head in a fine mist. He tried to groan but the blow to his nuts had taken away all his air.

From the corner of his eye Glenn saw Carl get up, turning over the table in the process, and rush toward him. Without letting Conley's head up he pulled the .45 and pointed it at Carl.

The bodyguard stopped short when he saw the pistol. He held his hands out to show Glenn he would stand still.

"Atta boy, Carl," said Glenn. "Conley only gets so much loyalty for so much money. I know he's not paying you enough to die for him."

He held the pistol steady, pointing it in the center of Carl's chest. "You picked a good spot. Just hold what you got over there."

He turned back to Conley and pulled his head off the bar. He stuck the pistol against Conley's head, trying to screw the barrel into the man's ear.

"Calling the parole office would be rough, all right." He pushed harder on the pistol. "Now either give me my money or I swear to God you'll pay twice that much in hospital bills. I'm the one who's tired of fucking around. It's up to you."

Conley's mouth worked like that of a fish out of water, trying to suck some air into his lungs. His eyes were tearing, and blood from the cut on his forehead ran over them. The first thing he did after getting his breath back was moan. The second was to tell Carl to go get fifteen grand from the office.

"Make it twenty, Carl," said Glenn.

Conley's head snapped around to look at Glenn. "I only owe you fifteen, goddammit."

"That's true, Bert. But you're a slow pay and you caused me trouble on top of that. Add carrying charges and interest for five years and you're coming out cheap."

He pulled Conley's head back as if to smash it against the bar again. "You want to argue some more, Bert?"

"Get it, Carl," said Conley, and Glenn released him. Conley pulled a silk handkerchief from his breast pocket and wiped at the blood.

"I won't forget this."

Glenn gave him a one-sided smile. "I don't want you to, Bert. But I want you to remember it in a way that'll do you some good. Let it teach you not to try and fuck people, Bert. And don't threaten me about what you'll do. You scare me, asshole, and I'll take you out one night when you're walking to your car." He raised the pistol until it touched Conley's nose. "Do *you* understand?"

Conley nodded. "Good. I'm not taking nothing you don't owe. Let it lay and we're through."

Carl came back and handed Glenn four packets of money. Glenn fanned through them and saw they were all hundreds. He stuck the money in a back pocket, then walked back to the door, still holding the pistol.

"Thank you, Bert. Carl, wash him off and put a bandage on that cut. Earn your keep."

He opened the door just as a dancer was coming in. Her eyes widened at the sight of the heavy pistol in Glenn's hand.

He held the door open and motioned for her to come in. She hesitated, clearly thinking about running, but fear got the better of her. She stepped through the door nervously, never taking her eyes away from the pistol.

Glenn nodded politely. "C'mon in, hon. No need for you to be scared. We were just talking business. You work for him so you ought to know how he is."

He walked outside and toward the car. He wanted to look over his shoulder but resisted the urge. Eddie would let him know if Carl came out. He opened the door and got in.

"Let's ease out of here, Eddie. The last thing I want is for that bastard to think I'm scared of him."

He pulled the money out and started counting. Eddie watched, eyes growing wide.

"How the fuck did you get twenty grand outta that tight-ass bastard?"

"You know how reasonable people can be with a pistol stuck in their ear."

"It don't sound like you've straightened up."

"Straightening up don't mean I'd let people fuck me out of what they owe me."

As they came to a Ford dealership Glenn told Eddie to turn in, and an hour later he owned a year-old Thunderbird. He came out of the building and walked around the car, rubbed his hand along the shiny black finish, then opened the door and did the same to the red interior.

"What do you think, Eddie? Like it?"

"You know I do. It's a sharp ride. But do you think you should've spent so much money? You're damned near broke now."

"No, I've got some left, came from somewhere else. Besides, you have no idea how many days I looked over that wall and thought about riding down the highway in one of these."

"Well, follow me home and I'll park mine, then we'll go have a few drinks, celebrate your getting out."

"Wish I could, Eddie, but I've got to go see the old man. I'd a helluva lot rather have that drink. Believe it."

CHAPTER SIX

GLENN TURNED off Perkins onto a small street in what had been East Memphis twenty years earlier. Today it was just a lower middle-class neighborhood, the fashionable east side having moved farther out as younger people moved up.

In the middle of the block he turned in a driveway, cut the engine but did not get out right away. Instead he watched an old man who, as the man himself would say, was piddling around in the garage. The man picked up a lawn mower, looked at the Thunderbird a few seconds, then put the mower on the workbench. He turned to look again, squinting his eyes. The set of his lips just before he turned away the second time told Glenn he'd be wasting his time waiting for an invitation.

The man was dressed in khaki shirt and pants. The only difference from those he'd worn for thirty years was that these had no "Light and Power" insignia. He was in his seventies and while he was the same height as Glenn he was a little stooped.

But the old bastard sure gets around good, Glenn thought, getting out of the car. He walked inside the garage and stopped.

"Hello, dad."

The old man went on removing the cowl from the lawn

mower's engine. When he had it off he laid it on the work-bench, then looked at Glenn.

"How long you been out?"

So it wasn't going to be easy, thought Glenn. Did you really think he might have changed? You haven't, and you're a part of him.

"Two days ago. You're looking good."

Walter Odom gave Glenn a sideways look. "It don't look like that place done you no harm. What're you gonna do now that you're out?"

Glenn's father had come to see him once after he was arrested, and the visit was not a pleasant one. He merely said he hoped Glenn was happy now. He'd finally hit the bottom he'd been sliding toward the last fifteen years. It was the last time either had seen the other until today.

"I hope to hell it put some sense in your head. Maybe now you'll get a job and make something out of yourself. It ain't too late."

His idea of making something of yourself was to get a job with a good pension and benefits. Plod away at it thirty years and then you get to piddle around with lawn-mower engines. You get to do that because the pension that once looked so good isn't enough to take you across town these days, let alone on a vacation.

"Dad, it's hard to work for somebody after you've been in business for yourself."

"Hah, you're forty years old and owned two different bars in your life, if you can call 'em that. Fronts for gambling and whores is what they were."

He was wound up and there would be no stopping him. Glenn leaned against the wall and lit a cigarette, prepared to let the old cuss run out of steam.

His father had been a taskmaster, a tyrant in his own house. Glenn's mother was scared of him to the end. They were from the generation where divorce was never consid-ered, so she was trapped. She put up with his instructing her on everything from how much makeup to apply to when to go to bed.

Then she got lucky. She died.

He tried to do the same with Glenn but he refused to buckle. Two weeks after turning seventeen he persuaded the old man to sign the papers so he could join the army, just to get away. Now his father brought those memories back.

"I don't know where your mama and me went wrong. We tried to do our best raising you. You were a hero. Your medals are still up in your old room and I know you ain't looked at 'em in—"

"They don't mean nothing."

Glenn had been decorated twice in Vietnam, three times if you counted the Purple Heart. Recommended for the Medal of Honor but ended up with the DSC and the Silver Star. There was even a senator waiting to shake his hand the day he stepped off the plane. Hugged Glenn and told him he was a hero, his breath stinking with gin. Said he'd appreciate it if Glenn would vote for him. Glenn didn't bother to tell him he wouldn't be old enough to vote for another year. . . .

His squad had been on patrol, coming down out of the mountains. Earlier the squad leader had pointed to a spot on the map as a likely spot for an ambush. He called it right but it didn't do him any good. He was one of the three killed. They were coming out of a saddle into an open area. The point man saw something and flashed a signal back in time for most to take cover. He was the first one killed. But because he was on the ball the VC were forced to start the ambush too soon. The radio man went next, a direct hit from a grenade launcher, taking out the radio too. And standing beside him had been the squad leader.

Glenn caught two rounds of rifle fire, in the chest and right leg. He couldn't really recall being hit in the leg, but he sure as hell could the one in the chest. He remembered lying on the ground, at first thinking he must have slipped on some loose rock. They were trapped, with no way to retreat that wouldn't get them all killed. A hundred yards back up the trail was another open area where Charlie could pick them off like ducks in a shooting gallery. The canyon walls sloped up gently for seventy-five feet on both sides, then rose straight up, which kept Charlie from coming in but it also kept them from getting out.

Glenn thought for sure he would die that day. So did the medic. Glenn instructed them to carry him up the left slope to where the cliff began. When they did, they fashioned as good a cover as possible and left him with an M-60 to cover their retreat.

The men, most of them kids no older than Glenn, drew fire as they ran up to leave most of their grenades with him. The regular machine gunner stayed long enough to fold extra ammo belts beside the M-60 so Glenn wouldn't have to waste time reloading. He'd been older than the rest of them, serving his second tour. He didn't waste his breath with false hope.

"Try to hold 'em as long as you can, kid. Don't die on us before we can get our asses out of this canyon."

Glenn watched them leave, laying a stream of fire down to cover them, tears rolling down his cheeks.

No, he sure as hell hadn't thought of himself as a hero. He was just a kid who thought he was dying. The squad couldn't carry him and make it. Besides, he would be dead before they could reach help anyway. Strong words for a kid to have to swallow ten thousand miles from home. All he'd wanted to do was get away from the old man. Well, he'd certainly managed to do that.

It took the squad three hours to get to a radio. There were two platoons in the air close by and they went in to get what they thought would be four bodies. But instead of finding Glenn dead they found sixteen Vietnamese bodies scattered across the canyon floor, and a lot of empty brass cartridge casings around Glenn. Blood dripped from his soaked fatigues as they carried him to the chopper, but by God, he was alive. That got him the DSC and the Purple Heart. The Silver Star came two weeks before his second tour ended. He ran sixty feet under heavy fire to bring back his wounded lieutenant. But only because the bastard was lying out there looking straight at him. And to show his gratitude, while waiting on the chopper, the lieutenant gave a stupid order that got one of Glenn's friends killed.

Yeah, he was a hero. Big deal. A shit-faced senator shook his hand. Kids his own age spit on him as he walked through the airport in his uniform. And they were right. He and the other hundred thousand combat troops were just stupid cannon fodder to make fat cats fatter. . . .

He lit another cigarette, which brought a fresh tirade from the old man. Righteous old bastard ever since he quit a few years ago.

"Didn't you read the surgeon general's report on what those things do to your lungs?"

"Yeah, I see those brochures all over the place. I breathed plenty of their Agent Orange too, but I don't re-member 'em putting out any brochures telling us what that shit would do to a man."

The war was a touchy subject between them. The father had never gone, so it was easy for him to be a flag-waver.

"What'd you come for?"

Glenn stared down the street, watching some kids build a makeshift ramp to jump their bikes off. One of them tried it out. He watched the youngster pump his legs to build up speed, the sun reflecting from the wheel spokes as the kid started up the ramp, which collapsed, to the carefree laughter of the other boys. The only other sound in the sleepy, sunny afternoon was the drone of a katydid.

Why did he come?

Because I catch myself sitting like you when I'm think-ing, staring off in space just like you, old man. I trim my beard, and I see more of you looking back than me. And it scares me to fucking death, old man. I came just to see how bad it will be later on, when I'm closer to your age.

"Just to check on you, see how you're doing. You need any money?"

Glenn knew what the answer would be.

"I'm doing all right, my bills are paid. If I did I'd get it somewhere else. One thing's for sure, whatever you got you didn't come by it honest."

"Why, you old son of a bitch . . . ." Let it go, he told himself, but decided against it. He'd held back long enough. "You stole for thirty years. Every time you cashed your paycheck you stole. Pop, you worked for the city, which means you didn't do a total of a year's work in the whole thirty. I just did mine more open, and you can't stand that."

For a moment he thought the old man would try to hit him with the wrench, but all he did was wave it in the direction of the Thunderbird. His blue eyes, eyes like Glenn's only more faded, shot sparks of anger.

"I'll not listen to that, Glenn. By God, I punched a time clock every day. Get out. Get in that fancy car of yours and enjoy it. I ain't got a son anymore."

Glenn opened his mouth to apologize, then closed it. Not this time. He stood still, waiting, hoping the old man would take the words back. But only the katydid broke the strained silence.

He got in the car, backed out into the street and drove away, his neck stiff in his refusal to look back. Yes, the father was in the son, all right.

He pulled into a Steak and Ale to eat but first he wanted a couple of drinks, needed them to untie his stomach before trying to put any food in it. The two stretched into four, one of them a double. And then he enjoyed a steak, his first one in five years. While he ate he eyed the waitress serving the tables around him. When she bent over, he had to restrain himself from bending his head to try and look the rest of the way up her short skirt. The hem stopped just two inches below her ass. He had to laugh. No, performing wasn't going to be any trouble. He'd get out tonight and find a willing partner.

But he didn't. Instead, he lay in the motel room and thought about Darleen. He might as well have still been in the joint. The only difference was he could get up and go see her again. He had to fight hard to overcome the urge.

Welcome back.

CHAPTER SEVEN

GLENN STOOD outside the car on the outskirts of Chattanooga trying to locate a spot on a road map. The glare of the noonday sun reflected from the slick paper. He turned it in a futile effort to shade it. Sweat fell from the tip of his nose onto the map. He folded it irritably and got back in the car.

He turned the air-conditioning on high as he got back on the interstate and adjusted a vent to blow directly on him, but his sweat-soaked shirt chilled quickly and he turned it back to low. He was on his way to see Frank Slater, a guy he'd known over twenty years. As he drove he wondered what kind of trouble Frank had gotten himself in. Going to see him and finding out was as good a reason as any for not staying in Memphis. It would also keep him from going back to see Darleen, something he knew he'd do if he stayed.

Out in the country now, he recognized an exit from the map that would at least get him in the general vicinity. He took it, turned left, and a curve later the interstate was out of sight.

He let the Thunderbird loaf along at forty, enjoying the scenery. The narrow two-lane asphalt road twisted and turned down the side of the mountain. On some of the curves there were two-hundred-foot cliffs, straight down.

Houses were infrequent and most of them sat well back from the road.

He knew that Frank lived in the county bordering Chattanooga, out in the country, and that he raised dogs. But that was about all he knew. He had Frank's address, but what the hell good was it if it didn't show on the map. He had Frank's phone number too, but that was strictly a last resort. It wouldn't be much of a surprise if he had to call.

He had met Frank in Nam, and a deep friendship had quickly developed between them. Sometimes months would go by without any communication, occasionally a couple of years without either hearing from the other. But the bond went beyond the need for letters or phone calls. The letters they did exchange were more like notes, short and to the point.

Glenn came to a crossroads now and turned right, which took him deeper into the country. He drove a few miles, trying to read the names of roads he passed, but most had none showing.

He passed an old country store, its tin roof turned silver in the bright sun, and turned around to find out where he was. He parked, got out and walked to the Coke machine, which looked to be as old as the store. He hadn't seen one like it since he was in grade school. He inserted two quarters—probably only took six cents when it was new—and pushed a handle down that rotated a Coke forward. He tilted his head back and took a long swallow, then nodded to an old man sitting in a cane-bottom chair.

"I wonder if you could tell me how to find Warrington Road?"

The man nodded, turned his head and spat a thick brown stream of tobacco juice several feet. He was spare, almost scrawny, dressed in faded bib overalls. Wrinkles, deep like ditches, lined his face.

"Who you lookin' for? Slater?"

Glenn's face registered his surprise. "Matter of fact, I am. What makes you ask?"

"Ain't but one other house on Warrington fer miles, and it's been empty fer months."

Glenn noted he still hadn't told him how to find the road.

"You wantin' a dog?"

"No. Frank's a friend."

"Didn't think you looked like a dog man. But if you was I got a couple, both of 'em good fighters. Jist didn't see no need to send you to another man if that's what you wanted."

The part about fighting dogs intrigued Glenn but he let it pass. The old man seemed a little too friendly and he was tired. He repeated that Frank was a friend.

The man grinned at him. "Well, you come a little too far fer Warrington."

Glenn sighed, prepared to backtrack several miles. "How much too far?"

" 'Bout a quarter mile."

The old man spat another stream, then turned and pointed in the direction Glenn had come. "See 'at road back yonder? That's Warrington. Slater lives about four miles from here, on the right. Keep a sharp eye out 'cause the driveway is hard to spot. He don't like fer people to know the place is there."

Glenn thanked him, got back in the car and on the right road. This one was gravel and narrow enough so he'd have to put two wheels on the shoulder if he met another car. But he had the road to himself.

The man was right about the driveway. Glenn didn't see it until he was past it and had to back up. Bushes grew thick on both sides, their branches almost meeting. Even the mailbox was almost completely hidden.

The driveway was dirt and turned sharply out of sight a few feet from the road. Ruts were deep enough to scrape the car's bottom. Trees covered both sides, making it impossible to see more than few feet into the brush.

At the sound of barking Glenn cracked his window, and a cacophony of barks hit him full blast. Another sharp turn brought the house in sight, and the dogs. Now he knew what the man meant—Frank was raising pit bulls.

The dogs were brown or black for the most part, but a couple were tan-and-white spotted. The barking increased to frantic yaps now that they could see him. They ran toward the car, only to be jerked to a stop by the thick chain all of them had fastened to their collars.

The house was a white frame, old, built in the shape of an I laid flat. A porch stretched across the front, with an old-fashioned wooden swing at one end. Flowerpots sat on each side of the steps, both of them containing plants that looked close to dead.

Someone behind the screen door stepped out when Glenn got out of the car. He was a huge man, six-six and probably weighed 285. As he walked down the steps he gave the impression it was all solid. Sandy hair fell past his shoulders, and an unkempt beard made him look like something wild. He wore a pair of bib overalls without a shirt beneath them.

He met Glenn in the yard, grabbed him and hugged him, hard. He pushed Glenn out at arm's length, looked him over, then shook him like a rag doll, grinning hugely.

"Goddamn. Glenn. It's good to see you, fella. You look good. When the hell did you get out?"

Glenn grinned and rubbed his upper arm, throbbing where Frank squeezed so hard. "Couple of days ago. How've you been?"

"I'm doing fine. How'd you manage to get out? I thought you said you'd be getting out around the first of next year."

Glenn explained about the early release as he followed Frank around the side of the house. Beneath a large red oak were some chairs and a table with an umbrella. Frank urged him to sit down, then went inside, returning with two bottles of beer.

"I got your letter telling about you and Darleen. Reckon I shoulda wrote back but you know how I am. I'm sorry to hear ya'll ain't together. She shoulda waited on you."

Glenn grinned, one corner of his mouth turned up, the other down. A grin a man gives to hide pain, the kind that fools no one.

"Don't blame her, Frank. She came and told me she was leaving and that was enough. They don't come any better than her so I'd be wrong to hold it against her."

He changed the subject before Frank could reply. "What did you mean you'd probably be coming to spend some time with me? It wouldn't have hurt you to be a little more specific."

Frank grinned. "Aw, I caught a little marijuana case a couple of months back. I got to go to court Monday, in fact. I'm gonna plead guilty for five years."

Glenn gestured toward the dogs. They were quiet now, most of them sleeping in the shade of their houses.

"I had no idea it was pit bulls you were raising. I didn't know you knew anything about them."

"Shit, Glenn, I grew up around it, that and roosters. My daddy fought dogs all his life. Ain't you ever been to a dog-fight?" Glenn shook his head. "Well, you're in for a treat, there's goin' to be one tonight. Dozer there is fighting."

Glenn turned his head to look at the dog. The animal lay flat on his stomach, asleep, head resting between his front legs. He looked over the large yard, counting the dog houses. Twelve. They were constructed from raw lumber, utilitarian and unpainted.

"You mean to tell me you own all these dogs and fight 'em all?"

"Naw. I own two, fight one of them. The rest are boarded out for me to keep in shape."

"What'll happen to them after you go to jail?"

Frank grinned. "Looks like you're fixin' to get in the dog business."

"What the hell are you talking about? I don't know anything about regular dogs, let alone the kind you fight."

Frank reached in a pocket and pulled out a joint. He lit it with a grin, then passed it to Glenn.

"What does a little pot case mean?" Glenn asked, holding the smoke in a few seconds before blowing it out. "Jesus, Frank. Where did you get this stuff? Tastes like what we used to smoke a long time ago."

"Tastes like Nam, huh? Grew it myself. It's some of what they busted, about two hundred plants. I didn't have much choice about copping a plea. Hell, they had pictures of me watering the plants."

Glenn's head was lit up like a Christmas tree by the fourth toke and his ass felt like it was weighted down with lead. It sounded to him like his words came out in slow motion.

"What were you planning on doing about these dogs before I showed up?"

"Let a guy who I don't really think would do a good job live here. It's a gravy train, Glenn. Rent's free."

"How come?"

"Fella that owns the place owns that white dog yonder. If there's a sorry one in the bunch it's that one. The rest pay two hundred and fifty bucks each. After feed, vitamins and medicine you'll pocket a thousand or better a month."

"What do you mean, medicine? I thought they were tough mothers."

Frank laughed. "Toughest fuckin' dog in the world. But you got to give 'em vitamins and heartworm pills in their feed every day. After a fight you'll have to doctor 'em up with antibiotics."

Glenn eyed the dogs. Each one had a ten-foot log chain around its neck, the other end connected to a stake in the ground. Jesus, he thought. Just pulling that heavy chain ought to make a dog strong.

"Aren't they supposed to be unpredictable?" He'd heard stories of pits sometimes attacking and killing both adults and children.

"Those stories are bullshit for the most part," said Frank. "There's one dog in that bunch out there who'll bite, and she's mine. You can train 'em to bite, but you'll have to damned near drive 'em insane to do it. Mama Sue is the only pit I ever had that turned mean on her own, and she waited 'til a couple years ago to start. I suppose I shoulda shot 'er, but she was a champion. Too old to fight now, but goddamn it, I love that dog."

He paused long enough to drain his beer. "A pit will naturally try to kill another dog. It was bred in 'em a couple hundred years ago and there ain't nothing you can do to stop 'em. But at the same time they were bred not to be vicious to man."

"Well, I've heard some stories about them."

"Don't pay any attention to 'em. Once in a while a dog will show signs of being mean. You need to shoot one at the first sign."

"Why?" Glenn thought of the money it cost to have a German shepard trained to attack. Killing a natural attack dog made little sense to him.

" 'Cause as a rule it means the dog is insane. And he won't just attack, he'll kill. Once you turn 'em loose there's no calling him back 'til he's finished. I can see you don't know nuthin' about 'em but I can teach you enough over the next couple of days to get by."

He pulled out another joint and held it up.

Glenn shook his head. "Damn, Frank. That one has me where I couldn't get up if I wanted to. I haven't smoked shit that strong in a long time. They growing that kind of stuff around here now?"

"Yeah, quite a bit. You know there was a lot of guys like

us over yonder. Some of our daddies made moonshine. We discovered it don't cost nearly as much to grow pot as it does to make whiskey. That reminds me, I better tell you something about this place."

He gestured to the north. "There's eleven acres here. Go any direction but that way."

"Somebody got a crop?"

"Yeah, and he's got it protected too. He learned a few tricks from Charlie, Glenn, so keep away. It's booby-trapped like you ain't seen in a while."

"Yours?"

"Naw, you know better'n that. If it was I'd take and show it to you. Just go on about your business of taking care of the dogs and you'll never even see the guy it does belong to."

"Frank, you talk like I'm going to do it. I don't know a damn thing about dogs."

"I can teach you enough to get by between now and Monday. Besides, there'll be somebody here to help you, at least for a while."

Glenn rubbed his beard. "I don't know. I don't think I'd like living way out here in the boonies."

"My ass. The boonies is having to walk two days just to find a grass hut with a water buffalo tied out front. You're twelve miles from the edge of Chattanooga."

"I drove farther than that coming out here."

"Only because you don't know the roads. I need somebody taking care of the dogs that I can trust. You gonna let me down?"

"You're putting me on a spot, you bastard, and you know it. Yeah, okay, I'll give it a shot."

Frank changed the subject abruptly. "You ever want to go back, Glenn?"

There was no need to ask where. "Not to the field. Hell, no, not that. Sometimes I think about the times we had, though." He looked closely at Frank. "What about you?"

"Sometimes I miss it. It ever bother you, the memories?"

"Once in a while I might have a bad dream. But nothing I can't push aside. You sound like it might be working on you."

Frank closed his eyes and rubbed them. When he opened them Glenn saw that old "thousand-yard stare" in them. He could have been seeing anything, but whatever it was, it was in his mind and not the woods his eyes were pointed at.

"That's when I want to go back the most, Glenn, when it's bothering me. Like maybe I didn't do enough and wishing I could go back and change it."

"We did what we could, Frank, all they'd let us do. We couldn't do more than that."

The pot floated Frank back to the first day he'd seen Glenn. He was in one of the helicopters that went in to pick up what they thought would be four bodies. Frank spotted him first, lying amid hundreds of spent casings glittering in the sunlight.

It was Frank's first combat mission. Bodies lay on the ground, arms dangling by strips of skin from a few, a leg all shot away from one. Heads were shattered, brainpans emptied, and intestines trailed from several of them. They were not lying gracefully like they did in the movies. These bodies had been picked up by bullets hitting with a force of more than two thousand pounds and flung to the ground. Only in Hollywood was there dignity in combat death.

Frank was also one of the first to reach Glenn. He could not believe anyone could be alive after losing so much blood, but Glenn was not just alive, he was conscious and talking.

The medic began feeding him morphine and plasma, asking where he was from to check for shock.

Glenn said Tennessee and Frank blurted out, "Hey, me too."

Glenn looked at him from the ground. "You know, I wish

to hell I listened to those folks back there who tried to talk me out of this."

He talked halfway to the chopper, his blood dripping from the stretcher, until the morphine knocked him out. Frank told him later it was the bravest thing he figured he'd ever see. Glenn said he kept talking because he was afraid he'd die if he stopped.

But it didn't stop Frank's belief that Glenn was double-barrel tough. He transferred to the same unit and was waiting on Glenn when he got out of the hospital.

"I never saw anybody else stay as calm as you were the first day I saw you," he was saying now. "I think I would've panicked."

Glenn looked off in the distance, not wanting to go back to those days. "Get that shit out of your head, Frank. Don't be afraid you'd have lost it if you were hit. Very few panic. Your mind tells you it won't do any good."

"Maybe so. But sometimes it bothers me, being so scared and always trying to cover it up."

"We were all scared, Frank. All of us that had any sense were. It was a shitty time, that's all. I wish I could help you with it but we both know there's nothing anyone else can do. I just don't let myself think about it. But I know that doesn't mean you can turn off your thoughts about it."

"You're right." Frank's eyes cleared and his mood sounded better when he spoke again. "Come on in and let me show you the house."

The living room took up all the front, dominated by a pool table in the center. It was obvious Frank lived alone. A light film of dust lay on everything and clothes were scattered about. Magazines, most of them *Soldier of Fortune*, lay wherever Frank had finished them. The furniture was mismatched. Two couches faced each other from across the room, the pool table between them. An easy chair of still another pattern sat a few feet from one of the couches. Glenn felt himself drawn to the place.

A bedroom off the kitchen was filled with women's clothes, and Glenn remarked on it. "Thought you said you lived alone."

"Well, I do, mostly. That's Tina's room."

"Who's Tina?"

Frank laughed softly. "Tina's Tina. That's who I said would be here to help you with the dogs. She knows damn near as much about 'em as I do. You'll just have to meet her, which'll be this weekend. I talked to her last week. She's in Tucson but she said she'd be here in time to go to court with me."

"You and her go together or something?"

Frank laughed again. "We did at one time but now it's just or something. When she's here we meet in the night once in a while. Nobody has a collar on Tina. She stays with some guy a while and then moves on."

"She a whore?" Glenn asked it matter-of-fact.

"No. She's just a girl who grew up in one foster home after another and knows there's a lot of world out there besides Chattanooga. She wants to see it but ain't got the money so she'll hook with a guy that does. Wait'll you meet her. You'll like her. She's good people."

Frank opened the refrigerator and took out two more beers. He handed one to Glenn and clinked his bottle against it.

"To tomorrow, Glenn. To hell with yesterday."

"I'll go for that. Yesterday wasn't worth a damn anyway."

CHAPTER EIGHT

DARLEEN SIPPED at a beer no longer cold, not trying to hide her irritation. She hated beer but couldn't order a mixed drink if she wanted to. Anything other than beer was illegal in Edwards County.

She hated this small tavern too, mostly because the air conditioner was too small to overcome the hot night. Never mind her feelings about the little hick town of Belton. Right now Darleen was also doing a pretty good job of hating Larry.

She glared at him as ZZ Top suddenly blasted from the speakers. He stood at the jukebox, tapping his foot, looking for other selections just as loud and rowdy.

The burglary was going down tonight, and here they sat drinking in a tavern. What went through his mind? she wondered. Okay, like Glenn said, he was a kid, but that was no excuse. She'd known not to drink before pulling a job long before she was Larry's age. The only reason she was here was to make sure he kept the alcohol to a minimum.

Darleen wished she knew how to open a safe. Then Larry could stay in this shitty little tavern as long as he wanted.

He came to the table and sat down, a fresh beer in his hand. With a wink he put his arm around her and tried to kiss her. Darleen shook his arm off and turned her head away.

"Behave, Larry. And I wish you wouldn't drink that. It's your fifth one."

He smiled. "Relax, sweetpea. I could be blind drunk and still open that cracker box of Sherill's. I'm good."

She decided to take the smile off his face. "Really? As good as you are at other things when you're drunk, I suppose."

"I'll tell you what I can do, drunk or sober, and that's whip your ass, Darleen."

She took a draw from her cigarette and exhaled slowly, looking at him. "Yes, you probably could. But I'll tell you what you *can't* do. You can't stay awake forever."

The ice in her eyes convinced Larry she meant each word. He might be too scared to bust her one but damned if he'd let a woman have the last word.

"To hell with you, Darleen. I'll be fine when it's time to do the job. Until then I'm going to find me some company that's more pleasant."

He got up and stalked to the bar, where he started a conversation with a bored bartender. Darleen lit another cigarette, glad to see him go. She thought better when he wasn't clinging to her side.

She wondered if Larry did what most small criminals did —see a bunch of ones and think it was a pile of money. If Glenn taught her anything it was to see for herself. She could hear him saying, "It's the number-one rule. Believe it." She pushed Glenn from her mind. She'd broken other rules of his and come out okay.

One thing was for sure. After this was over the first thing she intended to do was get rid of Larry. There was certainly no love on her part so there'd be no heartache. But there was still one little problem. She hadn't yet figured out how to split up with him and keep all the money at the same time. If that failed there would be plenty of heartache. Darleen had lots of love for money.

She checked her watch, then got up and moved past Larry without speaking. He came out a minute later, still sulking. He saw Darleen behind the wheel and opened his mouth, but closed it. The set of her jaw said he might not even ride if he pushed it.

They rode the few miles into the country saying very little. Tension was thick, but even if it wasn't there would've been little reason to talk. The job had been planned and discussed for months.

Darleen turned off on an old logging trail less than a quarter mile behind Sherill's house, parking a few feet from the road. She looked up the trail as she got out of the car, wishing she knew for sure if it led behind Sherill's house. She dreaded the trek through the dark woods much more than the burglary itself. She knew what was in houses, not woods. But the thought of the money waiting was enough to make her step out.

A branch whipping across her face startled her. Larry better be right about this, she thought. If there's nothing in that house I'll leave him, all right. I'll also hang his little ass by his balls and leave him hanging.

Shortly after they met, Larry had bragged about the money he'd seen in this Sherill's house. He told her he began dealing with the man while still in high school, selling him gold and jewelry. They went to look at the house, which ordinarily would have been easy to get into. But dealing with thieves on a daily basis had made Sherill smarter than most. The biggest hurdle to overcome was Sherill himself.

One, he owned a rough honky-tonk right across the road from his house. Two, the bastard was hardly ever gone, was either at home or at the bar. That problem, though, had solved itself; Sherill was on his twice-yearly fishing trip.

The house sat on top of a hill four hundred yards away

from the tavern at the bottom of it. Roy, Sherill's son, lived in a mobile home halfway between them. There was an alarm of sorts, crude, but until now effective. Since someone was always there, or close by, Sherill did not feel the need for an expensive system. Wires buried underground connected all three buildings, plugged to hidden microphones in each one. Turned full volume, a whisper would wake up Rip Van Winkle. When Sherill was in the tavern, the mike in his home was turned on, or vice-versa.

Actually, it wasn't a bad idea, since the speakers in the tavern were placed out in the open for anyone to see. Sherill made a habit of pointing out the speakers to those he was worried about. Fear of the man restrained any of the local boys from taking him off. That was one thing Larry had neglected to mention, just what a dangerous son of a bitch Sherill was.

Larry now knelt at the side of the house, where the wire went underground. One snip of the wire cutters and the microphone was dead, unable to snitch. He ran across the yard, back to the edge of the woods where Darleen waited. The tavern was still open. If there was a safety feature against such acts they'd soon know. Nothing happened.

An hour later the last customer came out. Music from the jukebox drifted up to where they waited. They watched a customer urinate beside his car before driving away.

Five minutes later they saw Roy lock up and walk across the road, carrying the day's receipts in a paper sack. He walked around to the rear of the trailer and went in the back door.

"How old did you say he was?" Darleen said to Larry.

"Thirty-two, thirty-four. I want a cigarette."

"He might see it. Wonder if he lives alone."

"I doubt it. But if he treats 'em like he did his wife you can bet they don't stay long." Larry got up and started through the woods back down the hill.

She followed, holding her arms crossed in front of her

face to keep from running into branches. When they were
out of sight of the trailer he stopped and Darleen asked him
what he meant.

"He beat the hell out of her. Put her in the hospital."

He took a draw on the cigarette, and the glow showed
him grinning. "Not because she pissed him off. He gets his
kicks that way. I was still living here when it happened.
She was in the hospital a month or more."

"What'd she do when she got out?"

He took a final draw and ground the cigarette beneath
his heel. "She left him. What do you think she did?"

"She should have shot him on the way out."

It was three in the morning before Roy turned off the
lights and went to bed, and Larry hurried across the yard
to a side door hidden from the road. Darleen followed close
behind him, glad there were no dogs to worry about. He
inserted a tension bar, followed by a pick.

Sixty seconds later he pushed the door open, bowed with
a flourish and swept his arm into the darkness of the house.
"After you, m'lady."

She sighed and pushed him forward. "Stop playing,
Larry. Let's get this done and get out of here."

The safe, an ancient square-door Mosler on wheels, built
back in the late Forties, stood beside a dresser in the bedroom. They hurried around the room pulling the drapes,
then hung blankets over them before turning on a lamp.

Larry wrestled the safe into the middle of the room, taking a break once to catch his breath. Even with wheels, a
four-hundred-pound safe won't be easy to move over carpet.

"Is it the kind you said was so easy?"

Larry heard the worry in her voice. "Like I said, a
cracker box. Relax and look around. Come back in five
minutes."

I bet I leave you alone, she thought. But she did get up
and look around the room. No antiques or good paintings,

just plain, practical furniture, the signs of an old man living alone. In place of paintings there were eight-by-ten black and whites of Sherill holding up a fish. She stepped in the closet that had suspenders hanging from the door, and stepped out quickly.

"Larry, come look. There's another safe in here."

He looked up but stayed where he was. "Is it like this one?"

"They look alike."

"Then I'll get it next. No sweat."

First out of the bag was a ten-pound, short-handled brass sledgehammer. Larry said they made less noise than lead ones. Next he pulled out a six-inch center punch and laid it to the side. He stood up and tapped the sledgehammer against the dial a couple of times, then drew back and hit it with everything he had. Darleen flinched at the noise, but said nothing because the dial flew clean across the room. He looked at her and grinned.

"Is it open?" she asked.

"Not yet."

He squatted and lined up the punch in the center of the hole the dial used to occupy. One hard whack with the hammer drove the tumblers through the plastic plate. The "dogs," the steel rods in the top and corner bottom that actually locked the door, fell back down inside the door with a click. Larry turned the handle and the door swung open like he'd used the combination.

They both caught their breath when the contents were revealed. Money was stacked in a row, tall stacks of it. Four hands began taking it out and stuffing it in a pillowcase.

Darleen scooped the money out eagerly. She could see it was a bigger score than Larry had estimated, and there was still another safe.

Larry pulled out a sack, looked in it and threw it on the bed.

"What was that?"

"Some kind of VCR tapes," he said, going back to taking out the money.

She retrieved the sack and put it in the pillowcase. "We want 'em. If they're in the safe then there must be something important on them."

Larry followed the same procedure on the other safe, but got only as far as knocking the dial off. He felt around in the hole the dial had occupied, swore and rocked back on his heels.

Darleen hovered behind him. "What's wrong? Can't you open it?"

"Not by punching it. This one's got a metal plate. These bastards came along in the early fifties. And they been getting tougher ever since. I'll have to peel it. No big deal."

He left the closet and came back with a medium-size crowbar. He raised the sledgehammer over his head and brought it down as hard as he could on the top corner opposite the hinges. The door buckled, not much, but enough to knock it out of flush with the rest of the safe. He inserted the crowbar in the gap, put a foot against the safe and pulled back.

Beads of sweat appeared on his forehead and for an instant Darleen thought it wouldn't open. But he found a little more to give and the rivets broke loose, popping like gunshots. He stumbled back and would have fallen if Darleen hadn't caught him.

The steel plate of the door hung by one row of rivets, revealing the concrete behind it. He knelt and used the punch to gouge out a hole in the same corner in which he'd inserted the crowbar. The concrete was more protection from fire than thieves, about as tough to dig through as plaster. It took only a few seconds to dig the concrete from around the dogs, then he reached in, flipped them back, turned the handle and opened the safe.

They stood there staring at what lay inside the safe, neither of them able to move. They had no idea how much money they'd taken from the other safe, but a glance told them this one was as good. Ounce bars of gold, stacked and gleaming in the dim light. A coin collection. Small, supple leather drawstring bags.

Darleen took one out, opened it and poured diamonds into her palm. She opened another one to find a dozen rubies. She didn't bother to open anymore. She just kept saying, "Oh, boy" as she emptied the safe.

CHAPTER NINE

FRANK TURNED the van into a narrow dirt lane a few miles from the house. The ruts here were even deeper than those in his driveway, and bushes scraped the sides of the van as they crept along. A man stood a few feet back in the woods, a shotgun leaning against a tree, invisible from the road.

"What's up?" Glenn asked. "Why all the security?"

A front wheel slipped into a deep rut, causing Frank to bump his head on the roof. He rubbed the spot.

"The law is down on dogfights." He hawked and spat out the window, then spoke again, looking disgusted.

"Them damned ASCPA, or whatever they're called, raise hell about mistreating the dogs by letting 'em fight. Like I told you, a pit is gonna fight, I don't care how you raise it. But they claim it's cruel. Now we have to be extra careful. Nobody gets in after the fight starts and nobody leaves 'til it's over."

He looked at Glenn with a sly grin, a lock of hair hiding one eye. " 'Course, the shotgun is in case somebody tries to rob the fight."

They reached the end of the lane that widened into a clearing. Cars and pickups were parked around an old barn that looked in danger of collapsing. Two wooden tables, each with a large tub on it, were fifty feet apart. A group of men stood around each table talking and laughing. Most of them wore jeans and work shirts. A couple even wore bib overalls and brogans. Glenn asked what the tubs were for.

Frank opened the rear doors of the van and pulled the dog cage to him. "Washing the dogs. That's what we got to do now. It's a safeguard. You got some that'll try something like soaking his dog in a nicotine solution. A dog ain't gonna bite once he tastes it."

"You ever do it?"

Frank looked at him calmly. "Nope. Ain't ever been accused of it either. I pity the poor bastard claims I do."

He opened the cage, grabbed Dozer by the collar and fastened a rope to it. The dog jumped to the ground, pulling against the rope. His ears stood up at the sound of the other dogs and his tail stuck straight out, quivering.

Frank beamed. "See what I mean. Dozer knows he's gonna fight. Look at 'im and tell me he ain't looking forward to it."

It was true, the dog was excited. Even Glenn, knowing nothing about dogs, could see Dozer knew what he was here for, and was more than willing to rush into it. He reached down and patted the dog.

"Dozer. That's a helluva name. Why'd you name him that?"

"I didn't." Frank picked Dozer up and put him in a harness to be weighed. Thirty-seven pounds and four ounces, three ounces less than the other dog.

Frank wore a satisfied look as he turned to the man writing down the weight. "Told you I'd bring him in under thirty-eight, Jim. Lookit that, twelve ounces to spare."

He turned back to Glenn. "You let a dog name himself, Glenn. When this'n was maybe four months old it was plain he had a lot of bulldozer in him. He'd just push his way through the other puppies with his chest. What else would you name 'im?"

He walked over and handed the rope to a gray-haired man in his fifties, then took a black dog out of a cage behind the man. Each man lifted the other's dog and put them in a tub.

Frank spoke in a low voice as he washed the dog. "Dozer's gonna whip this dog, Glenn. The odds are against him, but that's all the better in the long run. It's a good chance for you to add a little something to your bankroll."

Glenn looked the dog over, standing quietly while Frank poured rinse water over his coat. It was solid black with a chest wide and deep, and its jaw muscles stood out an inch past the mouth.

"What kind of odds?"

"Eight to five. Trust me, buddy. I'm giving you a lock."

Glenn pulled his money out. The wad was too thick to fold so he had rolled it and put a rubber band around it. He counted off five thousand in hundreds and offered them to Frank.

"You think you could get a couple of 'em to go together and cover five grand?"

Frank smiled as he took the money with wet fingers. "You really don't know nothing about dogfights. That's a nice bet, but it ain't no real big 'un either. The owner of this dog will cover it himself."

"That surprises me. To tell you the truth, it don't look like these guys could raise five grand between all of them."

"Well, they can. It ain't the kind of place you wear your good clothes to. It's a dogfight and things get bloody. But it's serious business. I reckon it'd be safe to say there'll be a hundred thousand or better change hands by the time the last fight is over."

"How much of your money's riding on it?"

"Fifteen hundred. I'd have more, but it's all I got left after paying my lawyer."

"Well, I just hope that lock is on good and tight."

Frank finished washing the dog, took Dozer back, then

walked a few feet to talk to another man. He looked to be in his late forties, dressed a little nicer than most of the others, wearing slacks and loafers. Glenn saw them glance in his direction, and the man gave a short nod. Frank waved him over.

"This is Ronnie Davis, Glenn. He's the owner of the house."

Glenn offered his hand and saw a diamond ring glint on Ronnie's little finger. "I'm glad to meet you, Ronnie."

"Frank was telling me you'd be a good man to stay there and take care of the dogs. Think you might be interested? I want somebody there I can count on. I'll be glad to give you the same deal I gave Frank."

"Yeah, I'd like to do that. I don't know what all Frank said, but I won't be running off and leaving you in a bind."

"That's what he said, and that's all I'd ever ask of you. The place is yours."

A signal Glenn missed must have gone out, because everyone began to drift inside the barn.

"That's us, Glenn," said Frank. "We're in the pit first. I'm handling Dozer so I'll be in it. Nobody else is allowed except the ref, but you stand close and watch. You'll probably be in there next time."

Glenn ducked under the low door, looking around as soon as he was inside. The pit turned out to be only three feet down in the ground. He judged it to be ten by ten feet, bordered by a wire fence eighteen inches high. A two-hundred-watt bulb hung directly over the pit, casting the rest of the barn in shadow.

On two sides were bleachers, three high, made of rough planking. Sixty, eighty people sat on them, and he was surprised at the number of women. Smoke hung in the air, thick dark blue clouds of it.

He saw large amounts of money being rapidly counted, changing hands and being counted again. Bets were called out, with heads nodding yes, others shaking no. The atmosphere was jovial; neighbors called greetings or jeered the other's choice of dog.

Someone called, "Gentlemen, face your dogs."

Glenn turned to see Frank already in the pit and facing him. He spun around, each hand dug tightly in the sides of Dozer's neck, straining to keep the dog between his legs.

Dozer tried to lunge forward when he saw the dog across the pit. He dug his hind feet into the ground and lifted his front legs, pawing the air. Frank's forearms bulged from the effort of holding the dog. He talked steadily, and his voice seemed to inflame Dozer even more.

"Get it, Dozer, get it. Work 'im, boy, gonna work 'im, ain'tcha. Yeah, you are."

The referee called, "Release your dogs."

Frank let go and Dozer ran forward, growling deep in this throat. Across the pit the other dog rushed to meet him.

Glenn, having seen only ordinary dogs confront each other, was amazed at how little sound they made. The average dog only wants to establish dominance, and usually it's done with more snarls and barks than actual biting. When the other dog submits, the aggression is withdrawn. Pits are different. They come to eliminate the threat forever.

The dogs met in the center, each rearing and trying to knock the other off his feet. The black dog, Tracker, hit first and hardest, forcing Dozer to give ground. His hind feet dug deep, trying to find a purchase as Tracker pushed him back.

The dogs whipped their heads back and forth, trying to get a good hold, so fast Glenn could not follow. Blood oozed from a half-dozen bites on each dog. Suddenly Tracker ducked his head beneath Dozer's and sank his teeth into Dozer's throat.

A roar came from the crowd. Glenn figured it would soon be over, nothing could live with its throat ripped out. Tracker's head, directly below Dozer's, pulled up, forcing

Dozer's head back. Dozer stood there, able to bite nothing but air, and Glenn saw his five thousand dollars sprouting wings.

But fifteen minutes later nothing had happened. Tracker still had Dozer by the throat, and now he walked him in a steady circle, bumping him in an effort to knock him down. But all Tracker had was hide, and for the last ten minutes his teeth could be heard grinding together.

Glenn listened as Frank and the other man argued about breaking up the dogs and scratching them again. It was plain Tracker could not seriously hurt Dozer, and after fifteen minutes a break could be made, provided both parties agreed.

Frank refused, grinning. "No way, Chuck. You know damn well Tracker'll have that piece chewed off in a—"

It happened then. Tracker's head jerked back, a chunk of skin and hair hanging from his mouth. The move surprised him. Not once had Dozer whimpered, and the flesh tearing loose did not faze him either. Instead, he was a blur, moving forward before Tracker regained his balance. Dozer turned slightly just before contact, enough to hit Tracker with his shoulder and knock him onto his back.

For a split second Tracker lay there, exposed from throat to nuts, and the second was all Dozer needed to sink his teeth where the kidney would be, going deep.

Frank slapped his thigh. "Goddamn, Glenn, look at 'im. The son of a bitch is locking."

Glenn watched Dozer shake his head back and forth, work his teeth deeper into Tracker, recalling what Frank had told him about a pit's bite. Their jaws didn't really lock, but they did exert between sixteen hundred and two thousand pounds of pressure per square inch. Almost three times the power of a ninety-pound Doberman.

It doesn't really matter, thought Glenn. With that much power he might as well be locking. It would be damned hard to pry loose that much force.

The crowd roared its approval, many standing for a better look. The appeal was lost on Glenn. He found himself watching the people instead of the dogs. Their expressions were the same as those worn at a prizefight when one of the boxers got hurt. Another roar called his attention back to the fight.

Dozer had chewed into an artery and the bright red blood squirted high in the air, spraying the referee and soaking Dozer's muzzle. Glenn turned away, pushed through the crowd and outside. He walked to a pickup and leaned against the hood, his back to the barn. He pulled a cigarette out and lit it, prepared to wait out the next three fights.

The one with Dozer was soon over. Frank and a couple of other men came out, the men congratulating Frank. Glenn saw the tall man looking around for him and called his name.

Frank came over, carrying Dozer in his arms, and Glenn fell in step with him. Dozer's tongue lolled from his mouth, which was still covered with blood, and Dozer would swipe at it with his tongue, then lift his head and try to lick Frank.

Glenn opened the rear doors of the van and Frank put Dozer inside, examining the wounds while Glenn held him. When he was satisfied none of the bites needed immediate attention he poured peroxide over them.

"That'll hold 'im 'til we get home and I can put a couple of stitches in the one on his throat." He looked at Glenn. "Where'd you go, buddy? I figured you went to piss but you never came back. Hey, how's that for makin' a quick eight grand? C'mon, let's put Dozer in the cage and get back in there."

"You go, I'll just stay out here."

Frank stared at him. "You mean you don't like it?"

"That's right."

"Why?"

"I just don't see any sense in it." He held up a hand. "I

believe what you say, Frank, about 'em naturally fighting. But there isn't anything natural about putting two dogs in a pit."

"But you done told the man you'd take care of the dogs, Glenn. We got to fight another one of the dogs tomorrow night."

"One has nothing to do with the other. I'll keep the dogs in good shape and take good care of 'em. But I won't ever watch 'em chew each other up again."

Frank looked perplexed. Glenn reached up and slapped him on the shoulder.

"Don't take it personal, Frank. I'm not going to join the protesters. If you like it, enjoy it."

Frank reached in his pocket and pulled out a thick wad of money. "Well, here. This is yours. I more or less forced you to make the bet and I'm sorry about it."

"Why? I got nothing against making money. Take it back with you. Try to make me another eight grand."

Glenn spent a minute petting and talking to Dozer, then got in the van to get a beer from the cooler. He left the back doors open and strolled to the front to lean against the windshield.

The moon was full and almost directly overhead, looking so cold on such a hot night.

He was on his fourth beer and had his head tilted back, looking at the moon, when a woman spoke behind him.

"Feeling better?"

He looked down and turned, up to now unaware of her presence. She repeated the question. There was enough light to see she was good-looking, in her thirties. She wore jeans that stretched across a generous ass, and a western shirt. A straw cowboy hat perched on top of short dark hair.

"I didn't feel bad. Just wasn't interested."

"I could tell it was your first fight."

He looked at her deadpan. "How could you tell that?"

The woman eyed him, fiddling with her hair, standing hipshot. Glenn looked her over now from boots to hat.

"From the way you were looking things over," she said, after he came back to her face.

"I guess that was a giveaway. I'm Glenn and you're . . ."

"Sharon." She leaned back on the van next to him, lifting her arms to run her fingers through her hair, stretching the shirt tight across her breasts.

"Why'd you come if you don't like it?"

"A friend thought I might. You come often?"

"Yes. But not here. My husband and I live in Georgia. His dog just lost the second fight."

Husband was a bad signal. "Is he why you come?"

"I said his dog. I've got my own, a better one. Mine won last week in Dalton."

She looked directly at him. "You got a cigarette?"

Glenn gave her one and lit it for her. "Why do you like 'em so much?"

She bent her head, looking up at him through the flame. "They make me horny as hell."

He turned to face her, propping an elbow on the van. "Really? Now that's something I could really get interested in."

She stared back. "I bet you could."

"*Sharon.*" His tone was pure don't-make-me-come-get-your-ass. He looked at her and shrugged. Husbands had first claim.

"I hate that," he said.

Sharon stuck the tip of her tongue out and licked the corner of her mouth. "Me too."

He watched her walk back to her husband, hips swinging. She linked an arm through her husband's and walked into the barn without looking back. Glenn looked up at the moon again.

"This shit's getting old," he told it.

CHAPTER TEN

GEORGE SHERILL stood in the doorway, hands shoved deep in his khaki pants, staring at the busted safe. He was tired, the result of a sleepless night and the flight back from his fishing trip in Florida. Anger mixed with exhaustion in the lines in his face. His eyes were near-slits, what little of them showed was the color of coal, and reflected about as much softness. He spoke without looking at the man standing in the hallway.

"I told Jackie to sleep in the house while I was gone. Why wasn't he in here?"

"I had 'im picking up a car in North Carolina. I thought it'd be safe with the mike on, daddy."

Sherill flinched inwardly. Why was he stuck with a son thirty-four who still said "daddy" with a whine? He considered pointing out that sending Jackie—who would have been totally useless if not for his car-stealing talents—to North Carolina had ended up causing the loss of hundreds of thousands of dollars. But he let it pass.

"When did they get in?"

"I ain't sure. Jackie woke me up when he come back with the car and I came up here to get some coffee. That was around nine and I called you as soon as I seen somebody had broke in."

81

Sherill turned and walked back down the hall, using his slight frame to shoulder his son out of the way. He sat on a couch in the living room and stared up at the massive oak beams that ran the length of the room.

Roy came in behind him, sidled in actually, and sat in a wingback chair. Except for the eyes they looked nothing alike. The son was tall and fat, with a beer belly that poked from under a T-shirt that hung over a pair of faded corduroy jeans.

"I didn't want to call the law and report it because of them tapes, daddy."

The old man said nothing. Roy picked up a tiny figurine of an elephant, its head tilted back in a soundless trumpet. He shifted it from hand to hand, to have something to do with them. Its intricate beauty was lost on him. After a moment he set it back down on the table.

"I tole you them tapes would cause more trouble than they were worth. As soon as Dodd finds out about 'em there'll be hell to pay."

Sherill shook his head. One good thing about dying, he thought. I won't be around to see it all go to hell when Roy gets his hands on everything.

"Dodd's the least of our problems. I put 'im in office." He looked at Roy sharply. "Who all knows about this?"

"Just Jackie."

"Then you talk to 'im. Let 'im know I don't want a word said to nobody about it."

Roy looked perplexed. "How you figger on gettin' any of it back, daddy, if we don't report it?"

"Whoever done it will be in touch with us. Wantin' to sell 'em back to us."

The sound of tires crunching across gravel came through the open windows, stopping further talk. Both men stood to watch a silver Buick make its way up the steep drive. Sherill stood in front of Roy and missed the shadow of fear that flickered across his face.

"What'n hell is Dodd coming out this morning for?"
Sherill turned and looked at Roy. "You sure Jackie ain't
said nothing to nobody?"

"He couldn't a tole nobody, daddy. He ain't left my place
since comin' back. He's down there asleep right now."

The tone was sincere but a current of guilt ran beneath it,
not missed by Sherill. "Goddamn it, Roy, you know more'n
you're telling."

He turned back to the window, speaking over his shoulder. "You go on down and open the bar. It shoulda been
opened two hours ago. I reckon I'll be finding out what
you've done in a minute."

He moved to the door while Roy went out a side door to
avoid the man in the Buick. Another move not lost on the
old man.

THE BUICK eased to a stop behind Sherill's black Lincoln
town car. The car door opened and a pair of size twelve
Italian loafers appeared on the ground below it. The man
wearing them seemed to unfold in stages until he stood
outside the car. In spite of the heat he wore a tan Dacron
sport coat, buttoned once.

Sherill opened the front door. "Morning, Phil. How'n
hell did you know I was back?"

Phillip Dodd, sheriff of Edwards County, nodded to
Sherill as he walked between the cars. "I didn't, George.
Truth is, I came out to talk to Roy."

Sherill pushed the screen door open and stepped back.
"Well, come on in anyway."

Dodd followed him through the house, sinking deeply
into the lush blue carpet, and into the kitchen. He took a
seat at the table and accepted a cup of coffee.

Both gave full attention to sugar and cream, one not
wanting to speak and the other not wanting to hear.

Dodd sipped his coffee, then cleared his throat. "I hate having to come out, George, but Roy's done it again."

Sherill said nothing. He stirred his coffee slowly while looking at Dodd.

Dodd gazed back, thinking it really didn't matter to him who that bastard hurt. He cleared his throat, and the act made him angry at himself, implying he was afraid to speak out.

"Roy and that Dotson boy, Jackie, raped Janice Kirk night before last."

Sherill smiled condescendingly. "Now, Phil, rape's an awful strong word."

Dodd held the level gaze, speaking flatly. "What they did was rape. They—"

"They got a little split-tail drunk, Phil, then put the make on 'er. Tell me you never done the same thing when you was a kid."

"What they did was fill a minor, a sixteen-year-old kid, full of booze and downers. Then they raped her."

Sherill held a hand up to interrupt, but Dodd went on, raising his voice to override Sherill's. "They raped her front and back, George. That little girl had to have stitches in her asshole, for Christ's sake. That sort of takes the edge off of seduction, wouldn't you say?"

He spoke again before Sherill had a chance to. "No. I never did anything like that when I was a kid. Did you?"

"Now you listen to me," Sherill said, "I've run that *innocent* little girl away from the Spoke a coupla times myself. Don't tell me them boys raped her. They mighta got a little rough, but that don't make it rape."

Dodd was silent a moment. He chose his words carefully, aware of how much power sat across from him.

"They fed her so much shit she passed out. When she came to she tried to get away and got one eye almost knocked out for her efforts. They also loosened a couple of teeth. Still want to call it seduction?"

"Why'd you come out?" Sherill asked. "You knew I was in Florida." He fixed his eyes on Dodd, with the same expression as when he looked at the safes. "I think you was planning on doin' more than just talkin' to Roy."

Dodd met his gaze. "Why aren't you in Florida? Roy call you about Janice?"

Sherill ignored it and he went on. "Yes, I was, George. I was going to take his ass to jail until you got back."

"Well, I'm here so you can forget about that."

Dodd crossed one leg over the other, resting his ankle on his knee. He clasped huge hands around the knee that stuck up above the table.

"You being here doesn't change what he did. Janice's daddy is plenty hot and wants him in jail."

"Naw, he don't. Roy might get outta hand once in a while but he knows what he's doin'. You go talk to Kirk, find out how much he wants."

Dodd showed his anger for the first time. His dark, thick eyebrows wrinkled together across a beaked nose. Blood rose to the surface, giving his deeply tanned face the coloring of an Indian.

"I've done that twice already, George, and each time I swore I wouldn't do it again. I didn't run for sheriff with the intention of giving Roy free rein. If he can't keep his dick in his pants something's got to be done."

Sherill slapped a palm on the table, rattling the cups and saucers. "Well, jail ain't gonna be one of the things you want done so forget about it."

A strained silence followed until Sherill spoke again, softer this time. "How much money have you made under the table this year, Phil?"

Dodd folded a napkin and soaked up the spilled coffee from the saucer. His stoic face revealed none of the bile welling up.

"A little over forty thousand." He was aware that speaking the words took away the power of his argument.

"I'll admit Roy goes too far now and agin, and I'll put the brakes on his ass. You got my word on it. But like you said, you've already made forty grand this year—because of me. Go talk to Kirk. The man's bin a cropper all his life. You show 'im two thousand dollars and he'll snatch it outta your hand. Peanuts compared to what you make."

Sherill paused, black eyes flat as a snake's. "Or were you figgering on just serving one term? You know damn well I can see to it that it works out that way."

Dodd reached inside his coat and pulled out a package of Life Savers. He wrinkled his nose at the green one, dropped it in an ashtray, and put a red one in his mouth. He crunched it a couple of times.

Everybody gets something, he thought. Roy gets his rocks off. Janice's daddy gets a little money. I get the job of giving it to him. Janice got raped. When he spoke, his voice was like his expression.

"That's true, George. And I'm the first one to know it. But we both know I could hurt you pretty bad on my way out. No, I'm not ready to give the job up, so don't push your weight around. It just might scare me."

He turned his head, and two pinpoints glowed in his eyes. "Running a chop shop and a couple of bootleg joints is one thing. Raping a kid is something else."

He stood up, and even from five feet away he towered over Sherill. "A lot of people are getting fed up with Roy's shit. If you don't bring him in line it won't matter who you back next time. Even you can't tell people who to vote for if they're afraid their daughters will end up getting raped across the road."

He turned, not giving Sherill a chance to reply, and walked through the house and outside. He walked down the drive, his six-four giving him long strides. The 245 pounds gave him a beefy frame and set his feet firmly in the gravel.

He got in the Buick, backed it around and started down

the long drive, riding the brake lightly. He stared at the building across the road. The Broke Spoke—honky-tonk supreme. The only bar outside the city limits in the entire county, and had been for almost the last forty years.

He turned left and gave the car gas, his foot heavy on the accelerator. He stared at the bar as he passed, thinking, One more, Roy. That's all it'll take and to hell with your old man. I'll come for your ass.

CHAPTER ELEVEN

Roy SHERILL slid a cooler open, pulled a Pabst for the one customer in the tavern and pushed it across the bar. The splayed fingers of a weatherbeaten roofer wrapped around the can.

"It started off hot today," the man said just before tilting the can for a long drink.

Roy swept the wrinkled five across the bar with sausage fingers, watching Dodd come down the drive. His small, oddly girlish mouth, emphasized by fat jowls, lifted in a sneer.

Dodd, in turn, sent the sneer into venomous hatred. As he drove past he extended his arm and fired an imaginary pistol. He could not see in the windows but Roy could see out, and Dodd knew he was watching.

And Roy knew he knew it.

The roofer tried for small talk again. "Yeah, them goddamned roofs take a lot out of a man when it's this hot."

Roy punched the register open. "Well, you ain't ona roof. Right now you're under one that's air-conditioned so quit bitching."

After giving the roofer his change he stepped through a door beside the register that went into a kitchen. To the right was a dining table, and he shook the shoulder of the person whose face was resting on it.

"Wake up, Jackie, goddamn it."

Jackie raised his head, eyes swollen with sleep. He was young, maybe nineteen. Bad teeth showed in a narrow, ferretlike face. Brown hair fell to his shoulders, a red bandanna tied around his forehead kept it out of his eyes.

"Damn, Roy. I ain't had two hours of sleep. What'd you get me outta bed for anyhow?"

"Dodd just left daddy's house. You know he come out here behind Janice."

Worry showed in Jackie's eyes. "What do you reckon'll happen?"

"Nothin'. Daddy's too upset about gettin' ripped off to be worried about her."

Jackie nodded, put his head back down on his arms and immediately dozed off, only to be shaken awake again.

"Daddy said for you not to say anything about the house gettin' broke in."

Jackie focused bleary eyes on Roy. "Is that why you got me outta bed to come down here? Who the hell do you think I wuz gonna tell up there asleep?"

Roy pulled a Kool from his shirt pocket and lit it. "Who you suppose broke in last night?"

A soft snore was his only answer. He stared at Jackie a moment, then shook him once more.

"Get up, candy-ass, and go on back up there and crawl in the bed. You're a helluva lot of company."

"Goddamn it, Roy, I'm tired. I need some sleep. You know I got to get up pretty soon and strip the car I brought in."

Roy waved a hand in dismissal. He sat there smoking, thinking. A couple of minutes passed and the roofer called out for another beer. Roy got one for him, then came out from behind the bar, taking surprisingly light steps for his size, and sat at a table in the middle of the room.

He pulled a deck of cards from his shirt pocket and started shuffling them. They seemed to take on a life of their own in his hands. His fingers were a blur, pulling the deck apart and sliding the cards back together from the side. A three-fold cut, followed by an innocent-looking thumb-and-finger riffle. The cards kissed together soundlessly.

He dealt a five-man hand, flipping the cards face up. They spun rapidly in the air, each card landing within an inch of the last one. All were cinch hands, trips, flushes, straights—his was a straight flush.

Sherill had put a deck in Roy's hands at eight, starting him off with a simple phony cut. By the time Roy was fourteen he could tell you he was going to hit you from the bottom and you'd still miss it. He could sit down in any game and bust it out in three hands. If he had someone to cut for him—and if he had the balls to sit down to start with.

One of the Spoke's customers, drunk enough to be honest, once remarked, "One of Roy's nuts is the size of a tomato seed and the other'n is a little bitty thing."

Roy gathered the cards, his fingers working independently of his mind, using that for Dodd. He did not like the sheriff, and vice versa. But Roy was scared of Dodd, and that wasn't vice versa.

He hadn't needed to hear their conversation to know Dodd came out about Janice, and he knew if daddy hadn't been there he'd have gone to jail. He realized whoever broke into daddy's house had also saved his ass.

He dealt again, thinking about night before last, getting a hard-on from the memory. He didn't know what all the fuss was about. The little bitch should've known what was expected of her when she took the 'ludes. But, no, she had to act all prim and proper when him and Jackie wanted to fuck. That had been okay too. It was better when they fought.

But Dodd didn't think so, that was for sure. Right now the sheriff belonged to daddy, but daddy wasn't going to live forever. And now daddy better get them goddamned tapes back if he didn't want Dodd making trouble for them, "them" being mostly Roy.

Dodd had left no doubts about how he felt, once telling Roy, "Your ass is gone the day after that old man is dead. I'll have your ass in jail before they get the dirt shoveled in his grave."

The memory was so clear his fingers slipped and he dealt himself a busted flush. If daddy's right I'll be okay, he thought. I'll make sure the son of a bitch that stole them tapes don't show 'em to nobody.

Anticipation cheered him into expansiveness. He kicked the chair across from him a few inches away from the table and looked over his shoulder at the roofer.

"Gary, go behind the bar and flip on the switch for the jukebox, then come over here. Ever time you see me cheat I'll buy you a beer."

DODD STOPPED at a small country store a mile from Sherill's. He walked to a cooler in the rear and selected a pint of orange juice. Three-fourths of it was gone when he reached the counter.

"You doing all right, Amos?" he asked, handing over a five.

Amos, bald as a cue ball, wiped his hands on an apron covering a generous stomach before taking the bill. He turned to the cash register, shifting a toothpick from one side of his mouth to the other.

"Can't kick." He counted Dodd's change back to him. He looked at Dodd with a thoughtful expression, clearly wanting to say something. He moved a display case filled with cheap plastic sunglasses a few inches, saw that it revealed a layer of dust on the counter and moved it back to where it had been. Finally he looked at Dodd, this time speaking his mind.

"What brings you out this way? Getting Roy out of trouble behind that Kirk girl?"

Dodd hadn't expected the incident to stay a secret but the man's bluntness bothered him. "I'm not the one getting him out of trouble, Amos."

The store owner gazed back. "Maybe not. But on the other hand, I don't see that fat son of a bitch in your backseat either."

The door opened and a young woman came in. She carried an infant and struggled to keep a dirty-faced toddler beside her. Dodd nodded to her and moved back. While she paid for her purchases he gave the toddler a Life Saver, a green one, and was rewarded with a smile from the youngster.

"Suppose I did arrest him, Amos," he said when the woman was gone. "You know damned well Sherill would just fix it in the courtroom. At least this way he'll have to shell out some money to the girl."

He finished the juice, crumpled the carton and leaned across the counter to throw it away. "Now which way do you think's best to handle it?"

"There's other things you could arrest him for, Phil, and you know it. Ain't a weekend goes by that some pore bastard don't get his brains knocked loose and rolled down there. And they're taking cars apart behind the damn place like they was Mr. Goodwrench."

Dodd shook his head and told his first outright lie in the conversation. "I've checked that out enough to know it's bullshit."

THE SHERIFF drove back to his office and buried himself in paperwork, putting off going to see Kirk. He knew the man would end up taking the money, more from need than a lack of morals, and Dodd did not want to be witness to it. It angered him that people like Sherill saw to it the Kirks of this world stayed needy. That Sherill owned him too made Dodd break his pencil in two and fling the pieces against the wall.

He got up and put on his coat, intending to go home, when a call came in. A semi carrying a full load of jet fuel had overturned on 129, trapping a car under it. It was something that required Dodd's presence and he welcomed the emergency—it was something he could handle.

He was on the scene until almost midnight, sweating a leak that threatened to erupt from the tanker. But the truck was righted without mishap, and the elderly couple trapped in the car were extracted without serious injuries.

News teams from all three Knoxville stations were there and Dodd talked to each of them. He enjoyed the exposure, knew he looked good on television and talked in a smooth, confident voice. He was very aware of the power of television and had the savvy to use his good looks to his advantage.

A soft glow showed behind his living-room drapes when he turned into the driveway. He entered through the kitchen, the room that had grown to be the most comfortable over the years. The walls were covered with needlepoint homilies done by his wife Ellen.

She turned now from the stove and put her arms around him, as petite as he was tall, and tilted her head back for a kiss, then steered him to the table, slipping his coat off and hanging it over the back of a chair.

"I saw you on the eleven o'clock news." She put her arms back around him. "You looked real good."

Dodd opened his belt and removed a holster holding a snubnose .357. He laid it on the table as he slid into the chair.

"Yeah, we had us a touch and go there for a while. Sorry it held me up so long."

He leaned back and stretched his legs out, watching Ellen bend over to look in the oven. Once again he found himself surprised she'd been with him since high school. Two grown daughters in college, and neither of them could match their mother's figure. A swath of gray two inches wide ran through the center of her hair. Otherwise it was as dark as his.

She set a plate in front of him and placed a hand on his shoulder. "I haven't expected you home early since you were elected, sweetheart. You ought to know by now I don't expect apologies either."

She sat across from him and watched him eat. After twenty-five years if anything was wrong it showed in the appetite first. He ate quickly, only half-chewing his food, ripping the bread.

"What did George say about Roy?"

Dodd got up and went to the refrigerator and took out a pint mason jar and a tray of ice. Into two glasses he poured the moonshine, the color of bonded whiskey because it had been aged three years in a charred oak cask. Its taste reflected that of a man with love for the craft of making whiskey.

He came back, handed Ellen hers, then sat down and loosened his tie. He took a good-sized drink that went down tasteless but exploded into liquid fire the second it hit his stomach. The faint taste of caramel, unique to sour mash whiskey, followed.

"Pay the, as he put it, little split-tail off." He looked at his wife. "That's the third girl I know Roy's raped this year. I don't know what I'm going to do about him." He took another drink, a bigger one this time. "Yeah, I do. I know. The day after that old man of his is dead."

He sipped his whiskey. Phillip Dodd, local high school football and basketball champion. Good enough for a scholarship, the only way he could have gone to college. He came from the same stock as the Kirks of the world. Dirt poor, with pride being the only thing they could claim ownership to. He'd been raised with the knowledge that his pride was the one thing no one could take from him. But he'd ended up selling his, and now the loss of it festered deep inside. He graduated ROTC, went into the army as an officer and on to Vietnam, to come home and to the sheriff's department. Sherill's power came over him gradually. Like taking money not to see Sherill's bootleg joints when he was a deputy. Such things could never be stopped, not as long as Edwards County stayed dry. People wanted such vices.

But the little things slowly became bigger. Once it's established you're a whore the price is all that's left to be decided on, he thought. For the thousandth time Phil Dodd wished he could start fresh.

Not that he wouldn't allow himself to be bought. That line about anybody being able to grow up to be president belonged in a Grimm Brothers fairy tale. You got in office one way—if you had enough money to get the votes—and he had nothing against such a system. When reelection time came around he'd get out and get enough honest people to contribute so that he wouldn't need Sherill. He'd do it without the bastard.

Fat chance, he thought. Now it's either stick with the son of a bitch or get out altogether. Everybody in the county knows who pays me.

Dodd drained his glass until the ice clinked against his teeth. The same thoughts were making the same old knots in his guts. To stop them he reached for Ellen's hand, his last and steadiest bastion against people like Sherill.

CHAPTER TWELVE

THE LATE afternoon sun streaked across Darleen's bare legs. She lay on her stomach on the floor of her living room, wearing a bra and red bikini panties. It was Sunday and they'd just gotten up. Exhaustion had kept them from counting the take until now.

She counted the last of the money, her fingers swiftly walking through it. She sat up and reached for the calculator on the coffee table, pushing aside the sack containing the VCR tapes.

"Three hundred and six thousand." She entered the numbers and looked at Larry, her eyes sparkling.

Larry nodded, sitting on the couch counting the one-ounce gold bars, his lips moving silently. He held onto the last one and joined her on the floor.

"Two hundred of these little things." He held the piece of gold out to the sunlight, watching its burnished surface reflect the light while Darleen worked the calculator.

"I can turn the gold to one man for forty thousand," she said. "That's what we'll do, not dole it out a little at a time for another fifteen thousand. The coin collection will bring another twenty-five thousand from the same man."

Her tone left no room even to consider whether or not Larry agreed. But he did not hear it anyway. He was seeing himself driving the new pickup he intended to buy, sitting on pleated leather seats, turning on the hundred-and-fifty-watt stereo. The cash alone was ten times more than he'd ever seen at one time. What was fifteen grand either way to a man as rich as he was now? Hell, he had money's mammy.

Darleen used a loupe to examine the jewelry with a critical eye, learned from Glenn. She thought of him suddenly now, wondering where he was. Too bad he wasn't here to see what she'd pulled off. He couldn't have done any better. In fact, he chose not to go in with her. His loss.

The stones were flawless, first rate. No yellow showed in any of the diamonds. Even the smallest of them reflected a blue fire from their depths. The rubies, not quite as many, were just as perfect. The jewelry would bring another hundred thousand. She started to cut the figure in half but didn't. Tell him the truth. It didn't matter anyway. She hadn't worked out how yet, but she had no intention of letting him have any of it.

There were still a few pieces left in their settings and she picked out a gorgeous emerald ring encircled with diamonds to keep for herself. She slipped it on and held it up to watch the sparkle when the light hit it. When she lowered her hand it slipped off her finger. A chill ran through her. Was it an omen? She pushed the feeling aside and went back to figuring out a way to keep it all for herself.

If she kept it all there was enough to set her up for life. Glenn had been right—Larry was and would always be a kid. He'd been fun but it was time to move on. And like she told Glenn, she enjoyed being in control and would be with the next man in her life. But this time she'd pick somebody closer to her own age, somebody at least able to carry on an adult conversation.

She leaned back against Larry, using a pencil now. He put an arm around her waist and watched the bottom line.

"Jee-sus Christ. You mean we're gonna pull four hundred and seventy thousand out of this after everything's sold?"

She remembered the two videotapes and took them out of the sack. One was marked DODD, the other MERRITT.

"Do you know anybody up there named Dodd?" she asked.

"Hell, yes. He's the sheriff."

"What about Merritt?"

He shook his head.

She got up and put the one marked DODD in the VCR and came back to sit beside Larry, folding her legs gracefully on the way down. She picked up the remote and turned it on.

The tape was poor, grainy and dim, but good enough to make out the features of one of three men. He sat on a couch, a tall, large man facing the other two. A briefcase, closed, lay on a table between them.

Larry squinted, then pointed. "Yeah, that's that son of a bitch Dodd."

"Shhh," Darleen said, running the tape back to the beginning. "Let me hear what they're saying."

Dodd's voice came from the television. ". . . You say you want to bring in two loads a month, right?"

One of the other men answered, the light too poor to see which one. "That's all, two loads. We set down, unload and take off."

"And what else do you want?"

"That bastard," broke in Larry. "I always knew he was crooked."

Darleen hit the reverse again. "Shut up, Larry. I can't hear you and them too."

She listened to Dodd ask the question again, to be answered by the other man. This one spoke with a high, reedy Spanish accent.

"We'd want you to have your deputies somewhere else when we come in. We won't be on the ground ten minutes."

Darleen and Larry watched Dodd lean back and prop up his feet on the table beside the briefcase. The lamp above his head was on and Darleen watched the man carefully, hearing the undercurrent beneath his casual tone.

"You boys are taking a helluva chance, coming in here trying to buy me. What's to stop me from busting your asses?"

The other men exchanged looks. The first one spoke carefully, his voice cultured, with no accent.

"You could do that, sheriff. But Mr. Sherill said we could do business with you, and you are here. Arrest us if you want. We'll make bail before you can get us out of the booking room. I'm not trying to scare you, Dodd, but if that happened there would be other people very upset. Including your Mr. Sherill."

"Nobody's going to bust you," Dodd said. "I just said it took balls to walk in here big as life with your money."

He swung his feet down and leaned forward, obscuring the other two from view, rapped his knuckles lightly on the briefcase.

"I take it this is the money."

"That's it," said the Spanish guy. "Twenty grand, the first two months."

"And all you want me to do is make sure my men don't come in the area."

"Or anybody else," the other man said. "I'll always call the afternoon of the night we're coming in. If you have any knowledge of the state or DEA being onto us we'd certainly expect you to pass that knowledge to us."

"How big will the loads be?"

"Big enough to pay you ten thousand dollars a month, Mr. Dodd," the cultured voice answered.

Dodd, staring at the briefcase, said nothing. Seconds went by. One man lit a cigar, and in the match's flare it was obvious he came from farther south than Mexico. He puffed a couple of times, then spoke.

"Try to look at us as businessmen, sheriff. So what if we bring in a couple of loads of coke a month. You have a lot of people right here in your county who like the stuff, don't you? You know those people are going to buy it whether it comes in here or a couple of counties away. Why not make it profitable for yourself, both ways? Keep right on busting the locals the way you've been doing and it makes you popular with the voters. We don't care. What we bring in won't be staying here."

"All right," Dodd said after a moment. "You got a place to unload. I can guarantee you won't be busted in my county as long as you keep your end. I want you off the ground the minute it's off the plane."

All three stood up and the American stuck his hand out. Dodd, standing a head above both men, simply looked at it. The man withdrew it.

"I believe we stated at the start here that's the way we'd handle it." He motioned at the table. "Enjoy your money, sheriff."

They disappeared from the tape and Dodd sat back down. He opened the briefcase, and Darleen counted as he lifted twenty packets of bills out, thumbing through each one. He closed the briefcase, got up, and both the case and Dodd disappeared. Darleen fast-forwarded the tape but nothing else came on, it might have been a still picture of the room. Then it went blank and she switched it off.

"Well, well," she murmured.

"Why'n hell would he be stupid enough to tape himself taking a bribe?"

She pulled the other cassette from the sack. "He didn't tape it."

"Well, I don't think them other two guys did. So who the hell did?"

She looked at Larry like a weary teacher might look at a slow pupil. "Whose safe was it in, Larry?"

"Well, why would that old bastard do it? You can bet he's getting his share too."

Darleen hushed him, intent on the second tape. Same room but a different man sitting on the couch, turned so that only a quarter of his face showed. He wore a suit and looked to be in his mid-forties, with salt-and-pepper hair.

Sitting close to him was a teenage girl Darleen judged to be fifteen, sixteen tops. Her voice was the first one heard.

"I like to never got away from home. I'll have to get back early tonight, Mr. Merritt. Mama's scared to death I'm gonna end up violating my probation."

"Don't worry about it, hon. As prosecutor I've got the final say on that. I don't see where that will be any problem as long as you keep me happy."

Darleen glanced at Larry with a smile. When she looked back at the television she saw Merritt reach in his pocket and bring out a thin round metal container. Evidently it was some of the product discussed on the first tape, because both of them put some of it up their noses.

Another hit of coke apiece and the girl stood up to strip, doing a very amateur bump and grind. Her lack of fullness in the breasts and hips confirmed her youth.

The light went even dimmer, but enough remained to see the mildly kinky action that followed. The attorney positioned the girl on her knees and shoulders, ran her arms beneath her body and tied them to her ankles. He didn't undress, just unzipped his pants and mounted her from behind. He spanked her ass as he fucked, hard, solid smacks that hurt.

It became painful enough for the girl to cry out and appear to really try to get away. Her eyes were squeezed shut, her lower lip sucked into her mouth as she bit down on it in an effort to endure the pain. But beyond this the expression on her face seemed to say she had already accepted her life and expected no more than such treatment.

Merritt laughed at her pain and stuffed her panties in her

mouth, then grabbed her around the hips and began to fuck harder.

Larry scooted next to Darleen and started stroking her thigh. "I want to try something like that with you, honey. Think you might enjoy it?"

Darleen pushed his hand away. "If there's any tying up done you can bet I'll be the one doing it. You think you might enjoy *that*, Larry?"

He pushed away from her and got up to sit on the couch, lit a cigarette, pointedly refusing to look at the tape.

Darleen went back to watching the film, feeling some pity for the girl, but she also recognized the passive acceptance, and in a moment her mind was traveling in another direction as the tape ended and she turned it off.

This changed a lot of things. What she was thinking now depended on Larry. If he could pull off the plan forming in her mind she wouldn't mind being generous enough to give him a little something before she sent him packing.

She got up and mixed a drink, making one for Larry almost as an afterthought. She watched him as she poured, slouched on the couch, the pout still showing. He certainly wasn't the one she'd choose if she had a choice. He wasn't hard enough. But she had a few days to coach him. She spoke from behind the bar.

"It was a good score, Larry, but how would you like to make it a better one?"

Larry stretched out on the couch, kicking his shoes off. "You thinking about selling the tapes to Sherill? I still don't see why he made 'em. The one with Dodd implicates him as much as it does Dodd."

She brought the drinks over and after pushing his legs off the sofa sat down beside him. She leaned over him, brushing his hair with her fingers as she talked in a soft voice.

"Insurance, sweetie. Like you said, he put them in office. Suppose either one decided he didn't want to take orders from Sherill anymore. What he's got on those tapes would do more than just bring them back in line. Both of them could end up in jail once it was known what's on the tapes."

"How much you think he'd pay to get 'em back?"

Until last night she'd only half-believed the strength Larry attributed to Sherill. The money convinced her he was powerful, and the tapes cinched it.

"Half a million." She looked carefully at Larry as she said it.

"Get real, Darleen. We just took damn near a million away from him. He'll never shell out that much."

"He'd pay all right. But we might be able to work both sides of the fence."

Larry wasn't following, but he kept quiet.

"You and I are going back up there, investigate this Merritt a little. Find out if he's worth anything. He might be willing to shell out some money for the tapes too."

"How you gonna give both him and Sherill the tapes?"

"Neither of them will get them. We'll just pull another version of the old pigeon drop, make them *think* they're getting the tapes."

"But Sherill's the one with the money. When we start to bargain with him what's the least you think we should take?"

She reached for a cigarette, lit it and blew out a long thin stream of smoke. Larry watched it change from gray to gun-barrel blue as it passed through a shaft of sunlight.

"No negotiating," she said. "You tell him the price. If he balks, then you ask him how much he thinks the sheriff and D.A. would pay for them."

"Me? Ain't you gonna be there too?"

She began to brush his hair again. "No. You'll have to do that part of it alone, baby."

"I don't know, Darleen. Sherill ain't nobody to mess around with. Those people know me. Goddamn it, I used to deal with 'em."

"All the more reason why you should go alone for the actual scam. They do know you. You're a man. I go and they'll automatically try to cross me out because I'm a woman."

That worked. Larry's chest swelled out. "Yeah, that's right, by God. But how will we give the bastard proof we've got the tapes without me taking one?"

"That's easy. We can buy all the equipment we'll need to make a copy. We've got lots of time for that, though. Checking Merritt out will take a couple of weeks. But that's all for the better. Wondering about the tapes will have Sherill all the more ready to deal."

"That still don't stop the fact that old bastard is gonna know who I am. You can bet he'll do his best to find me."

The smile Darleen gave him was sincere. "He owns that little county, sugar, not the world. And once we've got the money we can go one hell of a lot farther than his power reaches."

She pulled Larry's shirt out of his pants and unbuttoned it. She lowered her head and licked around a nipple of his smooth, hairless chest. Took it in her mouth and bit down lightly, speaking around it.

"I'm tense and tired from the job, sweetie. Make me relax and then after a nap we'll go on a shopping spree like you've never seen."

CHAPTER THIRTEEN

FRANK AND Glenn walked among the dogs, Frank filling their water bowls from a garden hose. Dew covered the grass, and it was early enough that the coolness of the night still lingered.

The dogs ran back and forth, all of them barking except for a brown male that simply stood there waiting for Frank to get to him. He accepted a pat on the head, then lapped up a drink of the fresh water.

"That's Senator," said Frank. "Probably the best dog in the yard. Look how proud he stands, just like a damned politician, full of himself."

The next dog ran up to Frank, rearing up and putting wet paw prints on his slacks. He picked the dog up and slung him as far away as the chain permitted. The slack ran out before the power of Frank's throw did, jerking the dog a half-flip while still in the air. The dog hit the ground hard but was up in a flash and running eagerly back to Frank.

"See what I mean about 'em being tough bastards? Zack thinks that just means you're wanting to play with him."

The next dog, a bitch, did the same thing she'd done the three days Glenn had been there. She rushed forward, lips lifted up to show her teeth, growling low. The charge, along with the vicious look on her face, made Glenn jump back although he knew the chain would stop her. Frank never slowed his step, just walked up and petted the dog. She changed instantly at his touch, licking his hand and weaving around his legs like a puppy, her tail going ninety to nothing.

Frank saw Glenn's fear. "Just give her a little time and she'll treat you like she does me."

"Let's say you're right. In the meantime, how am I supposed to feed and water that evil-looking bitch?"

"Just take a stick and push it to her. Trust me on this, Glenn. It won't take long for her to come around. And then you'll have a dog who'll die for you without blinking an eye."

He knelt down, pulled the dog to him and hugged her. The bitch licked his face, pushing against him, trying to get closer. The affection Frank felt for the dog showed in his eyes.

"Mama Sue, you act right. This fella is gonna take care of your sorry ass while I'm gone. Hurry up and get to know him, 'cause he's one of the good guys."

Glenn watched with a smile. To him, it seemed sort of silly to talk to a dog like it was a human.

Frank stood up. "Give her another week, then put 'er in the house at night. You won't know she's there and you won't need to lock the door. Mama Sue knows who belongs in there. They come in, fine. Anybody else and she still won't make a sound. But she'll sure as hell make the son of a bitch tell you he's there."

They watered the rest of the dogs, with Frank giving last-minute tips, telling their good points, their quirks. When they finished he took a long look around, turning his head slowly, uttered a long, drawn-out sigh and looked at his watch.

"Well, let's go. I don't know what happened to Tina but we can't wait around any longer. We'll be late for court if we do."

Frank looked back until the curve hid the house, then said, "I was sure glad to hear how bad the overcrowding is. Maybe I won't have to do all this time after all."

"Frank, you won't even make it to the joint, which is bad. It's better there than it's going to be in the jail. You'd have more freedom to move around in the joint. But the jails are just as full, so you'll only do eight, nine months and then they'll parole you out."

He cut his eyes at Frank. "Trust me."

GLENN LISTENED as the judge sentenced Frank, then spent a moment talking to him before they took him away. He assured Frank he would care for the dogs and come regularly to let him know how they were doing. He shook Frank's hand and walked out of the courtroom without looking back. He did not want to see the chains being put on his friend.

It was a little after one when he got back to the house and immediately noticed the air-conditioning in Tina's room was running. Four suitcases were piled just inside the front door, and the door to her room was closed. He wondered what it was going to be like sharing a house with someone he didn't know.

It was late, well after dark, when the door opened. Glenn was cooking supper for himself, eggs and bacon, and the quiet hello from behind startled him.

He turned, and caught his breath as he found himself looking at one of the most beautiful women he'd ever seen.

She leaned against the door frame, almost eye level with him, a mass of silvery blond hair piled loosely on top of her head. Large green eyes, set well apart, were watching him looking. Her mouth, wide and generous, had a slight cynical set to it. It sent him back to her eyes, and he saw a knowledge of life in them most women twice her age had not attained. He guessed her to be in her mid-twenties.

A nightgown T-shirt stretched to her knees, doing nothing to conceal that a nice body was under it. She pushed
away from the door, speaking before he could. Her voice
had a deep timbre to it.

"That smells good. Think you could spare another
plate?"

"Sure." Glenn opened the refrigerator and took out the
eggs. "All I need to know is how you like 'em cooked. I
figure you have to be Tina, and I'm—"

"Glenn," she said, nibbling on a piece of bacon, looking
him over. "Frank left me a letter telling me you'd be staying. Over easy on the eggs."

She crossed the small room and sat at the table. His cigarettes lay in front of her and she pulled one out, then used
his lighter.

"I hope he wasn't upset that I didn't make it in time."

Glenn flipped her eggs, waited a moment, then put them
on a plate and carried them to the table and took a seat
across from her.

"Not upset. Worried something might've happened to
you."

She laughed. There was some bass in it, like her voice.
"That's Frank, worrying about me, and him the one going
to jail. I didn't get in until ten-thirty. I thought about going
to the courthouse, but fourteen hours either on a plane or
waiting for one had me frazzled. All I wanted was a shower
and a bed."

"Fourteen hours? From Tucson?"

"No, Madrid. We left Tucson last week."

Glenn wanted to ask the hows and whys. Hell, he wanted
more than that. He wanted to know everything about her,
and wondered why. It wasn't like him to be curious about
people he'd just met.

She took small, almost dainty bites, and chewed slowly,
always swallowing before speaking. When she had finished
eating she got up and disappeared into her bedroom. She

emerged with a bottle and champagne bucket, filled the bucket with ice, then stuck the bottle in it.

"That will be ready about the time the food settles," she said. "How about turning on the outside lights. I haven't said hello to the dogs yet."

Mama Sue turned out to be the first dog she chose to greet. Glenn watched in amazement as the dog showed Tina the same affection she did Frank.

"According to Frank you've been gone four months but that dog remembers you."

She looked up at him, laughing at Mama Sue's frantic attempts to show her affection. "Sure she does. Most people think pits are dumb, which is a mistake. They're probably the smartest dog there is."

She stood up, brushing the dirt from her knees, and moved to another dog. "It's just a shame they're bred to fight."

"Yeah. I went to my first one the other night. I didn't care for it."

She continued to pet the dog, speaking without looking at him. "I know. Frank told me in the letter."

"What else did he say about me?"

"Not much. Not in the letter." She looked up now, and Glenn felt like she was looking inside him.

"But I know all about you, Glenn Odom."

He squatted beside her and rubbed the dog. Their hands touched and an electric tingle shot through him.

"If I believed that I'd already be gone."

Tina leaned over and kissed the dog on top of the head. Glenn found himself envying the big-headed bastard.

"The Glenn that Frank talked about never ran away," she said, looking at him.

"Well, tell me you never caught Frank lying."

She laughed. "Touché."

She suggested they stay outside and went back in the house, returning with the champagne. Glenn popped the cork, holding it away from the table until it stopped foaming.

"What shall we drink to?" he asked as he poured.

She held her glass up. "To your new occupation."

He looked over his shoulder at the dogs. "To an occupation I know nothing about."

"Then I'll teach you. A toast to our partnership."

He clinked his glass against hers. "I like that much better."

When the level in the bottle was down by half he rolled a joint from the stuff Frank had left him. The conversation was flowing freely but soon the combination of pot and champagne had them drawling their words slowly.

Each time Tina reached for the joint her fingers seemed to caress his. He'd been erect the past thirty minutes from just her closeness, and her fingers drove him crazy. He sensed it was an invitation, but his shyness was stronger than his sexual urge.

Tina also sensed it. When he passed the joint to her again she closed her fingers around his hand. She pulled him toward her and moved to meet him, opening her mouth slightly.

Their lips met, and Glenn's fears and shyness vanished. He pulled her to him exploring the inside of her mouth with his tongue. She responded, her tongue dueling with his.

Neither said anything when the kiss was broken. They stood up and she slipped her hand in his, to lead him inside to her bedroom. The full moon poured pale light through the windows, all the light that was needed.

With one swift move Tina pulled the long T-shirt over her head and off. Glenn heard his breath when she revealed her body to him. She stood there, pelvis slung forward a bit, allowing him to take in all of her. Her breasts were full and round, with thick, light pink nipples. Her rib cage narrowed to a tiny waist, then flared slightly at her nearly boyish hips. A sparse patch of silky hair covered her mound, lighter than the hair on her head.

After a moment she reached up and undid her hair, letting the pins drop to the floor. A toss of her head and it came cascading past her shoulders, shining in the dim moonlight. She got in bed and pulled Glenn to her.

"I just got out of . . . ," he began, a little hoarsely.

She put a finger to his lips. "I know where you've been. Don't apologize for something that hasn't happened yet. We've got all night."

He kissed her hungrily, then moved down to take a nipple in his mouth, feeling it grow even thicker. She smelled faintly of soap, different from Darleen, who always smelled of White Shoulders perfume. Then Darleen faded from his mind, to be thought of no more this night.

He moved down further, not stopping until his tongue found the moistness between Tina's thighs. He savored the musky fragrance, loving the taste of her. Gently he explored each crevice of her with his tongue until she forced him to concentrate in one spot by digging her fingers in his hair.

She climaxed, then again, and each one made Glenn want to give her another one. Finally she could take no more and pulled him up.

She reached between their bodies and guided him to her, more than ready to receive him. Glenn held back. He moved slowly, feeling her wetness and warmth surround him. Most of all he could feel her gripping him softly.

Then he was all the way in and had to stop or finish right then and there. He lay still, and Tina began to move beneath him, sliding her hips back and forth.

"Oh, God, don't or I'll come."

She looked at him, eyes wide in sudden understanding. "Why, you haven't been to bed with a woman yet, have you?"

She moved her hips again, and Glenn moaned, which

answered her question. She giggled and started grinding against him harder.

"You better stop."

She worked faster. "Then let it happen, Glenn. This won't be our only time." She wrapped her legs around the back of his, forming a cradle of her thighs for him to lie in.

"Now are you going to help or do you want me to do it all?"

Glenn began to move, and that was all it took. He felt his climax building up in his scrotum and then it spilled over. It was so strong he couldn't continue moving, just lay there, feeling like his balls were going to come out too. When he was strong enough he rolled off Tina to lie flat on his back.

She sat up, cross-legged, reached for the cigarettes, lit two and stuck one between Glenn's fingers. He let it stay there, breathing much too hard to attempt smoking. She bent over and kissed him lightly on the mouth.

"Good, huh."

He opened one eye. "Maybe that's all it was on your part. If it'd been any better on my end it would've killed me."

"How long have you been out?" When he said a week she looked surprised.

"Why did you wait so long?"

"Mostly busy. Taking care of this and . . ." He shrugged and admitted the truth. "Scared."

She snuggled next to him, cupping his balls in a cool palm. "I'm glad you were scared."

Glenn felt himself beginning to stir again. "Why are you glad?"

"Because it let me be your first one." She moved her hand up and started stroking him slowly, gently.

"I think you're about to be my second one too," he said, turning on his side and reaching for her.

CHAPTER FOURTEEN

THE PHONE rang just as Roy stepped out the back door of the tavern. He paused, then continued toward the windowless building sitting directly behind the tavern three hundred feet away. Fuck it. They'd call back if it was important.

He fumbled with the heavy key ring on his belt, found the right one and unlocked a heavy padlock, then opened one of the double doors only enough to get inside. A flick of a light switch revealed the cluttered interior of the chop shop.

A gutted Monte Carlo sat in the center of the shop, its frame resting on blocks, the rocker bars and springs about the only things still attached. The engine lay beside it, along with the bucket seats and instrument panel. The fenders and hood were lined up against the wall. Next to the Monte Carlo was a Ford pickup; the only thing still salable in it was the engine. A Corvette was alongside the Ford, untouched since it had only arrived during the night.

Roy ran his hand along the side of the Corvette, making a mental note to have Jackie bring the truck in when the sports car was dismantled. Daddy didn't like to have the parts lying around. He was still standing there taking a rough inventory when the door opened and Sherill came in. Roy grinned and gestured at the Corvette.

"This little baby here'll bring in a good fifteen grand after she's tore down, daddy."

Sherill did not even look at the car. "I just got a call about the tapes. Sumbitch wouldn't say who he was. Just said to meet 'im at the Waffle House on 129 and to bring a VCR. Said I'd know 'im when I saw 'im."

"How much he say he wanted?"

Sherill paced the length of the room, hands shoved deep in his pockets, rattling his change furiously. "He didn't say. Said we could talk about that later."

Roy watched the old man, able to feel the anger radiating from him. It had been three weeks since the house was broken into and now a thrill shot through him. Daddy would soon be turning him loose now that they'd been contacted.

"You goin'?"

"Hell no. You are." Sherill drew abreast of Roy and stopped inches from him.

"Now you lissen to me good, Roy. I don't want this fucked up. Take a VCR and go meet this bastard."

"I dunno, daddy. That might scare 'im off. He said he wanted to see you, didn't he?"

"I said lissen to me, goddamn it. You tell 'im I don't want to talk or meet 'im 'til you know for sure he's got the tapes. Make 'im play it for you and find out how much he wants. Then you call me, act like it's to tell me how much he's wantin'. Tell 'im all he has to do is come out and pick up the money. Whatever you do, don't let 'im out of sight. The important thing is talkin' him into coming back with you."

Roy's weak, feminine mouth formed a sneer. "Oh, he'll come back with me if I have to throw down on 'im."

"Goddamn it, that's the last thing I want you to do. I don't care what you have to promise 'im to get 'im out here, you do it."

"Well, shit, daddy. You sound like you're gonna pay the bastard off."

"If puttin' the money in his hands is what I gotta do to get them tapes back, I will." Sherill shook his head. "But we won't be payin 'im off. Once you get 'im back here he'll tell us who he's working with."

"After that do I get to make sure he don't ever tell nobody else nothin'?" Roy asked.

"Yeah, son. You can have that pleasure. Now get started. Call me at the bar soon as you see the tape."

LARRY SAT in the last booth, an untouched breakfast before him, watching the parking lot. He twirled a spoon between his palms, his armpits sticky with sweat in spite of the air-conditioning.

Fucking Darleen. Nothing to it, to hear her tell it. He wished her ass was sitting here, see how cool she'd be.

The bitch. She'd act like she was sitting on ice. Knowing that somehow failed to make him feel any better.

Now he saw Roy Sherill get out of a car and start toward the entrance, his eyes sweeping the length of the plate-glass front. He'd never liked Roy, had always been scared of him.

Roy now was inside, searching the faces of all the diners. His gaze swept across Larry and then returned, recognition coming into his eyes.

Larry lifted his hand to wave him back but wavered, and ended up running his fingers through his hair instead. He cursed himself silently for his lack of courage, then waved at Roy when his gaze swept past him again. He forcibly refrained from swallowing nervously when Roy sat across from him, his large belly brushing against the table. Roy grinned.

"Well, I be goddamned if it ain't Larry. Hazelton, ain't it? You're 'bout the last one I'da ever guessed. Looks like you done moved up out of the petty shit you was pulling the last time I saw you. I think you brought a couple of televisions down to the Spoke, didn't you?"

He waved the waitress away, keeping his eyes on Larry. "What'd we give you for 'em, Larry?"

"We ain't gonna talk about TVs today, Roy. I think I've got something a little better this time."

"I reckon you do at that. You done good, Larry. First time I reckon I ever seen the old man that shook up. You are the fella I come to see, ain'tcha?"

"I got the tapes, but it wasn't you I told to come. I'm fast starting not to like the way things are going."

Roy grinned again. "Relax, motherfucker. Nobody's fixin' to do anything to your ass. You know how daddy is. He ain't gettin' in nothin' 'til it's been checked out real good. So let's get down to the nitty-gritty. How much is it gonna cost us to get 'em back?"

Larry looked out the window, taking a moment to calm his nerves, then looked at Roy. "Half a million."

"I didn't say nothin' about the asking price, Larry. I asked how much is it gonna cost us."

"And I didn't say anything about negotiating. The price is half a million. If you don't want 'em somebody else will."

"Who you workin' with, Larry? You used to bargain with me ever time you brought something in."

Larry sensed he had the edge and gained a little courage. "Did you ever know me to work with anybody? Let's just say I've learned a lot since moving away from here."

"Either that or all that other shit you took from daddy made you get greedy." Roy slid out of the booth. "Well, come on. Show me what you got so I can call daddy. He'll pay it, but you better get your ass a long way from here. Just between me'n you, I think it's funny. You got 'im cold, Larry. You, of all people."

Larry got in his pickup and drove across the highway to the motel, Roy following. When they were inside the room he took the VCR from Roy and hooked it up. He felt beneath his clothes in a suitcase lying open on the bed and brought out a cassette.

It was the one of Dodd, and Roy, having only seen it once before, did not realize it was a copy. He picked up the phone, motioning for Larry to turn off the television.

"I've seen it, daddy," he said, watching Larry. "Oh yeah, it's the real thing all right. What you ain't gonna believe is who got 'em. Larry Hazelton. You remember him, don't you? Used to sell us TVs."

He paused to listen, then said, "I hope you're sitting down. He says half a million, take it or leave it."

He held the receiver out to Larry. "He wants to talk to you."

Larry listened a moment, then broke in, managing to put some insolence in his voice. "Sherill, it ain't just me on this. Now, I've been told how much to take for the tapes. You want 'em or not?"

SHERILL HAD no trouble recalling Larry. It enraged him to know such a small-time thief had taken him off. But there was no evidence of anger in his voice. It was silky smooth.

"What choice have I got? You're holding the best hand and you know it. You come on out with Roy and we'll work out the details. That okay with you?"

"How do I know I can trust you?"

"You got both tapes with you?"

Larry laughed. "Not hardly. I'm not stupid."

"Then I think you've answered your own question, Larry. I'll expect you in a few minutes."

Larry replaced the receiver and turned to see Roy unhooking the VCR. "He wants me to follow you back and talk to him."

"I told you that at the start. So c'mon."

Larry made a show of going to the suitcase and taking

out a small revolver. He flipped a pair of pants back and Roy caught a glimpse of something in a plastic case.

Larry stuck the pistol in one of his cowboy boots and gave Roy what he thought was a tough-guy look. "Just to keep everybody honest."

Outside, he started for his pickup, and Roy said it would be easier to go in his car. Larry objected, and for the first time Roy's facade slipped.

"Listen, fuckface, I'm gettin' tired of your shit. You gotta fuckin' gun and the fuckin' tapes. What the hell you think is gonna happen to you? How the fuck did you ever pump your nuts up to come back to start with? Now get in the goddamn car."

He drove a short way down 129 and turned onto a county road Larry well remembered. His nervousness eased, and within a few miles he was engrossed in the scenery of the rolling hills. Houses became farther apart as they drove through the remote countryside, and he failed to notice when Roy eased a .38 snubnose from the small of his back.

Roy swung his arm up from behind the seat to bring the gun crashing against the back of Larry's head. Drops of blood flew out to the side, one of which landed on Roy's cheek.

Larry grunted, put a hand up to rub the spot. He clawed at his boot with his other hand, and Roy slammed on the brakes, sending Larry's head crashing into the dash. When his head cleared, the car had stopped and he was staring down the muzzle of Roy's pistol.

"You dumb fuck, did you really think daddy'd give somebody like you money?"

"Oh, God, Roy, wait a minute—"

"No, you wait, shithead. You got that other tape. I seen it when you got your little gun out."

Larry opened his mouth, only to have Roy shove the barrel of the pistol in it. He could taste the oil on it and tried to pull his head back. Roy followed with the pistol, until Larry was against the window and could go no further.

"You shouldn'ta put that little gun so far away, Larry. Ain't doin' you much good, is it?"

Larry twisted his head to the side to get the barrel out of his mouth. Then he made his biggest mistake. In his panic he could think of nothing but begging for his life. He did not try to convince Roy he didn't have the tapes, and his failure to do that convinced Roy he did.

"Please, Roy, don't shoot me. Please. I'll do anything."

Roy was enjoying the begging. "I'll just save daddy the trouble of fuckin' with your ass."

Roy was tired of his old man always saying he ought to start thinking on his own. This would show him he knew how to handle things.

"Please, Roy, don—"

"Bye, Larry," Roy said, and pulled the trigger.

The bullet entered under Larry's chin, snapping his head up and back against the window, hard enough to put a six-inch crack in the glass. But Larry was past feeling any more bumps to the head. The bullet went in at an angle, straight into the brain.

Roy pulled the body below the window line and eased back onto the road. A mile further down he turned onto a smaller road, stopping as soon as he was out of sight of the other road. He opened the trunk, checked to make sure no one was coming, put Larry in it.

He got in the car, pulled forward, turned the wheels sharply and backed up until he was headed the way he had come. At the intersection he turned away from the tavern, going back to the motel. He was going to get daddy *both* of his precious tapes.

CHAPTER
FIFTEEN

SHERILL FORCED himself to calm down a little; it was either that or have a stroke. As it was, he could hear the blood in his ears. He turned and threw the tape at Roy, who did not catch it. It bounced off his chest and fell to the concrete floor of the chop shop with a clatter.

"A goddamn copy," he yelled with such intensity his voice cracked. "You killed the son of a bitch for a *copy*."

He bent through the open window of Roy's car and brought out a black plastic case. He threw it at Roy, who ducked this time. The case flew open when it hit the wall, and an electric razor fell out, breaking apart when it hit the floor.

"A goddamn copy. That and a fuckin' electric razor."

The grin was long gone from Roy's face. His small eyes blinked with each syllable that reverberated through the chop shop.

"I thought I saw the other 'un in his suitcase."

Sherill crossed the ten feet separating them with a speed that belied his sixty-odd years and slapped Roy open-handed. Roy's head snapped to the right, to meet Sherill's left hand coming so fast the two slaps sounded like one.

"No, you didn't. That's the goddamn problem with you.

If you'd just took the fuckin' time to actually think, none of this'd happened."

Roy started to speak but Sherill cut him off. "Shut up, Roy. I mean not a word."

Sherill glared at him a moment more, then walked to the open trunk and stared down at Larry's body. He tried to think, pulling at his lower lip with thumb and forefinger. After a few seconds he turned back to Roy, displaying something to his son for the first time—fear.

"Because of you we got no idea where them tapes are, or who's got 'em. Do you have any idea what kind of fix this puts me in? You had the big idea of killing 'im. Now see if you can think of a way to get 'em back."

Roy stared at the floor, missing the look of disgust on his father's face.

"I'm fed up with you, Roy. All I do is get your fat ass out of one scrape after another. All I ever asked was for you to listen to me. I ain't gonna be here forever. You think somebody like Dodd would put up with your shit after I'm gone?" He answered his own question. "He already wants your ass in jail. After this I don't know but what it ain't the best place for you. It might help to start you thinking."

He went back to pacing, his mind working from every angle. He was much worse off than before. When that punk Hazelton failed to show up, whoever had the tapes was liable to take them to Dodd or Merritt.

He wasn't nearly as worried about Merritt as he was Dodd. Merritt would be pissed about being on tape, but he was ambitious and greedy to the bone. He wanted to be senator and knew he'd never make it without Sherill's money. He dismissed the D.A. from mind and concentrated on Dodd.

There was no doubt in the old man's mind Dodd would use the tapes to get out from under his thumb if he got his hands on them. The man had an honest streak in him that came to the surface much too often to suit Sherill lately. He should've seen that in him long before now. And right now Dodd was the one son of a bitch who might be able to get them out of this mess.

He turned back to Roy, jerking a thumb over his shoulder at the trunk. "Take this bastard and dump 'im behind the Baptist Church on Tipton Road. They'll find 'im soon enough, tomorrow's Sunday. Take all his money and jewelry so it'll look like a robbery. And make goddamn sure he don't have no ID on 'im."

Roy started toward the car but Sherill stopped him. "You better lissen this time. When you get back I want you in the house. Don't show your goddamn face 'til I tell you to come out. I've got to call Dodd and tell 'im about this and you're the last one I want 'im talkin' to."

"That's one of our problems, daddy, you treat me like I was a fuckin' kid—"

"I treat you like you act, goddamn it. Start acting grown and I'll treat you that way. You don't even understand what you done. If them tapes fall into the wrong hands I'll lose every bit of power I've spent forty years building. You can throw it all away after I'm dead, but damned if I'll let you do it before then. I won't just sit back and watch it all go to hell."

Sherill walked up the steep hill to his house and called Dodd. After hanging up he poured himself three fingers of bourbon, knocked it back and poured again. He went outside to sit on the porch and wait for Dodd, taking the bottle with him.

He looked down the hill, seeing before him more than enough in property alone to make most men think they'd made it. Besides the tavern he could see three rental houses he owned free and clear. A quarter-mile behind the tavern a hill, higher than the one his house sat on, hid a trailer park he also owned. Not a dime was owed on the land or a single one of the twenty trailers.

He sipped the whiskey, his fear of the tapes receding, replaced with anger at Roy. He'd made it too easy on Roy as a kid. His wife dying in a car wreck when Roy was ten was the start. A boy needed a mama at that age and he had been too generous trying to make up for the lack of one. Well, it was coming home to him now.

He saw Dodd turn in the driveway, got out of the chair and went inside, coming back out with another glass before the car came to a stop.

Dodd got out, the Buick rising slightly with the absence of his weight. He walked around the rear of the car to the porch, giving Sherill a cursory nod.

Sherill poured generously in both glasses and motioned to the chair beside him. "Come on up and have a seat, Phil. I know you hated to come out what with both your daughters home for the weekend. I wouldn'ta called if it wasn't important."

Dodd took the glass but did not drink from it. "Well, I'm here. What's on your mind?"

"Phil, I'm afraid I killed a man a few minutes ago."

Hatred for Sherill and everything he stood for ran through Dodd but he kept it down. He looked at the glass in his hand and set it down, the whiskey still untouched.

"I reckon you better tell me about it. Start with who and why."

Sherill stood up. "Come on. I'll show you why."

Dodd followed him inside and down the hall to the bedroom.

Sherill stopped in the doorway and motioned for Dodd to go in. The safe still sat almost in the center of the room, the door open, the dial absent.

"That's what I came back to from Florida, Phil. They took damned near a million dollars out of here. There's another 'un in the closet that looks just like it."

Dodd turned to look at Sherill, who still stood in the door. "You have any idea on who 'they' might be?"

"Larry Hazelton for one. I found out today he was one of 'em."

"I take it he's the man you killed." Dodd was amazed he was talking so calmly about murder. "Who else was involved?" he asked when he got no response.

"That's another problem. I lost my temper and shot the son of a bitch before I could make 'im tell me."

Dodd looked at him. "That sounds like something Roy would do, not you. You sure you aren't covering up for him?"

"Goddamn it, Phil, you act like you're doing an investigation. Roy ain't done a damn thing, 'cept dump the body behind the Baptist Church on Tipton Road. And he done that 'cause I told him to."

Dodd walked to a window and stared into the woods on the side of a hill behind Sherill's house. It had been dry lately, and the combination of that and the heat caused the leaves to droop lifelessly. He put two Life Savers in his mouth, immediately crunching one into small bits. He turned back to Sherill.

"What else am I supposed to be doing, George?"

The arrogance in his voice brought the loss of the tapes home to Sherill again. Such behavior was the reason for them in the first place. He gestured at the safe.

"Help me find out who else was involved in this."

"You mean just ignore a murder."

Sherill's face flushed, his jaw muscles clenched. "Ain't nobody been murdered. One of the bastards just got what he had comin' for ripping me off."

"Why didn't you tell me about this when I was here a few weeks ago?"

A real look of disbelief came over Sherill. "And let it be found out how much shit I had here in the house? You know I couldn't afford that."

Dodd turned back to the window. "Why do I get the feeling you still aren't telling me all of it, George?"

Sherill's answer was soft but the menace in his voice filled the room. "You callin' me a liar?"

"I'm telling you everything I've heard so far has a bad smell to it."

Sherill crossed the room in two swift strides and grabbed Dodd by the shoulder, who allowed himself to be spun around.

"Lissen here, you bastard. This is twice in less than a month you've acted like I'm a nobody. Keep on and I'm gonna get worried."

"You threatening me?"

Sherill took a step back. "Yeah. Yeah, by God, I am. You better start rememberin' you're sheriff only because I wanted you to be, and I can see that you ain't just as easy. Your hands are plenty dirty, Dodd. If push comes to shove I'll use it."

He wagged a finger under Dodd's nose. "You want to be Mr. Clean all at once? I'll bury you in mud up to your ass. By the time I'm through, that wife and them girls will know all about their law'n order daddy sheriff. I don't think they'd have such a high standing in the community after the shit settled."

There it was. They faced each other, naked hatred in both men's eyes. Dodd felt the weight of the .357 riding high on his hip and resisted the urge to use it. But Sherill's threat had hit home.

"All right. Just what is it you want? For starters I hope you have something in mind to explain a dead body behind a church."

"That's easy, Phil. He's got no ID on 'im so you don't know who he is as far as your report shows. How long does it take to identify a body?"

"What about his car? Where is it?"

"I'll send Jackie to get it from the motel after it gets dark. That ain't no problem."

Dodd shrugged. "With no name to go on, a fingerprint and dental check might take a couple of months. And even then you might not come up with an ID."

"But you know who he is and that gives us an edge. I want you to run a check on 'im. He moved off a year ago or more. Find out where he went and who he was running with and that oughta lead you to who he was working with when he broke in here."

The feeling Sherill was holding something back grew stronger. "How'd you find out this Hazelton was a part of it?"

"Phil, all my business ain't yours. You'll just have to trust me on a few things. How don't matter. What matters is finding out who else was involved so I can get back what's mine."

Arrest him now, thought Dodd. He's giving himself to you on a silver platter, confessing to a murder. But he thought of his wife and daughters, and the shame they'd feel once Sherill made public just how dirty his hands were.

"I'm going to do this, help you cover up a murder and get your money back for you."

Sherill opened his mouth but Dodd held up a hand to cut him off.

"I'm changing the answer I gave you last time I was out here. This will be my only term. Even a man who's sold himself has a limit, and I've just reached mine. I don't want the office if letting you run loose is a requirement."

Roy came in after Dodd was gone. Sherill still stood in the center of the room, the difference between them never more obvious. The father showed a murderous rage, his son total fear.

"Daddy, you got to do something about that son of a bitch. I don't trust 'im at all."

"In due time, son. In due time. Right now I need him. He can find out things I need to know. The minute I get those tapes back I'll burn the one of him. And then I'll take him out of the picture."

CHAPTER SIXTEEN

GLENN COMPLETED his fourth set of fifty push-ups, holding his body up on the last one, his triceps straining. He lowered himself to the floor of the porch, exhaling heavily, his face red.

"Uh-huh," he grunted to his audience. "You thought I wouldn't make it, didn't you? Well, I fooled your ass. I could've done another fifty."

Mama Sue came over and licked his face. He closed his eyes and accepted her declaration of love until he could sit up, grabbed a handful of jaw on both sides of the dog's head and shook it back and forth.

"Mama Sue, your breath stinks."

Dozer barked suddenly, followed quickly by Zack. Most of the other dogs joined in, uttering deep, guttural barks of frustrated rage. Glenn scooted to the end of the porch and swung his feet off the edge, tightly gripping Mama Sue's collar. He pulled his cigarettes to him with a grin. The show was starting.

A gray-and-white tomcat slowly, disdainfully threaded its way through the midst of the dogs, looking neither left nor right. Tina had brought it back with her from a trip to the store a couple of weeks before.

At the sight of the dogs the cat had clawed his way down

Tina's leg and run under the house. There he sat for two days, staring at the dogs in shock.

Glenn didn't figure the cat was too damned smart if it took him that long to realize the dogs were chained. Tina named him Scooter, but Glenn called him Stubs because he had short legs.

He figured it wasn't really necessary to restrain Mama Sue. She no longer paid Stubs any attention, but then she wasn't chained up either. Three other dogs lay quiet, seemingly indifferent to the cat. Two of them were, having learned the cat knew exactly where each chain stopped.

But the third one, Rastus, was merely putting on an act. One of the smartest dogs in the yard, he tried to fake the cat out. Each day, a few minutes before Stubs made his appearance, Rastus would walk to the end of his chain, back up a couple of steps, then lie down on top of the slack. But Stubs wasn't an idiot either. He never wavered one inch closer to Rastus.

Glenn grinned at Bully Blue, the most stubborn of the dogs, the last one Stubs passed on his stroll. That didn't stop him from running full speed the second Stubs appeared until the chain jerked him to a stop. This usually meant getting flipped over in midair. It never fazed Blue, though. He'd simply get up, then back up to get another running start, barking frantically.

This afternoon the cat seemed to especially enjoy antagonizing Blue. He stopped directly in front of the dog, lifted a hind leg and began to lick his ass. When Blue's tongue was hanging in exhaustion he walked off, stopping to spray a bush before disappearing in the brush to attend to his nightly wanderings.

Glenn laughed softly. "Mama Sue, I bet that idiot would love me forever if I snuck out there one night and moved his stake over about eighteen inches. What do you think?"

"It makes me think you're losing it."

Tina stood behind him, wearing a short terrycloth robe. She pulled a comb through her hair, wet from a shower.

"Sometimes I do too," he said, still watching Blue. "But then on good days I realize there's no need to worry about it, because it slipped out of my grip a long time ago."

She came and sat beside him, swinging her legs back and forth, pulled a cigarette from his pack and lit it with the tip of his.

"And if I ever catch you doing something like that you'll find yourself sleeping out there with those dogs."

She leaned over and bit him on the shoulder. "Understand?"

He grinned and her teeth dug a little deeper, deep enough to make him answer. "Okay, okay. I swear I won't mess with the damn cat."

She released him and wiped her mouth. "You better not. You taste salty."

"Just good honest sweat. What're we having for supper?"

Tina smiled. "I was thinking a good restaurant would be nice. How does that sound?"

He stood up and put Mama Sue inside the house. "I've got a feeling if I said no, anything you cooked would be burned. Let me feed the dogs first."

He gathered up the bowls and Tina walked with him to the glassed-in back porch. He poured out the feed, then used a large eyedropper to measure out heartworm medicine, following that with a vitamin solution.

After feeding the dogs he went to the back porch again and opened the cage Senator was in, recovering from a fight. Seeing the dog had managed to tear the stitches loose from one wound, he took silk thread and a needle from a cabinet and began to close it up again.

"Senator, you dumb bastard. If you'd just lay still for one day I wouldn't have to do this."

Senator paid no notice to the needle piercing his tough

hide. The dog licked Glenn's hand as he worked, seemingly aware that he was helping him heal.

Tina sat on the counter, watching him use a simple loop stitch, his hands moving confidently and gently. Just as Glenn had a thing about eyes she had one about hands. And his fascinated her, they looked so normal. Hands she knew had killed so many men in Vietnam.

Frank had always been willing to talk to her about Vietnam—just the opposite of Glenn. But seldom without Glenn being a part of the stories—going down into tunnels, how calm he stayed under fire. The one he told most often was meeting Glenn and counting the bodies as they lifted him out. According to Frank, Glenn could claim at least twenty-five, maybe thirty kills. But Glenn absolutely refused to talk about it.

He would talk about his childhood and the years after Vietnam. He told her stories about the people he'd met in prison, making them funny. But the war was a subject off-limits with him. She knew he often played hooky as a child. Not because he was dumb. Glenn had been bright enough to finish first usually; his boredom made him aggravate the other kids. He'd also told her about the bitter feeling he and his father held for each other. When she asked why he began robbing jewelry stores he said because of boredom, as much as anything. She knew that was his way of saying normal life failed to offer any excitement after Vietnam. Trying to get him to admit that, though, was like pulling teeth. . . .

Glenn finished the stitching, then poured peroxide over the wound. He shook a finger in Senator's muzzle as it frothed.

"Senator, tear these loose and I'll have to put your ass in a smaller cage so you can't move around. And I don't want to have to do that."

Tina got down, came over and slipped her arms around

him from behind. "You're so gentle when one of them is hurt."

"That's me. Mr. Gentle."

She pressed her face against his back. "I don't think so. You're too gentle to be all gentle."

She pulled back and ran her finger lightly along the long scar that ran down his back. He jerked away.

"Don't do that."

"Why won't you tell me about that? You know I'm curious about it. I'd love to hear what you did to earn your medals."

Glenn turned, eyes angry. "You know what I think? I think people who want to hear about war and its killing are just wanting a cheap . . ." He stood there a moment, searching for words, then finished with "vicarious thrill."

Tina took a step back and opened her robe. She wiggled her naked hips at him. Her heavy breasts moved back and forth gently.

"I don't think you even know what vicarious means. But I could sure use one of those cheap thrills you mentioned, big boy."

He laughed, unable to hold his anger, reached out and pulled her to him, and using both hands reached around to squeeze the cheeks of her soft ass. He kissed her, at the same time slipping his fingers between her legs, finding her already moist. Her nipples pressed against his chest, warm and hard. He pushed the robe from her shoulders until it fell off.

Tina moaned, her hands busily opening and unzipping his cutoffs. He was already erect and she stroked him a moment, pushed the cutoffs down, then broke the kiss and stepped back. "I'll meet you in the bedroom."

She was gone then, leaving her robe lying on the porch floor. Glenn stood there a moment, his cock jutting out, the cutoffs bunched around his ankles, shook his head, amused, then kicked them away and followed behind her.

He joined her on the bed and pulled her to him, running a hand down her rib cage and over her hip. His touch contained the gentleness that intrigued Tina, but beneath it was also a firmness. The kind that said he was in control and would set the pace.

She ran her lips across his cheek, searching for his mouth, joyfully accepting the intrusion of his tongue. A spasm shook her body and she pressed tighter against him, seeking more of the pleasures his fingers offered.

He trailed his tongue down her stomach, but she clutched his hair and pulled him up, then scooted under him, opening her legs wide, too impatient to accept a slow, languid lovemaking session.

"We can do all that later," she whispered. "Right now I just want you inside me."

"Then let's see if I can't make you want it a little more."

He lowered his head to her breast and sucked the nipple into his mouth, his hands stroking her rib cage. After a moment he trailed his way down to her thighs and began to tease her, kissing, biting his way up her inner thigh, then working his way back to her knees, always stopping an inch short of where she wanted him to go. Only when she began to gasp in urgency did he stop.

He poised himself above her, supporting his weight on his elbows, wanting her as much as she wanted him.

Before he could do more the dogs began barking.

In the three weeks he'd worked with the dogs he'd learned that they gave different-sounding barks. They used one kind to announce someone coming, someone familiar. This one was the other, deeper, more urgent kind, telling him they did not know this person.

He stayed above Tina a second, smiling down at her. "Uh-oh, stranger coming in. Hold what you got."

He got up and began to pull on a pair of jeans. The barks became even more urgent, which meant a car was at the house.

"Damn," Tina said, also getting up and reaching for some clothes. "Whoever it is sure has great timing."

She reached over and grabbed his still stiff cock, shaking it back and forth. "Get rid of whoever it is as fast as you can. No sense letting this go to waste."

A powder blue Cadillac was behind his Thunderbird when he stepped out on the porch. A new one, the sticker still on one tinted rear window. He turned to Tina, who stood in the door. She shrugged, having no idea who it was either. He turned back to see the driver's window slide down.

"Oh, Jesus," he muttered.

CHAPTER SEVENTEEN

"Is IT safe to get out with all those damn dogs?" Darleen asked.

"Darleen, what the hell are you doing here?"

She made no move to get out. "Well, it's nice to see you too. I'd get out, even though you haven't asked me, but I'm scared of those dogs. They look awfully mean to me."

"Get out. They're chained up. Besides, I don't know but what they ought to be more worried about you than the other way around."

She stepped out of the car, wearing an expensive blouse and slacks that looked tailored. She smiled sweetly as she walked to the porch on three-inch spiked heels.

"Do I detect some hard feelings, Glenn?"

He moved off the porch. "Don't flatter yourself. How'd you find me?"

As she stopped less than two feet from him the faint scent of White Shoulders drifted past. He saw her eyes were red, with dark circles beneath them not quite hidden by makeup.

She gestured at the dogs instead of answering his question. "What in the world are you doing with all these dogs?"

"Making a living. How'd you find me?"

"I made Eddie tell me where you were."

"Looks like I'll have to say something to Eddie."

"Don't blame him. I know how you feel about Frank and narrowed it down that you'd probably be with him. Besides, I told Eddie it wasn't just curiosity that was making me ask."

She looked at the house. "Aren't you going to ask me in?"

"No. The dog in there isn't chained."

Mama Sue would behave as long as he or Tina was there and he knew it. But somehow he just didn't want her inside.

Darleen looked at Tina standing on the porch, dressed in a halter and faded jeans ripped at the knees. Her hair was mussed and she wore no makeup, a fact registered in Darleen's eyes, quickly gone. But he saw it and a flash of anger at her judging without knowing ran through him.

"Then how about introducing me," said Darleen.

Before he could speak she moved to the edge of the porch and extended her hand, slightly bent at the wrist. "I'm Darleen, Glenn's ex-wife. I'm sure he's had a lot to say about me."

Tina took a step forward and shook her hand. "I'm Tina. And he really hasn't had that much to say about you. Should he have?"

Score one for her, thought Glenn, turning his face to hide the smile he couldn't quite keep off. He saw Darleen's jaw tighten, but she quickly composed herself.

He turned and started walking. "Come on around to the side of the house, Darleen."

She caught up with him to whisper, "What was it you said about picking somebody closer to your own age? It was you who said it, wasn't it?"

He ignored the dig. "Want a drink? No vodka, just bourbon. Plenty of Cokes and I think there's some tea in the refrigerator."

"I could use one. Mix it with Coke, if you would."

He turned to go into the house but her voice stopped him.

"And put on a shirt, Glenn. That hairy chest of yours brings back too many memories."

Tina joined him in the kitchen, making no pretense of hiding her displeasure at Darleen being there.

"What's she doing here?" she asked, although it came out more of a demand.

He shrugged as he reached up and took a bottle of George Dickel from a cabinet. "Your guess is as good as mine."

"I don't like her."

"Well, keep it to yourself. Unless she's changed one helluva lot, knowing it would tickle her no end."

He left the room, returning a moment later wearing a shirt and sticking a bag of pot in his back pocket. He got out a tray of ice, picked up the whiskey, then looked at Tina.

"Get three glasses and a couple of Cokes and come on out. At least then you'll know why she's here as soon as I do."

He set a glass and the whiskey in front of Darleen, then took a seat across the table from her. Tina came out and took a chair, which put him between the two women.

Darleen poured quite a bit of Dickel in her glass, followed by considerably less Coke. She sipped a couple of times while looking around, then took a large swallow.

"I can't imagine you way out in the country like this, Glenn. Where's Frank, anyway?"

Glenn poured a couple of fingers in his own glass and added ice. He offered the bottle to Tina but she shook her head no. He picked up the glass and swirled it around to cool it, then drank off half of it.

"A month ago I wouldn't have imagined it either. But

damned if I don't like it. Frank's in jail. Five years for grow-ing pot.''

He pulled the weed from his pocket and rolled a large joint, lit it, inhaled and offered it to Darleen. She refused, wrinkling her nose, and he handed it to Tina.

"Why are you still smoking that stuff?"

"Why do I feel like I'm going to wish I had something a little stronger?" he countered.

She did not answer him. Instead she looked at Tina with a smile. "What do you do, Tina?"

It was an innocent question, but her tone implied she knew it couldn't be much. These two instinctively disliked each other, Glenn realized. He spoke up before Tina could form an answer.

"She's a citizen, Darleen. When are you going to tell me why you're here?"

She looked at Tina. "Could we talk in private?"

Tina started to get up but he motioned her to stay. "No-body's here but us."

"But you just said she isn't one of us."

"I didn't say I don't trust her. What's on your mind?"

She hesitated, clearly not wanting to talk in front of Tina. After a moment she saw he had no intention of changing his mind.

"Do you remember the burglary I asked if you wanted in on?"

He nodded, and Darleen then told about finding the tapes and what was on them. She briefly mentioned going back to Belton to find out how much Merritt was worth, then moved on to the part about sending Larry back to extort money from Sherill. He interrupted then, steering her back to Merritt.

"Why'd you care about how much money the prosecutor had?"

"I thought I might be able to get money from both him

and Sherill. After all, Merritt's a politician, and those tapes could hurt his career."

"Any particular reason why you didn't tap Merritt?"

"He wasn't worth it. He's pure politician, wants to run for something, but it's all Sherill's money behind him."

"How long's Larry been gone?"

"This makes the fourth day."

"When's the last time you talked to him?"

"He called the night he got there and said he was going to contact Sherill the next day. I haven't heard from him since. I stayed home until this morning and by then I was so worried I went to see Eddie. I left the minute I got him to tell me where you were."

"You think there's any chance he got the money and split?"

"No. To tell the truth, I don't think he's capable of thinking that far ahead."

Glenn took the joint from Tina, staring into the woods behind the house. After a moment he looked at Darleen.

"You think he could be dead?"

"Part of me does. But another part is afraid they've got him and are trying to get him to talk."

Glenn shook his head. "No. If he didn't split I'd say he's dead. I don't care how solid Larry is, which I doubt is very much, this guy could make him tell everything he knows. What you've got to worry about is whether or not he spilled his guts before they killed him."

"Maybe Sherill had him arrested."

"You don't believe that, Darleen. That guy's not the type who's going to do that. I told you that when you asked if I wanted in. No, reading Larry his Miranda rights wouldn't be part of the package."

Darleen appeared subdued, not as self-assured as when she stepped out of the new Cadillac. "Will you help me?"

"How the hell can I help you?"

"Try and find out what's happened to Larry. And if they

know I was with him. I'll give back the damn tapes if that's what it takes."

"In other words, you want me to take up where Larry left off."

She fished a cigarette from her purse and put it in her mouth, waited a moment, saw he wasn't going to light it for her, opened her purse again and took out an expensive gold lighter.

"I'll be glad to pay you. That is, if you can make sure they don't come looking for me."

"What was the take, besides the tapes?" he asked, watching her closely.

She hesitated for the merest fraction of a second. "Two hundred thousand in cash, two hundred one-ounce bars and enough stones to bring another hundred thousand, plus a coin collection."

"I take it you bought the car out of the two hundred thousand."

Another hesitation. "No, the two hundred is what's left. I've spent thirty-five, on the car and odds and ends. Will you help me?"

Glenn was silent. He gazed at the house, then the dogs, weighing them against getting involved. He'd told her no lie; he was happy with the life he was living. He and Tina were getting along well, her presence made it a home, and he was starting to like the dogs.

A cricket started up, its chirrups loud in the peaceful quiet of the dying day. The sound reminded him why he liked it so well. Did he really want back in that kind of crap? He didn't need to meet this guy Sherill to know he would be the kind who played for keeps. What the hell did he owe Darleen? He could feel Tina, silent all this time, watching him intently.

"I want an equal cut. Either a third or half—"

"No, that's too much," Darleen protested. "I said I'd pay you, not split it with you."

Glenn drawled his words out. "And I don't think you're in much of a position to bargain."

She tossed her cigarette away. The sun had set while they talked and the coal flashed brightly in the dusky twilight, twirling end over end.

"You really know how to squeeze, Glenn. What choice do I have? Okay, yes."

"Where are the tapes?"

"In the car. I suppose you want them."

"Yeah. I want to look at 'em and I'll sure as hell need 'em if I'm going to have any leverage against this guy you ripped off. Leave 'em with me and I'll drive up there tomorrow."

Darleen stood up. "Walk to the car with me and I'll give them to you. I don't think I'll say thanks. Not since you're doing a little ripping off yourself."

Tina spoke for the first time. "You're welcome to spend the night." Not really.

The smile Darleen gave her was almost sincere. "No thanks, you folks don't need me here. I'll get a motel in Chattanooga."

"By the way," said Glenn, "whatever you do, stay away from your house, in case he does know who you are. Just be sure and let me know how to get in touch with you."

"I'll call Tina tomorrow. I'll probably go to Berry Hill and stay with my sister."

She turned and started to her car. He walked with her and opened the car door for her. Her perfume wafted past him again as she got in.

"About the money. You got it in a safe place?"

"Yes. It's in—"

"I don't care where it is. Just make sure it's someplace where nobody can stumble on it."

"I've done that. Larry doesn't even know where I put it. Do you need any for expenses?"

He smiled. "I should make enough off this to pay my own expenses."

"What are you planning on doing, Glenn? Giving the tapes back to him?"

"How the hell do I know? I haven't got up there yet. I might do what you sent a boy to try."

CHAPTER EIGHTEEN

GLENN STOOD in front of the television, watching the tape of Merritt. When it was over he ejected it and inserted the one of Dodd. He stood there silently while it played, a frown creasing his face.

Tina lay on the couch, propped up on three pillows. Several more, in bold and bright colors, were scattered around the room. It was just one of the changes made in the room since her arrival. A shelf now sat in front of the window filled with plants, and plants also hung from ceiling hooks in two corners. She'd made the house look like someone lived there instead of just staying there.

She paid no attention to the television, her eyes on Glenn. Though nothing had been said she could feel a distance between them, as if he was already gone. She mentally cursed Darleen for creating the wedge. The film ended and she spoke, looking at his back.

"Have you asked yourself why you're getting into this?"

He turned. "Are we fixing to have Psychology One-Oh-One?"

She turned on her side, propping herself up on an elbow. Her long, slender fingers disappeared in her hair, holding it out of her face.

"Why are you doing it?"

"Didn't you hear me tell Darleen what I wanted?"

"Why are you answering my questions with questions? Are you doing it for the money, or because it's Darleen?"

"Would it make—?" He caught himself and bit the question off. He backed up a step and sat on the pool table. He rolled the cue ball in a two-corner bank, then caught it and did it again.

"That's a little tough." His voice was guarded, giving his attention to the cue ball. "You can bet your ass if it hadn't got screwed up I'd never have seen her."

He began rolling and catching the ball. After a moment he reversed the roll, sending it into a corner pocket at the other end. He looked at Tina, speaking in a neutral voice.

"I turned Eddie down on a job because I was through with that kind of stuff. But that wasn't really why I originally turned Darleen down. Because it was her, yes, I was interested. I said no to it because it was her job and not mine, so that means I was jealous. But another reason was I didn't know Larry and I thought he seemed too weak to trust. But I also told her this guy Sherill would kill her if he found out who took him off. She just laughed and said he'd have to find out who did it before he could do any killing."

"If you'd found out about Sherill yourself would you have robbed him?"

"I don't think so."

She waited a moment, then sat up, folding her legs under her. "Why is getting something out of you like pulling teeth? You were in prison for robbing a jewelry store. This was just a burglary. But like Darleen said, the man would have to find out who you were first, which wouldn't have happened if she hadn't tried to get something for the tapes. Why wouldn't you have done it?"

He shrugged. "Because I'd made up my mind to get out. But other than that, jewelry stores are insured, and you're dealing with clerks. A clerk doesn't own the stuff, which means he's going to help you all he can so you'll get that pistol out of his face and out of the store."

He jerked a thumb at the television. "But guys like that will bust their ass looking for you. The only safe way to take him off would be to kill him from jump. I never was into it that much."

He put a hand on the rail on each side of him and leaned back. "Darleen thought she could get away with it but she screwed up. She might need a good ass kicking, but she doesn't need killing. I'm getting in because I don't want that to happen." He allowed a grin. "But I'm also level-headed enough to make something off of it."

"So now you'll do what? Kill the man?"

"No. Yeah, maybe if it came to that. But I don't know what I'll do until I get up there. Maybe I can convince him the best thing would be to accept his loss."

"Just don't make the mistake of thinking you can trust Darleen."

"Wait a minute, you don't even know her. She can be a bitch but you can trust her—"

"Glenn, Darleen is a snake. And if you don't watch out she'll bite you."

He smiled, thinking of the scores he and Darleen had made together. "I don't suppose this assumption on your part could be blamed on a little jealousy."

Tina reached for a cigarette. "No. I'm much too smart for that, Glenn Odom."

She blew out a stream of smoke, holding the cigarette beside her cheek, running her thumbnail beneath a finger-nail. Her green eyes looked at him.

"If I thought it would do any good I would be. Jealous. But you're a long way from being ready to love anyone. Like it or not, Darleen hurt you deep."

He shook his head. "No good. Have I moped around, used your shoulder to cry on? You haven't once heard me say anything about my heart being broke."

"That's true. Like everything else, you hold it inside. Afraid to show any weakness. But the shoulder was there all along."

She got up to leave the room. At the door she stopped and looked back at him.

"You better wake up, Glenn. You're heading into something that's going to end up with people hurt, maybe dead. It could be you. And you're doing it for a woman you don't know anymore." She turned then and closed the door behind her.

Glenn went into the kitchen and made himself a drink. He filled a glass with ice, then poured until the cubes floated. He carried it and the bottle to the couch, feeling the warmth of Tina's body still on it. He sipped the whiskey steadily until he felt his lips start to tingle, absorbed in the thoughts Tina left him with.

He'd bet Larry was no longer alive. But he would have been if Darleen had been happy with the take from the burglary alone. The score was plenty big enough. His eyes narrowed, recalling the hesitation she'd shown when he asked how much they'd gotten. Had she lied about it?

Was Tina right about her? The question brought more questions and Glenn reached for the bottle, set it back down without pouring. The last thing he needed was to start tomorrow with a hangover.

No, Darleen might be a lot of things but he didn't think she would hold out on a partner. And a partner was what he'd become, happy about it or not.

Okay, he still had feelings for Darleen. Nothing he couldn't handle, and in time those would fade to where he could think about her without hurting. He supposed he would always have some love for her, nothing wrong with that. On the other hand, it didn't bother him that maybe there was a love in Tina's past still with her.

He walked to the bedroom door, opened it and stood there watching the outline of Tina's still form. After a moment she raised up and turned on the lamp, casting a soft glow across the room. She looked at him with a smile too damn wise for her years. She moved her arm, letting the sheet fall below one pale nippled breast.

"It's late, and it'll take a while for you to finish what you started this afternoon, Glenn."

CHAPTER
NINETEEN

BELTON LAY three miles east of 129, coming south from Knoxville, twenty miles distant. It was small, maybe five thousand people, nestled in the foothills of the Smoky Mountains. Glenn arrived in midafternoon and drove through the town, familiarizing himself with it.

It was a pretty town, clean, with Main Street turned into one of the semi-malls fashionable in small towns during the early Seventies. He drove through it, noting that like most other small towns, it had failed to lure business away from the shopping centers.

The two principal streets came together at the top of a hill and the light caught him. Immediately across the intersection, the street dipped sharply, leaving a panoramic view of the Smokies thirty miles away. The light changed and he went across and down, seeing the courthouse square three blocks ahead.

He circled it, a three-story building over a hundred years old. Attached to it was a modern two-story building that was the sheriff's office and jail. The customary Civil War cannon sat in front of the courthouse, and the four-faced clock with Roman numerals still worked. In back was the deputies' parking lot. The jail entrance was part of a parking lot that occupied half the ground floor. Glenn knew from experience the cars in it would belong to the sheriff, judges, chief detective and the like.

He turned back the way he came and pulled into the first motel he came to on 129, the Mountain View. After registering he drove around to the back side, where he was forced to park a few spaces away from his room. Tourist season was in full swing, and from the number of cars it looked like the motel was almost filled up. The view looked out across a set of gentle hills, dotted infrequently with houses.

He got his suitcase and carryall out of the trunk, brought them into the room, which could have been a generic Holiday Inn. The motif was pale green—the wallpaper, the bedspread, even down to the seat cushions on the two chairs beside the table in front of the window. He dumped the suitcase on the bed, hung up the carryall, then drove back to Belton.

During the night he had remembered a man from Belton who had celled a few doors down from him. A pool player, he shot and wounded a man for refusing to pay and did a ten-year sentence behind it. He'd gotten out six months or so before Glenn, and Glenn figured he'd be the one to ask about Sherill.

At the edge of town was a small tavern, the White Horse, and he pulled in. It was empty except for two men he took for salesmen at the end of the bar, arguing sports. Behind them was a pool table, its felt brushed clean. He took a stool at the other end of the bar, where the bartender stood reading a newspaper.

The bartender, about Glenn's age and wearing a greasy apron, reluctantly put the paper down and brushed back a lank of black hair. The hair looked like it had been rubbed with the apron. He didn't speak, just waited for Glenn to tell him what he wanted.

Glenn rested his arm on the bar, then moved it because it felt sticky. "Miller Lite."

He glanced down at the paper the man left behind, saw it was a local, the Belton *Herald*. An article seemed to jump up at him, something about the body of a man found shot and still not identified. He turned the paper toward him but the bartender was back with his beer before he could read it. The bartender took a five from Glenn, then picked up the paper and carried it with him as he walked to the register for change.

Sociable son of a bitch, thought Glenn, tilting his head back and drinking from the can. He set it down, leaving his change on the bar.

"I'm trying to find a fella, Stacy Denison. You know him?"

The bartender stopped reading to look at the change in front of him. "Name don't ring no bells."

It was a lie. Glenn knew it, and the man knew he knew it. The pool table told him that. In a town this small, Denison would be known in every bar that had one. He took another swallow of beer, refusing to buy the man into a better memory.

"Tall fella, mid-thirties, pool player."

All he got was a shake of the head. This time the man didn't even look up from the paper.

He took a napkin and scribbled a short note, giving his name, the motel he was staying at and his room number. He asked Stacy to call and signed it, writing "12/6" behind his name. It would mean nothing to the bartender unless he'd been there, and Glenn thought chances were good he had. It was his old cell number and walk. He pushed it in front of the man.

"Well, just in case you remember him get this message to him. He'd be mad if you didn't."

With the edge of his palm he scooped his change off the bar and got off the stool, took a step, then turned back and tapped the newspaper with his finger.

"Oh, yeah. About four years ago he shot a man in one of

these bars for not doing like he should. You might remember reading about it. Hell, it might've happened in here. If you really don't know him maybe you ought to ask around."

He found another bar a few blocks away, but there was no pool table. The barmaid was a friendly enough woman and he believed her when she said she didn't know Stacy. He stayed long enough to finish his beer and get directions to the one pool hall in Belton.

It was in the center of town, under the sidewalk, only a couple of blocks from the courthouse. He went down the short flight of stairs, reading a sign above the door that said a tournament would be held over the weekend. An odor of stale beer and smoke greeted him when he stepped inside. It was like the two bars he'd just been in, almost deserted. No tables were in use, but four old men were engaged in a domino game, two of them cussing each other over a bad move one of them had made.

The man behind the counter was smiling as he listened to the old men exchange insults. Short and overweight, he gave off an aura of being the owner as he greeted Glenn.

"Need a table?"

Glenn shook his head and handed the man a note he'd written at the second bar. "No. I need you to do me a favor. I won't even bother asking how to get in touch with Stacy Denison. Wouldn't expect you to tell me. But I'd really appreciate it if you got this message to him."

The man read it, shrugged and put it in his shirt pocket. "I don't see any problem with that. Care for a beer?"

Glenn refused, thanked the guy and left, knowing he would be talking to Stacy no later than tomorrow. Back on 129 he pulled into a small café, smiling at the name, Mama's Place. But inside he found himself treated with a friendliness that lived up to the name. After ordering he unfolded the paper he'd bought before coming in.

The paper was like the town, small, a twice-weekly. The

article told little, just repeated that the body was found behind a church early Sunday, shot to death. It gave a description that could have easily fit twenty-five percent of the men in Tennessee. But Glenn felt the article was describing Larry.

He pushed the plate away and accepted the waitress's offer of a second glass of tea. Was it going to be this easy to find Larry? A trip to the morgue would tell him that. The whereabouts of Larry were only part of the problem, and a small part at that. He sipped his tea and watched the traffic passing, wishing he could come up with a better plan. Several minutes later the glass was empty and he realized his thoughts had drifted to Tina. He got up, left a tip, paid for his meal and left.

He returned to his room, planning on staying there the remainder of the afternoon and night. The first thing he saw after unlocking the door was the red message light on the phone blinking. A call to the desk got him Stacy's number and he punched it into the phone. While it rang he opened his suitcase, holding the receiver with his chin.

"Hello, Stacy," he said after the phone was answered. "Glad you got my message. I'm sure you remember me."

The two had celled a few doors from each other more than three years, walked past each other three and four times a day. Neither did more than speak in passing, perhaps exchanged remarks about the weather. Yet both knew the other to be the kind to mind his own business and not care to know the next man's. They were quiet men, each for his own reasons, each with his own small circle of friends.

The voice that came back was deep, relaxed. "Hell yeah, I remember you, Glenn. I tried to call you fifteen minutes after you talked to Harold. Then I got a call from Moon. I got two different descriptions of you. Harold called you a son of a bitch, Moon said you seemed like a nice fellow."

"Moon must've been the guy at the White Horse," Glenn said. "Harold needs an attitude adjustment."

"He gets one every month or so. What're you doing up this way?"

"I need to find out a few things about somebody you'll know. It'll take longer than I want to go into over the phone. If you aren't too busy I'd like to see you. Do a little talking, drink some whiskey."

"Sounds good to me. I should be there in twenty minutes. It'd be easier than trying to give you directions." The voice was friendly but it was unmistakable that until he knew more Stacy preferred to keep his address to himself.

Glenn used the time to unpack. When he finished he took the ice bucket and filled it from the machine in the breezeway. On the way back he watched an immaculate dark blue '74 Chrysler Cordoba ease by and turn into a space a few doors past his room. Stacy Denison stepped out of it and waited for Glenn.

He was tall, slender, good-looking. Blond hair brushed straight back, long enough to cover his ears and fall just below his shirt collar. When Glenn came up level with him he extended his hand.

"You look good, Glenn. When did you get out?"

"Five, six weeks ago." He gestured at the Chrysler. "I like that car."

Stacy grinned. "I do too, so don't even think about asking how much I want for it."

"That was going to be my next question. Come on in and let's have that drink."

Stacy took a seat, stretching out his long legs and crossing his ankles. He said ice would be plenty since it was George Dickel they would be drinking. They exchanged small talk a few minutes and then Glenn asked if he knew Sherill.

Stacy looked at him, nodded. "Yeah, I know Sherill. Him and his son both. Why you asking about him?"

Glenn shrugged. "Suppose we were back in the joint and I was asking you for a character reference on him."

"I'd say stay away from the son of a bitch in there or out here. He's more poisonous than a snake, and can be trusted about as much as one."

Glenn pulled a cigarette from his pack and offered one to Stacy, who shook his head. After lighting up he asked another question, smoke drifting from his mouth as the words came out.

"You suppose Sherill might have any money in his house?"

"Yeah. No telling how much either. But there's plenty places that'd be easier."

Glenn smiled. "He'd get hot about it, huh?"

"He'd be pissed all right. I sure wouldn't want him to find out I did it."

"It's already been done." Glenn paused a beat. "And guess what? One guy has come up missing."

Stacy didn't blink, just sipped his whiskey. "Any doubt in your mind what happened to him?" Followed quickly by: "How much did that old bastard have in his house?"

"I didn't get it, but I know it was a good lick. One of the people who was involved came to me." He hesitated, then shrugged. "What the hell would you call me? Consultant? Anyway, the guy wants me to keep Sherill off his ass."

Stacy drained his glass, looked at his watch, then reached for the bottle. "Trouble-shooter would be a better name, 'cause trouble is what you'll get into if you aren't real careful. I'm going to make myself one more drink. That'll give me time to tell you about Sherill. It's a story."

For the next five minutes Stacy talked steadily. He spoke with a lazy drawl, using his hands to help express himself. The majority of his knowledge came from his father; Sherill was probably twice his age. . . .

George Sherill came over from North Carolina in the late years of World War II. Actually it was his wife who was from North Carolina. Nobody knew exactly where he came from.

He built the Broke Spoke and began doing good business from the start. At the time there was one other tavern in the county itself, the Sand Pit, five or six miles away. The two men who owned it then were almost as powerful as Sherill had become. Back then there was no such thing as dope in Edwards County, but they controlled all the moonshine and gambling. They made no secret of wanting Sherill to close down.

He refused, and inside of six months of opening there was a serious fire in the Spoke. Sherill repaired the damage and went about his business. A month after he reopened his tavern dynamite made a shambles out of the Sand Pit two hours after closing time.

Sherill was reputed to have walked up to the two men while they looked over the damage and said, "Boys, I intend to operate in this county."

Whatever he said, it must have been pretty strong. The men never tried to reopen, and no other tavern had operated in the county since. From the start it had been run like it was now, wide open. There was a band on weekends, in the section Sherill had added a few years back, and for the most part it was attended by husbands and wives. But the original part of the Spoke was open for business seven days a week. There was always at least one whore to be found day or night. Two pool tables and never less than one or two buddies of Roy's to play against. And if you won you'd probably get to test your fighting skills before getting to your car with the money.

Sherill used his money wisely. He was known for saying that unlike most thieves he saved fifty cents of every dollar he stole. Slowly but steadily he bought up the land around him. From the beginning he contributed heavily to whatever sheriff was in office for the privilege of operating the Spoke. He mixed in politics, at first strictly in the background, generous with his money. Then ten or twelve years back he had become entrenched solid enough to come out front with it, handpicking the top county officials.

Stacy told of a man doing like the snake, eating itself. Sherill had once been considered solid in the world of criminals. He gave a fair price for stolen goods, made bond for those he knew would pay him back. But as he became more involved in politics he changed. Still the fence, but more. No dope could be sold without him getting a healthy cut. Refuse and you'd find yourself doing a little time. Threaten him and you wouldn't be found. . . .

"That's the old man," said Stacy. "His son Roy is another story. I went to school with him. He was just a fat coward then—still is today, for that matter. But he's also mean, to make up for being a coward, I guess. Don't get me wrong. He'll shoot you in a minute in the bar or anywhere around it. Knows his daddy is strong enough to get him out of it. He's always got a pistol in his back pocket. The old man carries one there too. If you have to deal with either one you sure better watch your ass."

Glenn nodded, taking it all in. "How could I see Sherill without going to his place?"

"That's easy. There's a Denny's in the shopping center a mile down the road from where you're sitting now. Just watch for a black Lincoln with a guy in his late sixties driving it. He eats breakfast there every morning. Him and a couple of cronies, other political shakers and movers in Edwards County. Such as it is."

"What about that, Stacy? I know there's not enough action in this town just in pool. How do you make enough to get by?"

"I mostly play in Knoxville but I travel a couple of weeks out of the month too."

He stood up, ready to leave, and Glenn spoke again. "One more thing. Tell me how to get to his bar."

Stacy looked at his watch again. "I've got some time. Why not follow me and I'll drive you past it."

He shook hands with Glenn. "It was good to see you. Glad you're out. All I got to say is be damned careful around Sherill. I expect that old bastard's dug more than one grave back in those hollows."

CHAPTER TWENTY

STACY TURNED south on 129, then right at the first road intersecting the divided four-lane highway. He drove like he talked. Fast instead of slow, but just as relaxed, his right arm flung across the back of the seat. Shortly after turning he was doing seventy on the narrow, twisting asphalt road.

Glenn stayed with him, uncomfortable seeing how deep the Chrysler leaned going into the first curve. The road got no better and he slowed, unwilling to speed into something he couldn't see around. Stacy disappeared over a hill to reappear a moment later, slowing a little. Another couple of miles and he turned to the right.

This road took them about six miles deeper into a remote rural area of the county. Houses were plentiful but not what the tourist business would show to entice you to Tennessee. These houses, unpainted as often as not, were more along the line of shacks. Few had foundations, supported instead by large rocks set under each corner. The people living in them worked in the boat factories and meat-packing plants in the area, making fifty cents above minimum wage. Ingrained suspicion, combined with little or no education, made them reject the unions. "By gawd, I ain't givin' no son of a bitch part of my money jist to work." So they gave the companies the best part of their lives, and as a reward the companies gave them five bucks an hour after fifteen years on jobs that sucked the life out of them.

There were also plenty of ragged-assed kids, a lot of them playing under the houses. The setting sun glinted off the windshields of faded and dented "We tote the note" junkers parked in the front yards. Many of them were like the houses—no foundations, just resting on blocks.

They passed three churches, built only marginally better than the houses. Getting what the car lot, the finance companies and U-Can-Rent didn't. Glenn wondered if Larry had been found behind one of them. He no longer even entertained the notion Larry might be alive.

The road ended at a T-shaped intersection and Stacy got out and walked back to the Thunderbird.

"Here's where I turn right but you turn left. It'll be on the left, less'n a quarter-mile down." He straightened, slapping the door as he stepped back. "Good seeing you, Glenn. Just be sure and watch your ass."

"Same here, Stacy. And I appreciate it."

Glenn watched him drive away feeling just how alone he was. Stacy had talked freely and asked few questions, but he'd made it plain Glenn was on his own. He pressed the accelerator and turned left, before the thought of being in this alone could put down roots.

He rounded a curve, and there it was. No name on a sign, just a wagon wheel with a broken spoke hanging from a pole. He counted seven vehicles as he drove past to pull in and park at the end of the building. Only one of them was a car. The rest were Jeeps and four-wheel-drive pickups, transportation of choice for tobacco-chewing mountain rednecks.

Knowing he would be out of place inside, he stayed in the car a moment. Shit, Ray Charles could see this was a place a fellow might need a pistol. But he had left home without one. The last thing he needed as an ex-con was to get popped for carrying a gun.

He opened the door and got out, looking across the road past the mobile home to the house beyond it. Sitting at the top of the hill, a rambling split-level looking down at the world. Set it in East Memphis and it would sell for two hundred thousand or better. But it wasn't the kind of house he would have looked at and thought it would hold such a big score. As he started for the door of the tavern he recalled Stacy telling him the house had been built with inmate labor from the county jail.

The tavern was maybe seventy-five feet long with two narrow, darkly tinted windows set chest high. Bricked waist-high, the rest treated wood stained a dark brown by age and weather. The door was full plate glass in a wooden frame, decorated with cigarette ads, pretty blondes smoking Salems and rugged men with Winstons or Marlboros. Inside, immediately to his right, stood the jukebox, country music blaring from it. A poker machine on his left, with a man sitting in front of it feeding in quarters to build up the odds.

A nod at the man got him an uninterested one in return. He started for the bar twenty feet or so across the room, wondering if the guy had ever heard the maxim, "Beware of anything that puts its back against the wall and challenges the world." In between, slightly to his left, stood a large potbellied stove doing nothing but taking up space in the midsummer heat.

As he walked across the floor Glenn took in the signs hanging on the walls. All of them were made of metal, advertisements for everything from Coca-Cola to plows, old enough to be valuable. A Lydia Pinkham Tonic sign dating from the turn of the century hung above a door at the end of the bar. The model's blushing cheeks suggested she might have been willing to show you just what made the Nineties so gay.

He took a stool, more or less in the center of the bar, and the man he knew from Stacy's description to be Roy stood in front of him. "I don't know you" was written plainly on his face. Mixed with "And I want to know why you're in here."

But what Glenn heard was, "What'll you have?" asked in a friendly enough voice.

He said Miller Lite, laying a twenty on the bar. When Roy walked off he swung around to look the place over. Six tables and three booths, fairly crowded. Nine boys and six girls. At least they were to him. All of them ranged from ten to fifteen years his junior.

The dance area was closed, shut off by a folding partition, cutting the size of the tavern by more than half. In a corner stood two pinball machines. Like the poker machine, they paid off in cash. Beyond them, separated by a railing waist-high, were two pool tables. A game was being played on one of them, and both pinball machines were in use.

His call was right; he did stand out, and all eyes had watched him come in, marking him as an unknown. All were dressed in work clothes, T-shirts, jeans well-coated with dirt and grease, and work boots. Even Roy wore jeans, faded but clean. Glenn wore a pale blue Ban-lon pullover, gray slacks and a pair of loafers.

A girl at the end of the bar disengaged herself from two guys barely out of their teens and ambled toward Glenn, big-busted, wearing a halter top too small and cutoff jeans that were too short. As she came close he saw she was in her early twenties, heavy breasts etched with stretch marks from childbearing while still only a child herself.

She took the stool next to him. "Well, hello. This might turn out to be my lucky night."

Glenn smiled, scratching his beard below his ear. "What makes you say that?"

She raised and lowered one shoulder. "Them two down yonder ain't gonna spend no money. You look like you might."

She smiled, revealing bad teeth. He took a swallow of his beer, then looked around again.

"What's there to spend it on? I'll buy you a drink, give you a couple of bucks to play the machines. But I wouldn't exactly call that being a big spender."

She stuck one of her legs between his, rubbing his thigh with a knee. "You could just spend it on me."

"Where could we go? I don't live around here."

She nodded toward the door at the end of the bar. "There's a bedroom back there."

Apparently the door led into a kitchen; he could see a refrigerator and the corner of a stove. He was tempted to accept her offer, just to see more of the area, but shook his head.

"It's tempting, but to tell the truth I just stopped to get directions."

The girl made a face and got off the stool. "Hey, Roy. This guy wants you more than he does me."

Roy took his foot off the edge of a cooler beneath the bar and started in their direction. She smiled and patted Glenn on the leg.

"Get lost a little earlier next time, hon."

He watched her enter the restroom, a smile on his face. It was still in place when he turned to look at Roy, who looked back at him, suspicion in the back of his narrow eyes.

"I took a wrong turn somewhere. I'm trying to get back to Belton."

"Where you comin' from?"

He allowed the smile to turn into a sheepish grin. "Belton. I was out driving around, you got some pretty country around here, and didn't pay close enough attention."

Roy propped a foot up again, shifted around to get comfortable, then stuck a Kool in his mouth. "Yeah, it's pretty all right. What part of the country you from?"

All good-ole-boy country friendly, but Glenn didn't fail to

notice he was trying a lot harder to get information than give it. He lifted his arm and looked at his watch.

"Just the other side of Chattanooga. I'd appreciate it if—"

"Oh yeah," Roy said, lighting the cigarette. "You ain't lost, jist a little turned around."

Roy gave him directions that would take him back the way he came. Glenn thanked him and left.

As he got in the Thunderbird he felt Roy had sized him up as a man not wanting an ass chewing from his wife. Which pleased him, but on the other hand he hadn't learned anything useful either. Roy seemed no different from any man running a honky-tonk, no different from Glenn himself when he owned a bar. No, they'd been honky-tonks too. And he knew from experience that your real self was the one thing you never show to customers.

There was a Taco Bell on 129, and he pulled in, using the drive-through window, then taking the food to the motel. As he ate he thought first of calling Tina, then Darleen, and rejected both ideas. He undressed, got in bed, lit a cigarette and looked back over the past thirty-six hours.

What the hell was he going to do? Blackmail was out of the question. Larry was enough to convince him not to try that. He'd be satisfied just to give the tapes back. Question was, would Sherill be satisfied with that? He was going to have to do some strong talking to convince Sherill the best thing to do would be to cut his losses and be happy with the deal. But how could he convince the man there were no copies? Sherill was the kind of guy who would want to erase the copy from his brain, and Glenn strongly disapproved of the method necessary for that.

He fell asleep thinking of Darleen getting out of that fucking blue Cadillac. At least she had enough sense to know she couldn't get away from Sherill in it. At least she was acting like it anyway. Yeah, she really had control of things, all right.

CHAPTER
TWENTY-ONE

GLENN ATE breakfast downtown, looking out at Cedar Hills Hospital on the edge of town. Like Stacy said, easy to find. Just look for the tallest building sitting on the tallest hill. The morgue was located there, but he ate heartily in spite of having to go there when he finished the meal.

The receptionist in the hospital lobby gave him directions to the basement. The morgue greeted him too quick on leaving the elevator to think about it being the gloomy place it was. He stepped through the double doors and saw a man dressed in hospital whites behind a counter. Absorbed in a soap opera on a tiny black-and-white television, he waited until Glenn got to him before looking up.

The man chilled him where the morgue had failed. Fifty-ish, almost bald, wearing makeup and with a nose Glenn wished he owned filled with quarters. The freak batted his eyes, smiling with lips the texture of cooked liver.

"Can I help you?"

"I hope not." He unfolded the paper he'd bought the day before.

"I'm from Knoxville and my sister's husband's been missing over a week. She read this and insisted I come see if it might be him. He fits the description and it's got her worried."

The man studied him a moment, then got up, motioning for Glenn to follow him. He swished to the other end of the room and opened a door, turning on the lights as he went through it.

The room was small, with six storage lockers two high along one wall. The attendant walked to the top center one and pulled it out. With a snap of his wrist he flipped the sheet back to Larry's waist, watching Glenn, disappointed when he showed no reaction.

Glenn stood below Larry's head, so the first thing he saw was the bullet hole under his chin. It was small, round and neat, and black with dried blood. A thin blue streak of bruised skin circled it, and still another circle, this one filled with tiny black dots. Gunpowder, which he knew was a result of being shot point-blank.

He looked at Larry's face, at the grayness death brings. Wondered what it was that made someone appear so different in death. The face on the slab looked nothing like the Larry he'd met, but there was no doubt who it was. The scar was there, slicing through the eyebrow, and it flashed through his mind that Larry wasn't ever going to get old enough for the scar to make him look sinister. He just looked dead.

He turned and started out of the room, talking over his shoulder. "Never saw that guy before. Sorry to bother you."

When the elevator stopped at the ground floor he stepped out and walked through the lobby into the bright sunshine. The time spent in the morgue hadn't been long enough to really feel the chill; still, the sun felt good.

He walked to the car deep in thought. Seeing Larry was no surprise, it merely confirmed what he'd strongly suspected from the start. It also went a long way in eliminating hope that Sherill might be a reasonable man.

He unlocked the Thunderbird, got in and started the engine but did not put it in gear. First he lit a cigarette, dragged deep on it, then turned on the air-conditioning. He did not see the morgue attendant behind him, breathing hard from running up the single flight of stairs to memorize his license number.

All right, what was he going to do? Why the hell was he even involved in all this? Tina was right. He was in it because Darleen was in trouble, and he still carried a fucking torch for her.

Okay, well and good, but that ain't getting your own ass out of the fire. And the fucking tapes were going to keep that fire plenty hot until he put them back in Sherill's hands. The more he thought about it, the more convinced he became that Sherill wasn't going to be satisfied just getting his tapes back. Well, if Sherill acted too shitty he could give Sheriff Dodd the one of him and the other one to Merritt, let them fight it out with the old bastard. Glenn had understood immediately why Sherill made the tapes, to make sure those two stayed bought and paid for. The thought faded. Doing something like that might divert Sherill temporarily, but it wouldn't stop him from going after Darleen.

DODD LISTENED, scribbling on a notepad, his head tilted to the side to hold the receiver between his ear and his shoulder. After a curt thanks he hung up, ripped the page from the pad, got up and left his office located at the end of the hall. He walked the length of it, past the detective office, one large room containing four desks. Next to it was the station's only interrogation room. Across from it was the squad room, its tables and chairs moved about haphazardly.

He looked through the door of the squad room as he rapped on the door leading into the booking and jail area. The floor was littered with paper, cigarette butts and crumpled cups. While waiting he made a mental note to have a trustee clean it up. The buzzer sounded, unlocking the door; he opened it and walked to the small room where the dispatcher was.

Dodd laid the scrap of paper in front of the dispatcher, a man in his late forties. "Put out a local APB, just for our boys, for this car. Then run it through and find out who owns it."

The dispatcher sent the message, which was acknowledged by five of the six deputies on patrol. He listened to the sixth one, grinning up at Dodd.

"Is this guy considered dangerous, Milt?"

Milt keyed his mike, looking and sounding bored. "You know as much I do, Wilson. Keep an eye out and call in if you spot 'im."

The radio crackled back. "Well, what's this guy done that makes us want 'im?"

Dodd shook his head. "Tell him—never mind. Hand me the mike."

He leaned down, the mike all but invisible in his big hand, the desk low enough to make his ass stick up in the air. "Wilson, who said this fellow has done anything? Just watch for that car."

Wilson had a trait that either makes a cop a good one or a bad one—he was stubborn. In his case it worked against him.

"Well, sheriff, we must want this guy for somethin'."

"How do you know his mother hasn't died?"

Wilson changed tactics. "You sure you don't want me to pull 'im over and tell 'im? I handle those kind of situations pretty good, you know."

Dodd cursed under his breath and looked down at Milt. "I want you to listen to that. Coming from a guy who'd fuck up a two-car funeral." He keyed the mike. "Wilson, how would you like to pull some third-shift duty—as jailer?"

The radio went silent and Dodd handed the mike back to Milt. "What the hell. I'm not about to fire Ellen's nephew. I just keep hoping that Boy Scout enthusiasm of his will get him shot."

He returned to his office and a few minutes later Milt brought him the information on the license number. The Thunderbird was owned by a Glenn Odom.

Dodd put his feet on the desk and leaned back, his hands locked behind his head. The first link to Larry Hazelton he had and it came from Memphis, the other end of the state. He'd hoped, while not believing, that it would be a local boy behind the burglary. One thing was for sure, though. Larry Hazelton hadn't been the brains. A glance at his rap sheet proved that. He'd been arrested several times, all of it two-bit stuff like shoplifting and petty larceny.

There'd also been no luck on getting information about where Hazelton had been living. He'd left Knoxville a little more than a year back, no one knew where to. Criminals didn't leave forwarding addresses, they just left. As often as not they themselves didn't know where they were going when they took off.

So who was this Odom? Somebody who lived in Shelby County and felt like he needed to go to the morgue and look at Larry Hazelton's body. Why? A criminal didn't check out a morgue to see if his partner was there. He just kept his split.

Dodd dropped his feet and swung around to the computer. As he typed with two fingers he made a bet with himself that NCIC would have a file on this Odom.

GLENN SAW the green-and-white sheriff's car pull out of a mini-market and fall in behind him, watched it in the rear-view mirror, wary, but relieved some when he turned in at the motel and it went on.

Darleen was staying with her sister in Berry Hill, a Nashville suburb, so that was the number he dialed. Darryl, the sister's son, answered the phone. He hollered for Darleen, and it sounded like he didn't bother to take the receiver away from his mouth.

Glenn smiled, hearing the boy's voice start out deep, only to crack on the second syllable. He recalled the last time he'd seen Darryl and realized with a start that the boy would now be in his teens.

Darleen came on, sounding a little breathless. "Thank God. I've been worried to death. I was expecting you to call last night. Why didn't you?"

"Why? I just got here yesterday. Anytime I know something I'll call."

The tension in her voice came through the lines. "What've you found out?"

He hesitated. Maybe he hadn't cared for Larry, but she had. Enough to leave him. He spoke gently.

"Larry's in the morgue, Darleen."

A moment of silence and then her voice—containing no sorrow, sounding matter-of-fact. "Okay. I guess that makes it a two-way split."

The coldness surprised him. "The man is dead, Darleen. He was your boyfriend—"

"And all that won't bring him back. I was going to leave him anyway. I just hadn't got around to telling him."

Tina's words came back to him. It was looking more and more like she was right. Maybe he didn't know Darleen any longer. Five years could bring a lot of changes. Her voice came over the phone, so damned cool and impersonal.

"So what're you planning on doing? I don't want this man after me."

"And I'm working on that. Have you got the money and merchandise with you?"

"Damn right I do. You didn't think I was going to run off and leave it, did you?"

No, not hardly, but he kept the thought to himself. "Bring it with you and meet me at a place called Troy's Butcher Block in Chattanooga tonight."

"Why? Will it be over by then?"

"Just be there, Darleen. With the money."

Before she could answer he broke the connection. He looked around the room, decided not to pack, then went into the bathroom. A moment later he came out carrying his toothbrush and shaving gear. He carried them to the car and pulled out, stopping at the office to pay two days in advance.

When he pulled onto the highway he saw the same patrol car leave the drugstore across the road and fall in behind him. A glance in the mirror showed the deputy talking into his mike, which made him tense up again, but a couple of miles passed with no blue light flashing. At least he wouldn't be pulled over.

The game's started, he thought. So Dodd was wise to him, and it had to be from knowing about his trip to the morgue. It also told him Dodd knew Larry's identity. He just wished he knew how much else the sheriff knew.

The deputy stayed with him all the way to the Knox county line, where the cop made a U-turn and headed back to Belton. Glenn watched, smiling slightly. He'd be out of sight for a couple of days, which would make Dodd and Sherill wonder why, where he was and what he was up to. Not knowing was sure to make them nervous.

He turned onto the interstate, thinking he'd better smile now . . . when he came back somebody would be getting in touch with him. And he was willing to bet it would be a hands-on kind of touch.

CHAPTER TWENTY-TWO

GLENN SAW Darleen come through the door, picked his drink up off the bar and went to meet her. With a hand on her elbow he guided her into the restaurant, noticing most of the men watched her as she walked past. She was wearing a peach-colored, scooped-back mini-dress that showed off her legs, cinched at the waist with a white, soft leather belt. He didn't know what the material was, but it screamed expensive.

"I had hell trying to find this damned place," she said after they were seated. "I hope you didn't have me drive all the way up here just to have dinner."

Before he could answer, the waitress was there with their menus. He ordered a Vodka Collins for her and another drink for himself.

"Try one of the steaks, Darleen. I don't think I've ever had better than they fix here."

She looked at him, her mouth set in a thin line. "I don't want a steak. I want to know what's going on."

"You can't eat and listen at the same time?"

The waitress came back with their drinks and asked if they were ready to order.

"Yes. I'll have a Kansas City Strip, medium rare, baked potato, no salad." He looked at Darleen.

"I'll have a Chef's Salad." She took a big gulp of her drink, set it down and tapped the glass. "And bring me another one of these, but make it a double."

After the waitress moved away she said, "Okay, I've ordered. Now will you tell me what you found out?"

"They know I'm up there. After I went to the morgue a cop tailed me to the motel and then to the county line."

"How did you find out Larry was in the morgue?"

"I read the paper. There was an article about a body matching his description. According to the article the law doesn't know who he is."

"Maybe they don't know."

"When did you start going on hope? He had ID on him, didn't he? What happened to his car?"

"He drove a pickup truck."

"I don't give a damn if he rode a bicycle. They know who he is. Believe it. And by now you can bet they know all about me too."

"Why would they kill him? He didn't have the tapes with him."

"That puzzles me too. There weren't any bruises on his body, which there would've been if they'd tried beating it out of him. Only thing I can figure is he either gave them the impression he did have them or else they killed him accidentally trying to scare him."

She finished off her drink. "It seems to me I'm in more trouble than ever if they know your name. It wouldn't take much of a cop to hook us together."

"Your concern for Larry is real touching, lady. But at least it isn't necessarily true that your name will be hooked to his. If anything, they're going to figure me for his partner. I'm the one who's up there nosing around."

The food came and Glenn busied himself, cutting up the entire steak before taking a bite. She pushed her salad to the side and lit a cigarette.

"So what are you going to do?"

He split his potato, loaded it with butter, promising himself he'd do an extra set of push-ups as penance. "One thing I'm not going to do is try to extort money out of Sherill. You can bet your bottom dollar on that. Being greedy is what got your ass in the sling it's in now."

"You mean you're just going to give them back to him?"

"That's exactly what I'm going to do."

She struck the weak spot immediately. "Do you honestly think he'll let you do that? There's no way he's not going to think you don't have copies. He'll figure you'll be back wanting money."

"Yeah, I know. What you tried to do is enough to convince him of that. Giving 'em back would be a damn sight easier if you hadn't tried to blackmail him."

"It won't work, Glenn."

"I hate to admit it, but it's looking more and more like you might be right."

"Why don't you just kill him?"

Glenn took another bite, smiling as he chewed slowly. He swallowed and pushed the plate away, his appetite suddenly gone.

He looked at her a moment before answering, and in that moment the torch flickered, then died, like sticking a match in water. This greedy, selfish woman was not the Darleen he'd once loved. Or thought he did.

"Just like that, huh? Is that why you came to me, thinking I'd just waltz up there and punch the man's ticket for you?" He went on before she could answer. "Why is it that people who've never killed anybody always think it's such an easy thing to do?"

"No, I *didn't* come to hire you as a killer. I came because I'm scared they're going to kill me. But, yes, before that happens I'd like to see you kill him."

"Before I'd let him do that I guess I would. But keep in

mind you did rip that man off, knowing what he is. The
money alone was enough to make him want to do you in.
But the tapes represent his power over the sheriff and D.A.
I want to get them to him if I can. Killing him would bring
down lots of heat, heat that neither one of us needs."

She changed the subject and asked the question he had
been waiting for. "Why did you have me bring the money?"

"Because you're going to leave it with me."

She stared at him unbelievingly, then waved for the waitress. She ordered another double and he nodded yes when
she asked if he wanted one too.

"I certainly will not," she said. "I planned that job,
Glenn, not you. The money stays with me."

He leaned back and lit a cigarette, enjoying the moment.
"Yeah, and you did good. Larry's dead, and Sherill thinks
I'm involved. And you'll be just as dead as Larry is if he
finds out who you are. Seems to me you aren't very good at
controlling things, so I'm taking over."

She shook her head. "No. I hold the money and that's all
there is to it."

He shrugged. "No problem. All you got to do now is take
care of the man yourself, because I'm out of it."

Her expression said she would enjoy nothing more than
digging her nails in his face. "You bastard, you're doing
this just because I left you while you were in prison."

"No, you know I'm not that petty—"

"Then why? You know you could get killed and then
where would I be? Are you doing it because you don't trust
me?"

"In a way."

When she started to object he overrode her. "Hold on. If
it was any other job there'd be no problem. But we never
had to deal with something like this and it makes a difference. In the past the most we had to worry about was getting busted. This time we're playing for our lives—and
you're scared. Scared enough for me to think there's a

chance you might panic and run. If that happened where would *I* be? Either leave the money with me or I'm out of it."

She sat there a moment, drawing patterns in the table cloth with a fingernail. "If that's what you're worried about then let's just split it up. You take half and I take half."

Good point. There was really no reason not to agree, except it would weaken his being in charge. But refusing would make him look like he was doing it out of spite. He sipped his drink.

"All or none, Darleen. I want to make sure I get an equal cut, and there's no way I can judge what the jewelry's worth out there in the parking lot."

It was weak but he no longer gave a damn. Let her think what she wanted to. Maybe there was some revenge behind it on his part. So be it.

She snatched up her cigarettes and lighter. "You know I don't have any choice. If you've nothing more to say, then I'm ready to leave."

Her Cadillac was at the other end of the parking lot, so he backed his car up to it. After unlocking the trunk she stood to the side as he switched the suitcase to the Thunderbird.

"For God's sake, Glenn, be careful when you go back up there. That's a lot of money there." Her voice turned smug. "More than any score you ever made."

He slammed the trunk deck shut. "I see you're as concerned about my well-being as you were Larry's."

He opened the car door and then looked across the roof at her. "You wouldn't hold out on a guy, would you?"

She got in the Cadillac, her thighs flashing in the dim light of the parking lot. But no light was needed for him to catch her hesitation.

"What do you think, Glenn? You've known me for a long time."

"A long time ago I thought I did know you," he said, and drove away.

HE COULD see Tina standing behind the screen door when he got home, his arrival announced by the dogs. She came out on the porch to meet him, a sandwich in her hand. She wore her usual cutoffs and T-shirt. The jeans were old and faded, the T-shirt had holes in it but she looked better to him than Darleen had in all her finery.

He pointed to her bare feet as he got out of the car. "Girl, it don't take you long to go hillbilly when you get back to these hills, does it? What're you eating?"

"Don't you know you can't get above your raising?" she replied. "Or do you think I ought to dress high-fashion taking care of this bunch of animals?"

He took the suitcase from the trunk and moved onto the porch, using his free hand to hug her. When they kissed he could smell peanut butter.

She held the sandwich up. "Peanut butter and jelly. Want me to make you one?"

He snatched it from her and skipped a couple of steps back, laughing when she tried to grab it. "I've already got one. But feel free to make yourself one."

"You're a bastard," she said goodnaturedly.

He set the suitcase at the end of the couch, then sat down and put his feet on the coffee table. "You know, there must be something to that. It's the second time tonight I've been called one."

She sat beside him and put an arm around him. "I can understand why if you go around taking food out of people's mouths. Who else called you a bastard, and what's in the suitcase? It's not the same one you left here with."

"Darleen. And the suitcase is full of treasure." He leered at her. "Money. Gold. And pretty baubles to go on your fingers and hang from your ears."

She looked surprised. "What did you do? You've only been gone two days. Are you saying it's over and you've already got your end from Darleen?"

He shook his head and told her what he'd told Darleen, holding nothing back, including the moment he'd looked at Darleen and realized she no longer had any hold on him. When he finished she asked the same question Darleen had. What did he intend to do?

He shrugged. "Let Sherill stew a day or two. Then go back up there and talk to him. Try to convince him the best thing for everybody would be for him to take the tapes back, no questions asked. The chances of it working are slim, and that worries me. Being ass deep in this thing with a game plan full of holes is not the way I like doing things."

"You don't really even want to be involved in this at all, do you?"

He stood and unbuttoned his shirt. "No. But they already know about me up there so I am in it, like it or not. Too late to back out now. I'm going to take a shower."

When he came out, a towel wrapped around his waist, he found Tina sitting cross-legged in the middle of the bed, the suitcase open in front of her. A dozen or more rubies lay scattered on the bed. She held a large one up to the light, gazing into it.

He walked over, began gathering them up and putting them back in the leather bag. "Pretty, isn't it?"

She answered without looking up. "It's beautiful. I'd love to have one like it in a ring, with little diamonds around it."

He tossed the bag into the suitcase, then opened the other bags until he found one with diamonds in it. He selected five of the smaller ones and put them in her hand.

"Then keep it. And the diamonds. After this is over we'll take them to a jeweler and have you a ring made."

She shook her head and put the diamonds back, along with the ruby. "No, thank you."

He laughed. "Take 'em. I'm not stealing from Darleen. When the time comes to cut it up I'll tell her about them."

"You wouldn't have to. She'd know they were missing. I don't want them because they're stolen. But after it's over I'll let you buy me a ring like that."

He moved the suitcase to the floor, dropped the towel and slid beneath the covers. "You've lost me somewhere in the translation, sugar. The money's stolen too, but you'd let me use it to buy you a ring."

"Yes, but you didn't steal it."

He laughed, unable to follow her logic. Decided not to try and reached for her, running his hand along the smooth skin of her back.

"I reckon that's fair enough."

They made love, slowly and tenderly. It had always been good, but it was even better this time. No memories of the past got in the way, no reminder she was not Darleen.

When it was over she whispered, "I love you," so low he almost missed it.

He was almost asleep, Tina snuggled against his back, when she spoke: "Glenn, what made you an outlaw?"

"Uncle Sam had as much to do with it as anything."

When he said no more she prompted him. "You still aren't telling me anything."

"Tina, they took me when I was a seventeen-year-old kid, trained me in making war, then stuck an automatic weapon in my hands and said, 'Go get 'em, boy.' For two years I was allowed to run loose over there, loose in a way you better hope to God you never understand. The first rule of war is you throw all the rules away. Then they handed me my discharge and told me to go back to being a civilian again. After the things I'd done over there civilian life didn't make it for me."

"Then why didn't you stay in the army? What made you so cynical about everything?"

"Not everything. Just this country."

She pressed on, her breath soft against the back of his neck. "Why don't you like this country?"

"Go to sleep," he said quietly.

CHAPTER
TWENTY-THREE

THE TABLE was small to start with, and Dodd's bulk took up almost all of one side of it. Sherill and Roy sat at each end, Roy clearly uncomfortable in the sheriff's presence.

They were in the kitchen of the tavern, a long, narrow room less than nine feet wide. Dodd had parked behind the tavern and come straight into the kitchen through the back door. The place was closed but he still didn't like being there. His connection to Sherill was no secret, but he still entered the place as seldom as possible.

"A Glenn Odom went and looked at Hazelton's body this morning." Dodd looked at the old man as he talked. Roy's chair could have been empty for all the attention Dodd paid him.

"He gave the attendant some story about being from Knoxville and having a brother-in-law missing. The attendant said this Odom gave no sign he recognized Hazelton."

"What do you think?" Sherill asked.

"He lied. He drives a black Thunderbird, registered in Shelby County, where he's from."

Roy spoke, popping his knuckles. "Now that we know who Larry was working with we can finally do something."

Dodd pulled a notebook from his shirt pocket, speaking

as if Roy hadn't. "Tag number's TDG-seven-three-two. He's registered at the Mountain View out on one twenty-nine."

"What all've you found out about this guy?" Sherill asked.

Dodd opened the file folder that lay on the table and handed him a picture of Glenn. "Quite a bit. He just got out of the pen a little over a month ago. Get this. He did five years for robbing a jewelry store in Chattanooga."

Sherill studied the picture. "That means he was out when my house got hit. He sure as hell sounds like the man I wanna talk to."

Roy reached for the picture and his eyes widened in surprise. "This bastid was in here early last night. Come in actin' like he was lost. And the son of a bitch tole me he was from Chattanooga."

"Then he's damn sure the one we want," said Sherill, looking at Dodd. "You say he's stayin' at the Mountain View?"

"Yeah, but he left some time around noon. Paid two days in advance but told the clerk there was no need for maid service because he wouldn't be there."

"Where the hell's he at?"

"I don't know. One of my deputies followed him to the county line and he hasn't been seen since. A couple of things don't add up. Why would he bother to check the morgue? You and me both know criminals don't do that kind of stuff."

"I don't give a fuck why," said the old man. "All I want is to get my hands on 'im. If I think about it I'll ask 'im for you."

Dodd pulled a sheaf of papers from the folder and leafed through them. "Another thing that bothers me, why was he working with a petty motherfucker like Hazelton?"

Sherill looked at him. "I wouldn't exactly call Hazelton petty, not after what he took outta my house."

"Only because he knew you had something in there

worth going after. He wasn't the kind who could've found
it on his own, and you know it. On the other hand, Odom is
the kind of guy you might ought to be careful with. Listen
to his military record. He was in the Seventh Cavalry, same
outfit as me but different companies. The guy was a fucking
hero. Got the shit shot out of him once. He was recommended for the Medal of Honor, ended up with a DSC and
a Silver Star. Even pulled a stint as a tunnel rat."

"What the hell's a tunnel rat?" Sherill asked.

"A guy with balls, big balls. That's what a tunnel rat was.
It meant going into a tunnel with no idea where it went,
looking for gooks. You didn't know where the gook was or
how many of 'em were down there. But you can bet your
ass they always knew the second you went in and where
you were."

Sherill, used to ruling his small enclave for more than
forty years, dismissed it with a wave of his hand. "I don't
give a fuck what this shithead did twenty years ago. He
ripped me off and I want it back. That's the only thing I
give a damn about."

Dodd looked at him with something like pity. "George,
this guy isn't like the nickel-and-dime junkies you're used
to. Didn't you hear me when I said he was put up for the
Medal of Honor? They gave out less than two hundred fifty
of them during the ten years we were in Vietnam. You have
no idea what kind of action Odom had to go through even
to be considered for it. That kind of man won't be easy to
buffalo. This guy went through way too much over there to
ever let someone like you scare him. And he isn't the kind
to work with someone like Hazelton."

"Mebbe so, but explain what he was doin' goin' to the
morgue—and comin' in here last night. He's the one I
want. And when he shows back up, by God, I'll have 'im."

Dodd got up and went to the bar, where he helped himself to a Budweiser, popped it open and drank it as he
leaned against the door frame. "That's the other thing that

bothers me. What would he have to come back for? He's got all the money now. That is, if he was Hazelton's partner."

Sherill simply stared at him.

Dodd drank the rest of the beer and tossed the can in the trash basket. When he turned back to Sherill he wore a bland expression. "What is it you're not telling me?"

"I told you before, Phil, don't worry about it. There's some things you're better off not knowin'."

"And there's things I don't want to know. But I think you're holding something back from me. And I've got a feeling it's something I need to know. Hear me good, George. I realize I'm up to my ass in shit with you, but I won't sit back and give you free rein to murder."

Sherill grinned. "And I wouldn't expect you to. Not what with you bein' sworn to uphold the law and all. But wait'll you got proof of me doin' all this murderin' you're talkin' about 'fore you start chargin' me with it."

Dodd gathered up the folder. When he spoke, ice water should have dripped from his voice.

"If the proof's there, George, count on being charged."

After the door closed, the old man looked at Roy. "Put Jackie in that motel. I want to know the minute that son of a bitch comes back."

CHAPTER
TWENTY-FOUR

GLENN EASED out of bed the next morning, leaving Tina sleeping soundly. He moved quietly out of the room, taking the suitcase with him. After dressing on the back porch he sat outside on the steps long enough to smoke a cigarette and enjoy the soft light of morning.

When it burned down to the filter he flipped it away and went back inside, got several plastic trash bags from the kitchen, then stepped out the back door again. A moment later he came around to the front of the house carrying a shovel and the suitcase. A couple of dogs barked a greeting as he put both shovel and suitcase behind the front seat of the Thunderbird.

HE TURNED in the driveway of the empty place a couple of miles away. It sat a couple of hundred feet or more from the road and he parked alongside the house. Anyone passing by would have to be looking hard to see the car. The yard was overgrown with weeds that rose to his chest, soaking his clothes as he waded through them. Every window he could see had been broken, and the small front porch was littered with rocks. As he moved up on the porch he wondered what it was about empty houses that drew kids like a magnet. He could remember riding his bike for miles just to hear a window glass shatter.

The front door hung by one hinge and groaned when he pushed it open. Wallpaper hung in shreds in all the rooms, and in places there were holes in the floor. Signs of field mice and other small animals were plentiful. He stepped carefully to avoid their fecal droppings. There were five rooms, and he walked through each of them, ending up back in the front room, choosing the spot he'd noticed coming through the door as a hiding place. One where he wouldn't need the shovel, which suited him fine.

He squatted in front of the fireplace, took two thousand out of the suitcase, closed it, then stuffed the bills in three of the garbage bags. Turning the suitcase lengthwise he pushed it up the chimney until it was out of sight. He pulled his head out of the fireplace, tilted the suitcase, then hit the bottom of it until it was wedged tight, while a cloud of soot came billowing out, forcing him to hold his breath. A hard pull downward locked it in place.

He released his breath as he stood up and wiped his hands on the bricks above where a mantel had once been. At the front door he stopped and looked back, acutely aware of how much money he was leaving for anyone to find. After a moment he shrugged and went outside. If the fireplace hadn't been used in all this time it wasn't likely to be in the next few days, he told himself.

TINA WAS up when he got back, so he used the water hose to wash his hands and arms. It wasn't that he didn't trust her. He just put more trust in the axiom, "You can't tell what you don't know."

When she opened the back door the smell of bacon floated past her. "Morning, early bird. How does eating out there sound?"

"I like it. I'm hungry enough for you to double up on however many eggs you're fixing."

He opened Senator's cage and checked the dog's wounds. All but one were healed up enough for the stitches to come out. Glenn clipped and pulled them out between wrestling bouts with Senator to keep him still. The dog sensed his imprisonment in the cage was over and was anxious to get started.

When finished, he put a leash on the animal and started for the dog's house. Senator walked a little stiffly, favoring his right hind leg enough for Glenn to check it out. Senator offered no protest to his probing fingers so he decided it wasn't anything to worry about. He scratched the dog's hard muscled chest and stood up.

"I know how you feel, fella. Got one myself that gets stiff now and then."

He brought Zack back and hooked him to the walker, sharing a joint with Tina while the dog exercised. One of the first things he'd learned was that keeping a pit bull in shape was about the only thing one could do. You couldn't teach a pit how to fight; one was either game or it wasn't.

Zack trotted for an hour in a circle, twice managing to clamp down on the bit of cloth bait Glenn thought he had put a few inches beyond his reach. Zack was the smartest dog when it came to snatching the cloth and Glenn liked watching him in action. Instead of just trotting around and around trying to bite it, Zack would get a fast pace going, then suddenly all but stop, which would cause the piece of cloth to rock back and forth. He would repeat this until it swung far enough back for him to clamp his teeth on it. Each time he caught it he stopped, dug in with his hind feet and shook his head, trying to rip the cloth loose. His tail would stick out, quivering wildly, and he'd sit there until Glenn reset the bait.

Glenn encouraged him when he showed signs of slowing. "Get it, Zack, get it. Work it, fella, work it."

He sat now at the table and measured an ounce of weed into a baggie, then folded five one-hundred-dollar bills in with it. After that he rolled the baggie between his palms, getting it as compact as possible, then stood and rolled it back and forth across the table, putting his full weight on it, working it down even smaller.

Tina came out as he was wrapping plastic electrical tape around it. By then the ounce was compressed to a cylinder an inch in diameter and three inches long.

"What are you doing?"

"Making a gift for Frank."

She waited a moment, then twisted his ear. "You going to tell me what it is or will I have to feed this to Zack?"

He groaned from real pain. "Damn, girl. You twist any harder and we'll be able to see if he'd eat it. Anybody ever tell you you're nosy? I'm going to take him a little weed. Make the days go by better."

"You planning on sticking it through the phone?"

Glenn had been right in his prediction about overcrowding. Frank was doing his sentence in jail, and one drawback to it was the no-contact visits. They had to talk on a phone, looking at each other through a small Plexiglas window.

"No. I'm going to have his lawyer go see him this afternoon and go with him. Lawyers get contact visits."

"Good. I'll go too. I'd like to be able to see all of Frank instead of just his head."

He put a final wrap around the package and stood up. "You can't go. What I'll be talking about is just for him to hear."

"Glenn Odom, you are the damnedest man I ever saw. Are you saying at this late date that you don't trust me?"

He unhooked Zack. "I trust you, Tina. But that has nothing to do with it. You aren't involved in this. Let's keep it like that."

She stuck her lip out in a pout. "I'll get mad."

He took Zack back to his stake, returned with Bully Blue and hooked him to the walker. Stood there a minute watching, then came back and sat down. "Well, you'll just have to get over it. Or else be mad an awful long time."

The phone call to the lawyer ended with Glenn agreeing to his fee of a hundred and fifty dollars an hour and to meet him in front of the jail at one o'clock. The attorney was there when he arrived, sitting under one of the several large shady trees on the courthouse lawn. He was in his late sixties, with a full head of silver hair.

Glenn, having seen him at Frank's sentencing, introduced himself, shook hands, then handed the man three hundred dollars. "I seriously doubt it will take that long for what I've got to say."

The attorney passed him off as an associate to the jailer. They were frisked, the guard merely going through the motions, then locked in a little room with steel walls. The only fixtures were a little metal table and two metal chairs. The door had a small window for the jailer to glance in every so often.

After a wait of some five minutes, Frank's face appeared in the window, looking puzzled about why his lawyer wanted to see him. Pleasure washed away the puzzlement when he spotted Glenn. The guard let him in, locked the door again and walked away. The two men shook hands, then embraced.

"It's good to see you without a piece of fuckin' glass between us, Glenn."

"Yeah, it is. You doing all right?"

Frank shook hands with the attorney while answering the question. "Yeah, I'm fine. Bored to death. How you, Mr. Thompson?"

"Fine, Frank. Anything I can do for you?"

"Nothing I know of, 'less it's a way to speed up these next seven months." He turned to Glenn, who pointed at his belly.

"Well, it don't seem to exactly disagree with you. Hell, you haven't been in here a month yet and you've already put on pounds."

"That ain't hard when all a man has to do is eat and lay on his ass. How're the dogs doin'?"

"They're in fine shape. I worked Zack and Blue this morning."

"Tina? How's she doin'? Ya'll getting along okay?"

"She's fine. Wanted to come but I told her I needed to talk to you about something alone. That's why I got Mr. Thompson to get me in like this. As far as getting along, we're doing good. I like her. She's a helluva girl."

Frank grinned. "The day you drove up I thought you two would hit it off. I knew if I could get you to stay long enough to meet her you'd hang around and help take care of the dogs."

They took the chairs and Thompson stood at the opposite end of the room in an attempt to be discreet—something a little hard to pull off, since the room was maybe eight by ten. Frank leaned back and looked at his old friend. "What's up?"

Glenn looked to the lawyer. "How freely can I talk?"

Thompson's face flushed. "Mr. Odom, I resent that. Anything said in this room will be treated as privileged information."

"Mr. Thompson's all right, Glenn," Frank said. "Hell, he was my daddy's lawyer for twenty years. What's on your mind?"

Glenn told Frank everything from the moment Darleen showed up. The big man sat with his hands folded across his stomach, listening intently, saying nothing until Glenn had finished.

"You made a mistake gettin' in it, but you did so there ain't no gettin' out. You know what you better do to that bastard. You don't and he'll waste your ass."

Thompson had begun to pace when Glenn was halfway
through his story, hands clasped behind him.

"That's what Darleen said, and wants me to do, but I
think I can get around having to do it. Who wants that kind
of heat?"

"I won't say you can't. You can do a selling job when you
want to. You used to talk us into going into the bush with us
knowin' the area was hotter than the hinges on the gates of
hell."

Glenn pulled the attorney's legal pad to him and scribbled CHIMNEY, EMPTY HOUSE DOWN THE ROAD.
Held it up to let Frank read it, then tore the page out,
folded it and put it in his pocket.

"The money's in there. Understand?" Frank nodded.
"I'm going back up there tomorrow. If anything happens to
me I want you to get it out. If Darleen's still around, split it
with her. My end will belong to you."

Thompson stopped pacing and looked at Glenn. "Young
man, I've had no desire to overhear your conversation. On
the other hand I've had no choice. I hope you'll believe me
when I say in no way am I trying to force my services on
you. But from what I've heard I cannot impart this strongly
enough. You would be well advised to take an hour before
leaving and stop in my office to make out a will."

Glenn looked at Frank, then back at Thompson. "I'm satisfied that I've just done that, counselor." He got up and
peered out the tiny window. "The weed situation getting
any better back there?"

"Hell no. You might be able to get it three days a week if
you're lucky. And five bucks only gets you enough for a
half-ass decent joint."

"Being able to draw only twenty-five bucks a week sort
of puts a crimp in getting stoned, doesn't it?"

Frank laughed. "Yeah, you could say that."

Glenn ran his hand down the crotch of his slacks and
withdrew the weed. He turned and tossed it to Frank.

"Then you ought to appreciate having this ounce. There's also a few bucks in it to buy some when that runs out."

Frank caught it one-handed. "Boy howdy. Man, you're hitting right on time. Except how'n hell can I take it back with me? The guard that's got our tank is a real bastard. He'll feel it for sure when he frisks me."

"Hoss, there ain't but one sure way. You know where it's got to go."

"Damn it, I ain't got no grease."

"Use spit and persuasion. When it hurts just say I love you to yourself. Tell you what, I'll turn around."

Frank unzipped the gray jail pants. "Fuck you. If you didn't turn around I'd start to really worry about you."

He stood in front of the door to make sure the guard didn't come back and look in while Frank took care of business. From the corner of his eye he saw Thompson also turn and stare at the blank wall.

When he heard the zipper again he turned back around. "That about takes care of it, Frank. I'm going on back to the house now. You take care of yourself. Tina'll be here this weekend and I'll be back when this is over."

Frank took a step and stuck out his hand, smiling when he saw Glenn hesitate. "Take it, dipshit. I used my left hand." His face grew somber, matched by his voice. *"You* be careful. Where I'm at is safe as a church compared to what you're messing with. Listen, in case you don't know it, Tina's falling head over heels in love with you. She's all but told me that much in her letters. I ain't trying to tell you what to do, but you'll never find better'n her. Watch your ass on this deal so I can come be best man for you."

"You've got my future all mapped out for me, haven't you, dude? I'll be careful. Believe it."

CHAPTER TWENTY-FIVE

DODD SPENT his morning in court testifying in the trial of a woman who had killed her husband. As sheriff he, of course, testified for the prosecution, but in his heart he didn't blame the woman. The husband, a drunk, had beaten on her for entertainment and Dodd wondered why she hadn't shot him ten years ago. In fact, he'd spoken with Merritt, trying to get him to persuade the grand jury to return a no true bill against her.

After Merritt finished questioning him it was the defense lawyer's turn, and Dodd allowed the jury to see where his sympathy lay. When asked if he'd ever arrested the husband for beating his wife Dodd answered yes. He wasn't required to elaborate, but he did, going on to state without being asked that the man had beat her severely numerous times. That got him an angry glare from Merritt, but Dodd could care less. Merritt was only pushing the case because a murder conviction would look better politically than justifiable homicide.

After leaving the courtroom Dodd drove to the Mountain View and got the key to Odom's room from the desk clerk. A search of it told him nothing. The only things Odom had left in the room were his clothes.

Tossing the room only took a couple of minutes and he

was back in his car, headed to the motel office. Parked close to the end of the building was an old beat-up Mustang that looked like Jackie Dotson's. He stopped and backed past it to verify.

In the office he asked the clerk, "When did the fellow in one forty-three check in?"

"About three hours ago. Why?"

"Let me have the passkey for that room."

"You know I'm not supposed to do that. It's one thing when the guy ain't there, but the man's in one forty-three right now."

"Good. It'll give me a chance to talk to him."

The clerk nervously pushed his glasses up a long, bony nose. "What's going on, sheriff? I don't want any trouble here, it's bad for business."

"And that's what I'm trying to make sure don't happen. Now let me have the key."

The clerk shook his head. "If I let you just walk in there he could sue the pants off me."

"Funny you say something about pants being off, Jerry. It reminds me of something. You still sing in the church choir, don't you?"

Jerry nodded and Dodd said, "If I'm not mistaken, Betty Morgan sings in it too. Reckon your wife knows about the singing the two of you do after choir practice?"

That got him the key, along with a weak threat. "Don't count on my vote in the next election."

"Sure I will, Jerry. Yours and Betty's. After all, she's married too."

The chain wasn't on the door and he was inside before Jackie could do more than stand up. Dodd nodded at him and smiled, which did nothing to offset the fear that spread across Jackie's ferretlike face.

"Since when did you start staying in motels, Jackie?"

"What're you doin' here, sheriff?"

"What are *you* doing here? That's the question that needs answering."

Jackie was more scared of Dodd than Roy was, but he decided to try using Sherill's name anyway, hoping the protection extended down the ladder to him." I don't think Mistuh Sherill'd want me talkin' to you."

It only took a single step to put Dodd squarely in front of Jackie. He outweighed him by at least a hundred pounds, and anyone standing behind him could not have seen Jackie.

"Since you spent money for the room make yourself comfortable, Jackie. Sit down."

As he spoke he reached out and pushed against Jackie's narrow chest with his fingertips. It was enough to make him stumble backward, the backs of his knees bumping against the chair. It also caused him to lose his balance and fall backward, his ass landing on the seat with a thump.

"I gotta right to be in here and you got no right comin' in like you did. I'm tellin' Mistuh Sherill about it."

The words sounded tough, but not the way he said them.

Dodd sucked on a Life Saver. "You're right, Jackie, Sherill would probably get mad about it."

Moving deceptively fast for his size, he bent slightly and closed his immense left hand around Jackie's throat, then lifted him out of the chair, using no more effort than if Jackie were a rag doll. He kept on lifting until Jackie's toes barely touched the floor, and did not speak until Jackie's face glowed a bright red.

"Let me explain your rights to you, tough guy. You got the right to piss me off. And opening your mouth to Sherill about this would do that faster than anything else. It would piss me off to the point where you'd have the right to try swimming back from the middle of Loudon Lake with a set of log chains wrapped around your skinny ass. Now, do you understand your rights, Jackie?"

Jackie managed a weak nod, and Dodd flung him back in

the chair. "Good. Now let's start all over. What're you do-ing here?"

Jackie rubbed his throat, speaking hoarsely. "I'm sup-posed to call Mistuh Sherill when the guy in one fifty-one comes back."

"Why does he want to see this guy so bad?"

"He's the one who broke in his house, sheriff."

"So why is he coming back? You hold out on me, Jackie, and it'll be a mistake you'll regret making for a long time to come."

"I dunno, sheriff. Honest." A giggle escaped from him, from nervousness, not amusement. "I'd be gone forever if I wuz 'at guy."

Dodd towered over him, nodding gravely. "That's some-thing you ought to give serious thought to yourself, Jackie. Getting gone forever. I'm going to arrest you one of these days, and we both know it. But you know what? I've got a strong feeling I'll have to shoot your sorry ass on the way to jail for trying to escape."

CHAPTER TWENTY-SIX

GLENN ARRIVED at the motel in midafternoon, and after unpacking opened the drapes. For the next two hours he sat by the window, watching, expecting to see a patrol car cruise past. The fact that one didn't did nothing to diminish his feeling that something would happen soon.

Supper was had in the motel restaurant, the food good enough that he spent a leisurely hour with it. It was dark when he went back to the room, so he closed the drapes and turned on the television. He lay on the bed, watching its images while his mind drifted to what would happen next, and when.

The wait wasn't a long one. Shortly after nine a knock sounded at the door. He got quickly to his feet and hurried to a corner of the window farthest from the door. Lifting the drape an inch allowed him to peer out and see Roy with a skinny young guy standing behind him.

He moved back to the center of the room and hollered out, looking around as he did, "Hold on a minute until I can dress. I just got out of the shower."

The lamps had heavy wooden bases, perfect for what he needed. He quickly took the shade off one and stood by the door, holding the lamp above his head. Just as he got in position Roy knocked again, and he saw the doorknob move slightly. It was locked, but all Glenn needed to do was turn it from his side.

He reached out, opened the door and flung it open. Roy was still holding the knob, and the move caused half his arm to come inside the room. Before he could pull it back, Glenn grabbed his wrist and snatched him inside. Roy stumbled through the door, off-balance enough to almost fall.

As soon as Roy came through the door Glenn brought the lamp down with all his strength, catching Roy on the back of the neck and sending the fat man crashing to the floor with a thud. He stepped across Roy's legs and slammed the door shut. Before it closed, Glenn caught a glimpse of the skinny guy still outside, frozen at what he'd just witnessed.

When he turned back around, Roy was on his hands and knees, shaking his head. He put his foot in the center of Roy's big ass and shoved, sending him back to the floor. Sticking out of Roy's back pocket was the handle of a re-volver, which Glenn snatched out, ripping Roy's pants in the process.

The slamming of the door seemed to galvanize Jackie into action, because he started to pound on it. Glenn ig-nored it as he grabbed Roy by his collar and hauled him up, stuck the pistol behind Roy's head and shoved his face into the wall.

"Tell him to quit beating on the door."

Roy pulled his head away from the pistol. "Man, what's wrong with—"

He rammed the barrel in Roy's ear and cocked it. "Tell 'im, motherfucker. *Now!*"

Roy yelled for Jackie to stop, without taking his eyes off Glenn, then began to protest his innocence. "Hey, man, I just came to talk to you."

"I bet you did. Put your hands on the wall, high as you can get 'em."

When he did Glenn kicked Roy's legs apart until he was

standing at a forty-five-degree angle to the wall. The muzzle of the pistol moved down Roy's spine as Glenn frisked him with his free hand. In one pocket he found a pair of handcuffs and a two-inch wide roll of duct tape in another.

"Talk, huh? Don't look like you were planning on letting me say very much."

He switched the pistol to his left hand and pivoted on the balls of his feet, driving his fist into Roy's kidney. The man went to the floor with a groan, and Glenn pulled him up to slam him against the wall again.

"One more time, you fat son of a bitch. *I've* got the gun now so I don't care if this takes all night. One thing about it, I'll be a helluva lot more comfortable than you will. Now, what were you planning to do?"

No answer, just a sullen look from Roy.

He tore off a strip of tape and put it across Roy's mouth, then kicked his feet still further from the wall. He stepped behind him and brought his fist straight up between Roy's legs.

Roy's eyes rolled up out of sight and the tape cut his scream off, making his cheeks bulge out. He fell hard against the wall, smashing his nose, then crumpled to the floor. Glenn pulled Roy's arms behind him and put the handcuffs on his wrists, then went into the bathroom, coming out with a strip of toilet paper. He squatted beside Roy and stuffed a piece of it up each of Roy's nostrils.

"Don't bleed on the floor, you inconsiderate bastard. Here, let me help you stop it."

When Roy managed to blow the paper from one nostril Glenn stuck a thicker wad into it. "I told you not to bleed on the floor. I know you were raised better than that."

He waited until Roy started to turn purple. When he panicked and began to flop around, Glenn spoke conversationally.

"Want your breath back?"

Roy nodded frantically, on the verge of passing out. His eyes were bulging and already bloodshot.

"Will you talk if I take the tape off?"

He nodded again, and Glenn ripped the tape away.

Roy drew in breath in gulps, so relieved at being able to breathe he didn't even notice the pain from the tape removing the first couple of layers of skin.

"My daddy knows you stole them tapes. I wuz gonna take you to 'im."

"Your daddy assumes I stole the tapes, Roy. And guess what? I don't care nothing about going to see him."

He stood up. "Your buddy got a gun?"

"No."

He stuck the revolver down the front of his pants, then pulled Roy to his feet. At the door he stopped, grabbed a fistful of Roy's hair and jerked his head back.

"Take this back to your daddy. You tell him that I will be talking to him, but it'll be at my choosing. Not his. And I'd best not get any more visits in the night. Let me see you around here one more time and he can forget about ever seeing the tapes again—and I'll kill you, fat boy."

He opened the door and shoved Roy outside, straight into Jackie's arms, the two men doing a clumsy little dance to keep from falling. Glenn pulled the pistol and held it alongside his leg.

"Take your lard-gutted buddy back home, fella."

He stood and watched until their car disappeared around the corner of the motel. Back inside he debated whether or not to find another motel and decided against it. Leaving would show fear, and he didn't want Sherill to think he had him on the run.

After putting the shade back on the lamp he picked up the phone, then put it back. He was willing to bet someone had been in the room while he was gone. They could easily have bugged the phone. He left the room and called Tina from the pay phone in front of the office. He said nothing about his encounter with Roy. "I've got enough sense to cover my ass," he told her when she said she was worried about him. "How's everything going back there?"

"You must not have hooked Zack up right," she said. "He managed to get loose a few minutes after you left. First thing he did was lock horns with Senator."

"Either of them get hurt?"

"Not really. They made enough noise that I heard them and got out there in time. Zack got a nasty bite on his nose. Senator didn't get a scratch."

When the operator broke in to tell them their time was up he fumbled in his pockets and inserted more quarters.

"Why are you calling from a pay phone?"

"Just to be safe."

"Are you sure nothing's happened?"

"You worry too much. It's better to be safe than sorry, that's all."

"Be glad I do. No telling how much trouble you'd get in if somebody didn't worry about you."

"Well, you're doing a good job. I'm almost out of quarters and I've still got to call Darleen."

"I worry because I care, Glenn. That's more than you can say about her. . . ."

Darleen answered the phone herself and he told her about the events of the night. She showed concern too, but hers was about what Sherill would try next.

"I'm not going to give him enough time to plan anything," Glenn told her. "I know how to see him without going into his territory and I'm going to do it tomorrow."

"When do you think this will be over? I'm about to go crazy wondering what's going to happen."

A semi pulled in and stopped at the office, the hiss of its air brakes making him miss what she said.

"I can't say when," he said after she repeated herself. "But stay by the phone tomorrow. I'll call after I talk to Sherill."

Back in the room he filled a glass with ice and Dickel, stopping a half-inch from the rim, then stretched out on the bed, setting the drink on the nightstand right beside the pistol.

He figured he'd told Darleen right, it wouldn't be long now. Things were fixing to start jumping. Sherill was losing face, something that ate up a man like him.

He turned his head and looked at the pistol. Keeping it could mean trouble, but damned if he was going to get rid of it. A visit from the law wouldn't surprise him any; after all, Sherill owned it around here. For all he knew it was the law that killed Larry. Yeah, he'd keep the pistol. At this stage it was better to be caught with than without it.

The semi that had stopped at the office or one just as loud woke him when it pulled out at six o'clock. He showered, staying under the stinging spray twenty minutes. Even the Dickel gave him a headache, something it didn't do before he went to prison. He decided to wear a sport coat, and put the pistol in the right pocket.

At seven-thirty he was parked in the parking lot of the Denny's Stacy had told him about. An hour later there was still no sign of a black Lincoln and he told himself he'd leave if Sherill didn't show up in the next thirty minutes.

WHILE GLENN waited at the restaurant Dodd was pushing his food around on his plate at home. The burglary was on his mind; he'd been able to think of little else since Sherill told him about killing Hazelton. Something really had that old man upset, something more than just the loss of money. Instinct told him it affected him in some kind of way.

The phone rang and he could hear Ellen tell whoever it was to wait a minute. She stuck her head in the door. "It's Sherill, Phil. He wants to talk to you."

"Tell him I'm already in the car, hon."

She talked to Sherill a moment, then came in and sat

across from him. "What's wrong? You haven't eaten a decent meal in three days."

"Just off my feed. Nothing for you to worry about."

"You mean nothing you want me to worry about."

He stood up, pulled his belt out of two loops and put his pistol on. "No. I mean it's nothing for you to worry about."

He held out a hand, pulling her up from the chair, and hugged her. "Seriously, it's nothing important, but you go ahead and worry if it'll make you feel any better. Here's something you can fret about. Worry that I won't be able to get home early tonight. Just in case I can't, why don't you sit around and take it easy today. I want you to have plenty of energy for one of the things on my mind."

When he got to the office his secretary greeted him by saying Sherill wanted him to call as soon as he came in.

"I don't have time to talk to him, Doris. He'll be calling back, and when he does tell him you haven't seen or heard from me."

GLENN SAT in the parking lot for two hours. The headache had faded away, allowing him to smoke the first cigarette of the day. Now he was hungry, his stomach grumbling, and he thought about going into Denny's to eat, then decided not to. He cranked the engine and drove back to the motel restaurant.

If Sherill ate breakfast at that place every morning, then what happened last night had to be the reason he didn't show up today. Well, it showed he was upset anyway. But Glenn realized upsetting the old man wasn't helping his case any. On the other hand, it would allow him to point out to Sherill that he wasn't up here to fool around. When he did get to talk to him he'd say, Old man, I could've hurt your boy. Not doing it should show you I just want to give the tapes back. Yeah, that sounded pretty good. It would give more weight to telling him he'd be a lot better off if he took them and forgot about the rest.

The breakfast rush was over and only a few customers were in the restaurant, lingering over coffee. He took a table beside the window and ordered country ham and scrambled eggs. When it came he dug into the tough, heavily salted meat with relish. Tina fussed at him for eating it so often and he knew it did play hell with blood pressure. But it tasted so damned good. It was one of those things he intended to give up, like smoking, or drinking too much. But later, not today.

He was almost finished when he saw a silver Buick ease past, then stop and back up. It came to a stop behind his Thunderbird, the driver obviously reading the license plate. The Buick backed up once more until it was clear of the Thunderbird, then pulled in and parked beside it. It came to a stop with the front bumper no more than five feet from where he sat.

Glenn had no trouble recognizing Dodd when he got out, buttoning his coat. Their eyes met and he saw Dodd knew who he was too. We've both got pictures of each other, he thought.

Dodd came straight to Glenn's table. "Mr. Odom, I'm Phillip Dodd, sheriff of Edwards County."

Glenn reached for a slice of toast and spread jelly across it. "Congratulations. You make a habit of knowing everybody who isn't from here?"

"No. Not everybody. Just the ones suspected of burglary." He gestured at the chair across from Glenn.

"Mind if I sit down?"

"If I said yes would that mean we'd be going downtown?"

"We might be going anyway, Mr. Odom, but such an answer would remove all doubts."

"Then by all means, have a seat."

Glenn could not help but feel a little intimidated by the

man's bulk. Jesus, his shoulders damned near spread from one corner of the table to the other. The waitress called from across the room, asking if Dodd wanted a menu, and he said coffee would be fine. He appeared willing to wait until it came before saying anything, so Glenn spoke up.

"I imagine you get your share of burglaries up here, sheriff. Which one am I suspected of?"

"How about the one that got Larry Hazelton killed?"

The waitress came with his coffee and Dodd poured in cream and sugar, looking at Glenn as he stirred. Glenn said nothing, returning his gaze.

"Will that do for starters, Mr. Odom?"

"I don't know anybody by that name."

"Acting cute isn't in your best interest either, Odom. I know all about you, and you know I do."

"Oh, I don't doubt you've checked my record, but how does that tie me to a burglary this Hazelton supposedly pulled? He tell you I was with him?"

Dodd held up a hand and began to tick off the reasons with a disgusted look. "You just got out of the joint for robbing a jewelry store. You were a suspect in at least eight robberies over the last fifteen years and they finally nailed your ass. That's one. Hazelton leaves Knoxville last year with nobody knowing where to. A man gets ripped off in a big way and Hazelton shows up shortly after it happens. And who comes all the way from the other end of the state to look at his body? Nobody but you, Odom. That's two. Enough to make me think he was your partner."

Glenn didn't fail to notice he'd said the other end of the state. At least he doesn't know where I really live, he thought. "Tell me something, sheriff. Why are you officially saying you don't know who Hazelton is?"

"Why are you denying that you know him?" countered Dodd.

"Let's quit playing games with each other, Dodd. Last night Sherill sent his boy to get me, wanted to *talk* to me.

When I sent his ass packing I figured he'd send you next, and he didn't waste any time doing it. Now you go back and—"

"Nobody's sent me. I'm here on my own. Sherill never filed a report on the burglary so that means I don't have to arrest anybody for it. But that don't mean you just get away with it. That old man will kill you, and I'm the only one who can save your ass."

Glenn stayed silent, and after a moment Dodd continued. "Give me what you took and I'll see to it Sherill doesn't fuck with you anymore."

Glenn couldn't quite suppress a snort of laughter. He'd been approached by crooked cops before, but this was the first one to try and get all of it.

"And just why are you so willing to help me?"

Dodd drained his coffee, pulled out the pack of Life Savers and stuck two in his mouth, looking thoughtful as he sucked on them.

"I've seen your military record, Odom. Very impressive. I was in the Seventh myself but I didn't come back with any medals. I respect anyone who did."

"We both know those medals and five bucks would just about pay for my meal," Glenn said. "You can freeze the flag, mom and apple-pie crap. I know about you, too. That means I know you're as crooked as one of these mountain roads around here. What's your real reason?"

"I want whatever it was you took out of that house that's got Sherill so upset."

Glenn was silent a moment, studying the man across from him. "If there was something in there besides loot, what makes you so sure you want it?"

"Because I think it would be something I could use as a weapon."

"Yeah? Who would you point it at?"

It was Dodd's turn to hesitate. He held his cup up for a

refill, then sipped it while staring out the window. When he turned back to Glenn his brown eyes were honest.

"Well, you've all but admitted there is something. If whatever it is would let me change a few things around here, things long overdue, I'd do it. And the first thing I'd do is put that fat son of a bitch Roy where he belongs, in the penitentiary."

Either he was telling the truth or else they were pulling out all the stops trying to get the tapes back. It gave Glenn something to think about, but later, not while he sat here playing word games.

"I haven't admitted anything, sheriff. There's been a what-if in this whole conversation. I wish I could help you but you're barking up the wrong tree. I haven't pulled any burglary. Not in your county, not anywhere."

Dodd gave a sigh and stood up. "Have it your way, hard-case. But I'm telling you now I can't protect you from Sherill if that's the way you want to act. You're on your own, which is another way of saying you'll probably be dead before the week's out. But just for the record, what I said about respecting guys like you wasn't bullshit, Odom. I was over there in it too and I know those medals didn't come easy. But there won't be any medals handed out for what you're getting into up here."

CHAPTER
TWENTY-SEVEN

THE FIRST thing out of Dodd's secretary's mouth was "Sherill," saying he had called several times. Pulling his tie down a couple of inches, he told her to put him through the next time.

A folder lay on his desk containing the monthly feeding budget for the prisoners. He opened it, stared at it blankly, closed it. He swung his feet up on the desk and locked his hands behind his head, trying to put together a puzzle he didn't have all the pieces to.

Sherill was holding something back, no doubt about it. The conversation with Odom cinched it, but the what part still wasn't answered. His thoughts centered on Odom. A cool bastard, or at least he gave a good impression of one. Not even a blink when he threatened him with jail. What was he doing up here? He had taken something out of that house the old man thought was valuable enough to kill for, had already done so once. All the signs pointed to blackmail. If that was it then Dodd damned sure wanted to know what it was that Odom knew. It stood to reason that if he had such information he could use it to break away from Sherill. Odom had to know how powerful Sherill was in these parts. So if his game was blackmail, then he'd certainly realize the risks involved.

His mind jumped to another track. Maybe Odom intended to kill Sherill because of Hazelton. But it didn't take
long to discard that idea, more wishful thinking than anything. Odom wasn't the kind to seek revenge, not behind a
job. His kind accepted that getting killed was the chance
you took. But it would let me get out from under Sherill's
thumb, Dodd thought. The phone rang as he was asking
himself if he'd really try to bust Odom if that proved to be
the case.

As expected, it was Sherill, who wasted no time with pre-
liminaries. "Phil, that goddamn Odom's gittin' to be a pain
in the ass."

Dodd recalled Glenn saying he'd sent Roy packing, and
the mental picture of it made him smile. From the anger in
Sherill's voice he must have done a real job of it. "I told
you he wouldn't be easy."

"Well, something's got to be done about 'im. I want you
to go git 'im and bring 'im out here so I can talk to 'im."

Dodd said nothing, and when the silence lengthened
Sherill spoke again. "Are you still there, goddamn it?"

"I'm here. What makes you think he'll want to come with
me? Sounds to me like he doesn't want to talk to you."

Sherill's rage came over the line, the man speaking so
loudly Dodd held the receiver away from his ear.

"Goddamn it, I want you to go to that motel and arrest
his ass. Ain't you still the fuckin' sheriff? Have I got to tell
you how to do ever damn thing?"

"He hasn't done anything I can prove to arrest him for,
George. What you're wanting me to do is kidnap him so
you can kill him."

"So what're you sayin'?"

Dodd hesitated a fraction of a second, then spoke firmly.
"I'm saying I won't do it. You said there were things I
didn't need to know. A man who sits down in a game where
he don't know all the rules is asking for a fucking."

"You better think about what you're sayin', Phil."

"I have thought about it. You're on your own with Odom. It'll be interesting to see how you come out."

He hung up before Sherill could reply. He looked resigned, like a man who cuts his own throat and waits patiently for his life to drain away. A numbness spread through him; he was all too aware that at best his political career had just ended. He'd done the "right thing," so where was the good feeling that was supposed to go with such an action?

Good feeling, my ass, he thought. As mad as you just made that old man you'll be lucky to get out of this with your life.

The phone rang, startling him. He picked it up, surprised at who the caller was.

"I'll be there in two minutes."

He moved through the outer office, not bothering to answer when Doris asked when he'd be back. The elevator door stood open and he stepped inside it, punching the ground-floor button. When the door slid open he stepped out, and there stood Glenn Odom, leaning against the Buick.

He nodded once, pushed himself off the fender and walked around to the passenger side. "Let's you and me go for a ride."

"Why not come up to my office?"

A smile flashed across Glenn's face. "Sheriff, I'm closer to a jail right now than I've ever come voluntarily. Let's go for a ride."

Dodd unlocked the car and got in, releasing the lock on the other side so Glenn could get in. "Where to?"

"Well, I don't think it'd be a good idea to be seen riding around together so that only leaves the country." He hesitated, then added, "It'll be one way to see just how much Sherill controls you."

"What're you talking about, Odom?"

"I think you know. Once you get me out of sight it'd be a good time to take me out."

"I know my saying it won't take the thought out of your mind, but for what it's worth, I don't play that way."

Glenn lit a cigarette, cracking a window to let the smoke escape. He sat his lighter on the windowsill, ran his finger and thumb down it, then reversed it and did it again.

Dodd was eager to know what was on his mind, but sensed he wasn't ready to tell it. After a moment, when Glenn still hadn't spoken, Dodd did, keeping his eyes on the road. "What happened between you and Roy?"

Glenn shrugged. "I turned the tables on him."

Dodd looked over at him. "Roy's a helluva lot bigger than you. You must've taken him by surprise."

"You know a better way to do it? From the way you talked a couple of hours ago it sounded like you don't care much for him."

"That's an understatement. I'd like nothing better than to lock his ass up."

Glenn took a final draw, then slid the window down a couple more inches and flipped the cigarette out.

"Let me tell you about a movie I saw the other day, sheriff. You know the actors. The light was bad but you could tell one of them was from somewhere down in South America."

Dodd's head swung around sharply, his lips set. "What're you getting at?"

"I'm talking about you being on film. Taking twenty grand to let coke be unloaded in this county. Yeah, you're on film all right, in living color."

Dodd's intake of breath was audible in the silence. So that was it. His mind quickly grasped Sherill's logic for having a tape of the transaction.

Glenn spoke again, bringing him back to the present. "There's two tapes, Dodd. The other one shows Merritt getting freaky with a young girl. I don't know how old she is, but it's easy to see she's a minor."

"I'll be damned." That part surprised him and he drove in silence, mulling it over. The fact that Merritt was also owned by Sherill was something he'd always known, and that Merritt was happy with the arrangement. But he hadn't known the man went for underage girls. "So why are you telling me this? Why not go ahead and use it to blackmail Sherill? Or are you trying to make something off all of us?"

"I didn't pull that burglary. And I never had any intentions of blackmailing Sherill. But there's no way he'll believe it."

"Then how did you get hold of the tapes?"

"From the person who did make the lick. Larry Hazelton was trying to extort Sherill. When he got killed this person got scared and brought 'em to me. The person just wants to stay alive."

"You still haven't said why you're telling me. Why not just give them back to Sherill?"

"That was my original plan, but he's already made it plain he's not going to be reasonable about it. Besides, if you were him would you believe me if I said I wanted to give 'em back, no strings attached?"

"No, not if I was Sherill. He's fucked over so many people in his life he'd be convinced you had something else up your sleeve."

"Right. The only way I can make absolutely sure this person will be safe is to kill the bastard. I'm still looking for a way to avoid that."

"This person is your wife, isn't it?"

Glenn stiffened. "Why do you say that?"

"Because you never say guy, fellow or man. Just person. You know I ran a deep check on you. She's mentioned often."

"Ex-wife," said Glenn. "Now, I want you to explain

something to me. Why are you wanting to put Roy in jail all of a sudden? You've been in cahoots with Sherill all this time. Why the sudden change of heart?"

Dodd took his time answering. He felt in his pockets for the Life Savers but came up empty-handed. Obviously some kind of decision would be made behind his reply and he wanted the words to be right.

"I wasn't brought up like that," he said. "Everybody knows there's no such thing as honest politics, and I'd love to get out there and run with the best of 'em. But people like Sherill are the wrong ones to bed down with. I did, and it's been eating at me ever since." He gave Glenn a brief glance, speaking after he looked back at the road. "I know it sounds corny, but my family looks up to me, thinks I'm really something. If I don't break away from Sherill now I know the day will come when my family won't look at me like that any longer. Sherill needs to be put out of business, but right now he's got more on me than I do on him. He's got enough, he could arrange to have me put in my own fucking jail."

Glenn turned sideways in the seat, watching Dodd closely. "And if I gave you the tapes I suppose you'd use them to bust him?"

"I don't know, I haven't seen them. Hell, from the way you described them it sounds like it's just me and Merritt with our asses hanging out in the wind."

"Sherill's name gets plenty of mention in the one of you. And it shows enough of the room to prove where the tape was made. A house trailer, right?"

"Yeah, and it belongs to him."

Both men were silent then, the only sound the low crackle of the radio. It was Dodd who spoke first.

"I'd like nothing better than to bust him and his boy, but I want to be honest with you. I don't know if I'll be able to or not. But I will do everything in my power to put him out of business. I will see to it Roy goes to jail."

"What makes you think you can do that?"

Dodd was thinking of Janice Kirk, and the expression on her daddy's face when he accepted the two thousand dollars. A look of hatred, mixed with defeat. It wouldn't take much leaning on Kirk to get a statement from both him and Janice, but he didn't tell all this to Glenn.

"I've got a couple of things I could use, and if I had the tapes to go with 'em it'd be enough."

When Glenn spoke, his tone was harsh. "Look here, Dodd, I don't give a good goddamn if you run coke in here or not. And I'm damn sure not trying to crowd in on your action. I don't feel that way about Merritt, but then I'm not in a position to bargain. Bottom line, what's in it for me if I give you the tapes?"

"Sherill won't ever be a threat to you or your ex-wife again. I'll guarantee that."

"A *guarantee*? Sounds real good. Answer this. How in the hell are you planning on guaranteeing your own life?"

"I'll put the originals in my safety-deposit box, then show Sherill a copy. I've got a will made out. My lawyer will be instructed to open the box if something happens to me."

"Merritt's a fucking lawyer too, Dodd. How do you know you can trust yours?"

"Because he's honest *and* because he'd like to be D.A. He'd make a good one too. The film would be enough to make sure Merritt doesn't run again—for D.A. or anything else." He looked at Glenn. "You have to trust people somewhere along the line."

Glenn lit another cigarette, taking several deep draws in silence. It was only half-finished when he cracked the window and threw it out. "Well, I reckon I'm going to start with you, Dodd. I'll give you the tapes."

Dodd sighed with relief. "Today?"

"I don't have them with me. Believe it. But I'll have them tomorrow and I'll call you. Good enough?"

Dodd put on the brakes and turned into a driveway. He

nodded as he put the car in reverse to go back the way they had come.

"You're doing right, Glenn. This way there'll be no more trouble for you or your ex-wife. And I'll get the pleasure of going after Sherill."

"You really think you'll be able to bring him down? How long has that old bastard been buying and selling politicians in this county?"

"Hey, I'm not a Boy Scout. I know it won't be easy, and maybe I won't be able to. But after I get those films I'll damn sure have some ammunition to go after him with."

They rode the rest of the way in an almost comfortable silence. At the edge of town Dodd said, "Correct me if I'm wrong, but Nam really fucked you up, didn't it? I mean, that's the reason you went the way you did. Right?"

Glenn started not to answer. After all, he'd never talked about it before. But it wasn't like he'd be seeing Dodd after tomorrow. "Yeah. I was mad at the way the people felt about soldiers. Plus I was bored, and pulling robberies looked exciting."

"I was bored too, and being a cop looked exciting to me. Know what? It has its moments, but for the most part it's the most boring thing in the world."

Glenn laughed softly. "So is crime. It gets you sent to prison. And you don't know what boring is until you spend a few years in there."

"So what are you going to do next? Another jewelry store? I don't really care, just want to give you that old warning not to do it in my territory." The look he gave Glenn was friendly. "Sounds like TV, doesn't it?"

Glenn returned the expression, actually liking the man. "A little, but I've heard it before. I don't expect you to believe it, and don't care, but I'm through with that shit. I just want to get back home and raise my dogs."

"What kind of dogs?"

"Pits. Damnedest breed of dog I've ever seen."

Dodd frowned. "I hate dogfights. They fight 'em in most counties around here except mine. I make a point of busting every one I can."

"Good for you. I won't go to a fight either. But I like the dogs."

"That's an odd way of thinking."

Dodd swung into his parking space and Glenn opened the door to get out, talking over his shoulder. "No more than the way you think, Dodd."

Dodd got out and looked across the car at him. "Why am I so odd?"

"Because you're worse than a Boy Scout, you're a fucking romantic. You feel guilty for selling out so now you're going to put on your white cape and wipe out crime. You're doing it because your conscience is bothering you, and it'll take one helluva lot more than a bad conscience to destroy Sherill."

He walked off a few steps, then turned around. "You'll never do it, and we both know it, but good luck anyway. If you don't do nothing else, make sure you keep that bastard off my ass. You don't, then I'll do it in a way that will make sure he don't come after me."

CHAPTER TWENTY-EIGHT

TINA MOVED around the living room straightening things halfheartedly, restless. Laundry needed doing but she wasn't in the mood. She sat down on the couch, took a shoe box lid from under the coffee table and started cleaning seeds out of the pot lying in it. After a moment she put it back. Nothing would get done if she got high.

Mama Sue sat in front of her, panting softly, her tongue hanging from the side of her mouth. She looked at Tina, then uttered a short, low bark, bringing it from down deep in her massive chest.

"I'm bored too, Mama. Wish I knew what was going on up there where Glenn is."

With a sigh she stood up, pulling at the back of her shorts, sticky with sweat. Outside she bent down to check on the health of a rose bush beside the front steps. She'd transplanted it a few days ago and now the leaves were brown and curled at the edges. In spite of having little hope it would live, she got the hose and watered it.

Some of the dogs began barking when they saw her come out in hopes of getting some attention, but just as she started in their direction the phone rang. She got back inside in time to pick it up on the sixth ring.

The operator wanted to know if she would accept a collect call from Glenn.

"Just hearing you makes me horny, girl."

She laughed, her mood already better. "Well, don't waste it on anybody up there, big boy. Bring it on home."

"I've got a better idea. Why don't you get on a plane and come up here."

"Are you serious?"

"Never more so. Bring the tapes with you. I've worked it out. It'll be finished first thing in the morning."

"Glenn, I could drive up there almost as fast as waiting around for a plane."

"You're probably right, but it would mean having to drive two cars back. Get somebody to water the dogs in the morning. We'll be back in time to feed 'em tomorrow night."

"How did you manage to convince him you don't want anything?"

"I didn't. I'm going another route. I'll tell you about it when you get here. After I've had my way with your body. Hurry."

Her voice dropped an octave. "I'm afraid you're going to have to keep your pants on until tonight. I've got an appointment to have my hair cut this afternoon." She turned serious again. "But if you really want me on the first plane I'll cancel it."

"No. The deal won't go down until tomorrow anyway. I guess I can wait. But it'll be hard. I'll call back in an hour to find out what plane you'll be on."

"If it gets too hard, big boy, just get a grip on yourself until I get there."

SHERILL CAME into the chop shop, his face registering the turmoil swirling through his mind. Jackie, busy stripping a new GMC pickup, nodded to him. He didn't receive one in return, but with the way Sherill looked that suited him just fine. The truck had come in during the night but it was already only a shell of itself. The only thing left to remove was the interior, and Jackie climbed in to start on that.

Whoever this Odom was he sure had the old man's bowels in an uproar, he thought as he pulled the knobs off the stereo. Dodd's too. I'd sure like to know what he's got on that old bastard.

A glance at Sherill was enough to make him change his mind. No, I don't. I don't give a fuck. That's dangerous information. I got more'n enough to keep me busy right here. He had half the screws out of the instrument panel when Sherill spoke.

"Leave 'at for the time bein', Jackie. It's almost four o'clock and Roy'll be coming down in a few minutes. You go up there and work the bar in his place. Tell 'im I want to see 'im back here."

Sherill paced back and forth, his leather heels clicking on the concrete floor. His anger flowed in two directions, at both Glenn and Dodd.

He had been top dog in the county almost forty years, unchallenged almost twenty. In the past few weeks he'd been ripped off by a punk, and told to go to hell by the sheriff. The same goddamned sheriff who wouldn't have gotten elected without his money. Dodd he could take care of later. First things first.

One son of a bitch thought he could come waltzing in here and blackmail him for those damned tapes. Now his partner was back here running around trying to play head games with him. He'd show this Odom head games. One thing about it, he didn't get to be top dog by sitting around scratching fleas off his ass.

One of the double doors opened and Roy came in, his sullen look exaggerated due to a puffy nose. "Jackie said you wanted to see me."

"Yeah. We're fixin' to put an end to Odom, Roy."

He walked to a corner and picked up a paper sack. He pulled four sticks of dynamite taped together from it and handed them to Roy. Back down in the paper sack again, this time holding a blasting cap when he pulled his hand out.

"What about the tapes, daddy? We still don't know where they're at."

"I ain't gonna worry about 'em no more. It's time to stop this guy. Dodd's stepped too far outta line anyhow. If I had 'em they wouldn't do any good. That means Dodd's gotta be next."

Roy looked at the dynamite, handling the sticks gingerly. "I dunno, daddy. We might oughta try'n get them tapes back first."

"Hell, Roy, Hazelton was his partner, and he's dead. Who else is left to do anything with 'em?"

"How you figgerin' on using this stuff?"

"You're gonna wire up his car tonight."

Roy took a step back. "I don't know nuthin' 'bout no dynamite. Doin' somethin' like that and not knowin' how is a good way to get killed."

"There ain't nothin' to it, son. I'm fixin' to show you how it's done."

He walked to the pickup and tore two wires from the firewall, each about five feet long. Next he stripped the insulation from the ends with his pocket knife and twisted them to the blasting-cap wires. He talked as he wrapped tape around the naked wire.

"All you gotta do is tape the dynamite to the frame, right under his seat."

The GMC's engine lay on the floor and he walked over to it to demonstrate. "You just push the cap in the end of one of these sticks and then wrap the wires around the coil here. See what I mean?"

Roy half-nodded. "One of the coil wires goes direct to the starter so there's no need to take either one of 'em loose.

Just wrap the blasting cap around the bolts they're hooked to. The second he turns the key it'll go off."

He grinned, showing yellowed teeth. "And then we'll see just how tough this big war hero really is. They'll pick up parts of 'im all over that parking lot."

TINA ARRIVED at 10:45. Glenn leaned against a column, smiling as she approached, watching her nipples jiggle beneath her blouse.

He took the small suitcase from her, then kissed her. "This has been a long twelve hours."

As they walked she slipped an arm around his waist, then let her hand drop down to squeeze his ass. "I know what you mean. I had a little trouble sitting still while I was getting my hair cut."

She reached up and flipped the back of her hair. "Like it?"

He pulled away to look. Damned if he could tell any difference but he bet himself she paid twenty bucks for it, plus a tip.

"Uh-huh. How're the dogs?"

She sighed. "No need to carry on so much about it, Glenn. You're starting to sound like Frank, worrying about the dogs before anything else. They're fine. You just left them, what, forty-eight hours ago?"

He smiled as he looked at his watch. The airport was the one place in the county you could get a mixed drink legally. But only because it actually belonged to Knoxville, which was in the next county. The Baptists controlled the rest of Edwards County with an iron fist. The bartender had explained all this to him while he was waiting for Tina's plane.

"You want a drink?"

She bumped him with a hip, her green eyes twinkling playfully. "I could've had a drink at home."

Once they were in the car he told her about the deal he'd struck with Dodd.

"Okay, big boy. I admit I was wrong. I didn't think you'd be able to pull it off without somebody, namely you, getting hurt. Congratulations. You did a good job."

"Well, it's not over yet, but I do think I'm going in the right direction." He shook his head. "Damned if I ever thought I'd work with a cop."

There was a parking spot open directly in front of the room and he swung into it. Inside he put the chain in place and turned around to see Tina standing in the center of the room, turning in a circle to look it over.

When she saw him looking at her she slowly unbuttoned her blouse and slipped it off her shoulders. The cold from the air conditioner made her nipples stiffen. She had on a denim skirt that zipped up the front that she unzipped and allowed to fall to the floor. There was nothing else to take off.

Glenn sat down on the bed, taking her in, as she walked over to stand in front of him, her breasts level with his face. He leaned forward and sucked a nipple into his mouth. He ran a fingernail lightly down her belly, watching her face, and felt her shiver. When he slipped his hand between her legs she moaned and pulled his head back to her breasts.

"I love you."

"No, you don't," he said, his voice muffled. "You're just in lust."

She shoved him back on the bed and got on top of him. "Yes, I do. And you know it, you bastard. You just deny it so you won't have to say it back to me. If you keep it up, one day I'll stop saying it to you."

He looked up at her and realized what she said was true. If she trusted him enough to reveal her feelings, he owed her no less.

"Yes, I'm falling in love with you."

"Then why do you have such a problem saying it?"

He eased her off and they lay side by side, their faces inches from each other. She stroked his hair, waiting for him to speak.

"For one thing, I'm quite a bit older than you."

"I won't accept that. When we're together I never think about our age difference. You shouldn't either. All I know is you fill a part of my life that's always been empty. That's enough for me."

"There's another problem. What about your habit of just taking off? I don't want to wake up one day and find you gone."

"I was just looking for you, Glenn. Now I don't have any need to go anywhere. Any other reasons?"

"I guess not, other than not being sure I can handle you."

"You've been doing a good job so far." She straddled his chest, turning playful again, rubbing her moistness along his chest. "I've got something here you can handle as much as you want."

They made love twice, stretching out the second time, sharing their feelings along with their bodies. Afterward they talked in low voices, and Glenn fell asleep listening to her soft deep voice, contented with just the sound of it.

SHE GOT up with the sun, and though she tried to be quiet, Glenn woke up. He stirred and opened one eye to see her putting on a pair of jeans.

"What're you doing up so early?"

She wiggled her hips to ease pulling the jeans over them. "I woke up wanting some fresh doughnuts and coffee. Doesn't that sound good?"

"Not this early."

She came over and kissed him on the forehead. "Then go back to sleep until I get back. The smell of them will change your mind."

Through half-closed eyes he watched as she brushed her hair. She switched the brush from hand to hand, making short quick strokes. While she put on eye shadow he dozed off, unaware of when she left the room.

Tina unlocked the car and got in, turning the key to the accessory position, letting the wipers clear the dew from the windshield. Next she fumbled beside the seat until she located the button that moved it forward. Rather than strain the battery she decided to wait until the engine was running to engage it. She turned the key to the right.

The explosion roared out, destroying the early morning quietness.

The window of the motel room shattered, imploding inward, the shards ripping the drapes. The shock wave tore the pictures from the wall, flung the chairs over backward, toppled the television to the floor.

The force of it slammed into Glenn and sent him flying across the bed into the wall. He realized what had happened even while still in motion. Wedged between the bed and the wall, he lay there stunned, trying to force his limbs into action. He opened and closed his mouth rapidly to stop the terrible ringing in his ears.

A moment later his head cleared enough to stand, and he managed to stagger to the door. There was no need to open it. It lay on the floor, tiny bits of glass embedded in it. What he saw outside made his knees buckle. He had to grab the door frame to keep from falling.

A thick cloud of oily black smoke drifted lazily up over the Thunderbird, which was completely demolished. Both doors were blown off, along with the hood and trunk deck. The roof was ripped from its support posts and folded back like it was made of tinfoil.

He turned his head to the right, and saw one of Tina's arms on top of a car forty feet away. A part of his mind registered it was her left one.

A few moments later the piercing wail of a siren penetrated the ringing in his ears and he saw the first patrol car rounding the corner of the motel. A deputy got out, his mouth open in disbelief at the sight in front of him. Two more cars pulled up and Glenn watched the deputies get out and begin to question the bystanders. When one of them pointed at him he turned and went back in the room. He was putting on a pair of slacks, as if in a trance, when one of the cops came in.

Glenn watched his lips moving. "Speak louder."

The deputy came closer. *"I SAID, DOES THAT CAR BE-LONG TO YOU?"*

Glenn nodded, turned a chair upright and sat down to put on his socks.

"WHAT HAPPENED?"

"You don't need to yell."

The man lowered his voice a little. "What happened?"

No answer.

The deputy flushed. "Who was in the car?"

"Dodd?"

"What? I'm asking the questions, mister. Start answering 'em. Who was in that car?"

"Fuck you. Call Dodd."

The cop undid the safety strap, lifted his pistol strap and pulled his pistol clear of the holster. Dodd now spoke from the doorway.

"Let him alone, Bob. I'll handle it."

The deputy looked relieved at the sight of Dodd. "Sheriff, he—"

"It's okay, you go on outside and talk to the people out there."

Dodd's hair was uncombed, and sleep still clung to the corners of his eyes.

"Who was it, Glenn?"

Glenn tried to speak but his throat closed up. He sat down and rubbed his face with both hands. The acrid stench of dynamite filled his nostrils, so thick he could taste it. He lit a cigarette with shaking hands to take the taste away. It didn't help.

"Was it your ex-wife?"

"Tina. Tina Newman. A girl I lived with . . ." He looked at Dodd. "She brought the tapes to me. She didn't have one thing to do with any of this."

"I'm sorry, Glenn."

"That doesn't help her."

"Where are the tapes?"

Glenn looked out the window, seeing the ambulance pull up. His eyes looked at Tina's small suitcase still standing upright against the wall. The tapes were in it but he wasn't ready to tell Dodd.

"There aren't any tapes. Not anymore. They were in the car."

"Then come to my office with me and make a statement."

"That I think Sherill did it?"

"If you'll cooperate I can build a case against the son of a bitch. I can't do it without your help."

Glenn turned his head slowly and looked at Dodd, blue eyes blank. "I said I'd help you yesterday and it got an innocent girl killed. I can't help you anymore.

He got up and began to pack.

"What do you think you're doing?"

"I'm leaving."

Dodd grabbed him by the shoulder. "You're just going to walk away and let Sherill get away with killing your girl-friend? What are you saying, that you didn't care anything about her, you just lived with her?"

Glenn shook free. "I'm not going to give you a statement."

"I don't want you trying to go after him on your own."

"You'll do it for me?"

"Yes, goddamn it, I will. I haven't changed my mind since yesterday. It's my job."

"And so far you've done a fine one."

"Listen to me. When I broke with Sherill I told him I would come for him if there were any more killings: That was before I even knew about the tapes. Now I'll keep my word. But the same goes for you."

Glenn finished packing. He closed the lid, walked over and picked up the other suitcase.

"Where you going?"

"I told you, I'm going home."

At the door he stopped, watching the ambulance attendants walk around the parking area. Both of them carried body bags. He turned back to Dodd.

"What funeral home will they send her to?"

"Thompson's Mortuary."

"Then you do this for me. Pick out a nice coffin for her. I'll make arrangements . . . to have her sent home."

Dodd called to him as he walked away. "Stay at home, Glenn."

Mama sue walked to the door of Tina's bedroom and stood there, scratching at it. She looked back at Glenn, who sat on the couch staring at the wall. She scratched again, keeping it up until he looked at her.

"She's gone, Mama Sue. She can't come back."

Mama Sue came over and stood between his legs, nuzzling his hand. When she got no response she crawled up in his lap and whined. The sound broke through, a sob erupted from deep inside him. Tears came next, down his cheeks, hot from the anger inside him. Mama Sue licked them away as they fell.

CHAPTER TWENTY-NINE

THE RAIN was moving from the east, alternating between a soft drizzle and hard, driving sheets. Dodd pulled the plastic slicker tighter around himself.

A jagged streak of lightning lit up the sky and he used its illumination to look at his watch. Eleven o'clock. Another hour before the tavern would close. Even then he couldn't go home, but at least he would be able to sit in the jeep. He looked back at it longingly, but the trees were too thick to get it any closer.

Six days had passed since the car bombing, and he had hidden on this ridge behind Sherill's house each night. It gave him a direct view of the tavern four hundred feet away. All of his instincts told him something would happen and that it would be at the tavern.

Sherill obviously thought the same thing. His black Lincoln was in the same spot as the other five nights, backed in, sitting right in front of the door. Their routine was the same every night. Thirty minutes after closing the two would come scurrying out, get in the car and shoot across the road up to the house.

Dodd knew he wasn't the only one hiding in these woods some of those nights. Glenn had been here too; he could feel him out there.

Ten minutes after midnight a van pulled in at the tavern, driving without lights. Dodd watched through a pair of binoculars but the rain made it impossible to see who it was that got out. There was no need for identification, he knew who it was. He got up and hurried to the jeep, wishing he could drive down the side of the hill instead of back-tracking down the logging trail.

It was Glenn, dressed in a black leather coat and black jeans. He wanted to be as hard to see as possible. In his right hand was a twelve-gauge pump with a pistol grip in place of a stock. It was only twenty-six inches long end to end, made for close work.

He walked to the door and took a second to peer inside. The lights in the bar itself were out but light flooded from the open door going into the kitchen. He stepped back and kicked the door, hard as he could. The wood around the lock splintered some but failed to give. As he drew his foot back for another kick he saw Roy suddenly appear in the kitchen door, his bulk blocking out most of the light. He could see Roy's arm coming up and quickly stepped to the side.

A shot sounded, blowing out most of the glass in the door. Glenn hugged the side of the building and waited for the next one. It came before the echo of the first one had died away. He watched as a spider web magically appeared in the rear window of the Lincoln.

Twenty years seemed to melt away, bringing back all the instincts he'd used in Nam. Without thinking about it he found himself timing the shots like he had done in the tunnels. He had even armed himself with the same kind of weapon he'd used back then.

Two more shots quickly followed, taking out the last of the glass in the door. When a moment passed without a fifth one, he stepped to the other side of the door. He fired as he passed the center of it, working the slide to chamber another round.

Once again he pressed himself against the building but there was no return fire. At the count of four he stepped back in front of the door, fired again, seeing it was unnecessary even as he pulled the trigger.

Chunks of flesh clung to the side of the refrigerator, a large smear of blood trailed down it. He could see one of Roy's legs sticking out from the end of the bar, motionless. His second shot tore into the side of the refrigerator, at least one pellet hitting the door. The impact flung it open, a jar of mustard shattering on the floor.

Now there was no need to kick open the door. Roy's shots had made an opening for him. He moved through it, sweeping the shotgun from side to side. He hurried across the room and saw the rest of Roy, lying with his head propped against the refrigerator.

The .00 buckshot had done its job. Eleven pellets per shell, each the size of a .32, and it appeared that most of them had hit Roy in his chest and belly. He was still alive but Glenn could see he would only last a few more seconds.

Roy held both hands pressed tight against his belly, his pistol a foot away. All he seemed to care about was the blood flowing across his fingers. His eyes were already losing the life that gave them color.

"You've killed me . . . ," he said in a dull whisper.

Glenn stepped over him and kicked the pistol away. He looked at the dying man, and the image of Tina's arm on top of the car went through his mind.

"Yeah. I did. And before it's too late I'd like to thank you for the privilege."

He stepped into the kitchen, the shotgun moving in a steady arc. Taking two shells from his pocket he replaced the two he'd fired. Money, the day's receipts, lay scattered across the table. A chair lay overturned a few feet away. The back door stood open, but the one to the bedroom was closed. He walked up to it and shot through it, letting the pellets open it for him. No one was in the room.

He stepped through the back door onto the porch and saw the chop shop for the first time. A light was on above the double doors, showing one standing partly open, and Glenn figured he'd find Sherill there. He started for it at a jog and was halfway there when the roar of an engine made him stop.

Suddenly the doors were knocked back as a Camaro came rushing out, the rear wheels spinning in the gravel, spewing rocks. It was headed straight at Glenn.

He raised the shotgun but waited a second, bathed in the headlights, wanting Sherill to see him as long as possible. When it was forty feet away he fired, but his aim was low. The right headlight blinked out.

No time for another shot. He tried to jump to the side but the fender brushed against his leg and sent him tumbling. He rolled over in the mud, making sure he held the shotgun out of it.

Trying to run Glenn down meant getting out of the gravel, and Sherill had lost control of the car. It crashed into a pine tree, hard enough to raise both front wheels off the ground. He jumped out and started running up the side of the hill. Behind him the Camaro's engine roared a moment longer, then died.

Glenn worked the slide and fired while lying on his stomach. The buckshot hit Sherill in the legs, knocked them out from under him. He tried to stand, couldn't. He began to crawl, still trying to make it up the hill.

Glenn got to his feet and started after him, chambering another round as he went.

The storm had increased and lightning now flashed almost continuously. It showed Sherill looking over his shoulder, Glenn less than ten feet behind him.

"I'm still here, old man. Helluva way to meet, ain't it."

Sherill rolled over on his back and pulled out his pistol.

Glenn saw the move, ran forward in a crouch. Sherill fired. Glenn heard the bullet go past his head buzzing like a hornet. Another step put him close enough to kick the pistol out of Sherill's hand. He jammed the shotgun's muzzle beneath Sherill's chin.

"You won't get another chance, bastard."

Sherill clawed the muddy ground with his fingers, scooting backward. Glenn moved with him, keeping the shotgun against his chin.

"Don't kill me, please . . . I'll give you anything—"

"Anything? How about that girl you killed?"

"I'm sorry, I didn't mean to kill her, you know that—"

"She's still just as dead."

"I'll make it up to you, I've got money, all you've got to do is tell me what you want—"

"I didn't come for money. I came for your life."

"Odom . . ."

The voice was faint, coming from in front of the tavern. Hope flared in Sherill's eyes. A few moments later the voice came again, from inside this time. Sherill started to grin.

DODD STEPPED inside the tavern, moving his pistol with the same sweeping motion Glenn had used. They'd been taught by the same teachers. He stepped over Roy, needing no more than a glance to realize he was dead. He looked at the kitchen, taking in the damage done to the refrigerator and the bedroom door.

Once more he called out Odom's name. A shotgun blast from somewhere outside was his answer. Dodd flinched and his stomach lurched. He knew what it meant.

He stood there a second, then forced himself to walk out the back door. The Camaro was the first thing he saw, its remaining headlight angled toward the sky, raindrops sparkling as they fell through the shaft of light. The only sound was raindrops falling on the car. He walked toward it, turning in a complete circle twice on the way, his pistol held at the ready.

Where the hell was Odom? Dodd inched forward. He was five feet from the Camaro when Glenn stood up. The shotgun he held was pointed across the hood, leveled at Dodd's chest. His hair was plastered to his skull and water glistened in his beard.

Dodd looked first at the shotgun, then at Glenn.

"Hello, Dodd. I figured you'd be close by."

"Where's Sherill?"

Glenn jerked a thumb toward the hill behind him.

"Why, goddamn it? Why'd you do it? I told you I'd take care of both of 'em."

The shotgun wavered slightly. "Your way of taking care of them would be to put them in jail. Not good enough."

The two men stood in the driving rain, guns pointed at each other. Dodd broke the silence.

"Drop the gun, Glenn. I'm going to have to take you in."

"Okay. You made the effort. Now holster your weapon."

"I mean it. I can't just let you walk away from two murders."

"The hell you can't. You said you wanted to put 'em out of business. I've done it for you."

Dodd shook his head. "I warned you to stay at home."

"And you knew I wouldn't when you told me. Holster your weapon."

"No. We'll just have to shoot each other."

"That's not a very good idea on your part, Dodd. You're holding a maybe. I've got a definite here, and you know it. Do you really want to die for the likes of those two ass-holes? I won't tell you again."

It had been many years, but he had seen the look Glenn wore often enough never to forget it. It was the killing fever that came during a firefight, when death was a simple muscle action against the trigger. Right now that fever was running high in Glenn Odom. Dodd put his pistol away.

"So leave. But it won't stop anything. There'll be a warrant out on you within the hour."

Glenn shook his head and motioned with the shotgun. "No, there won't. Walk. Stay in front of me and go around the side of the building. I've got something to give you."

When they got to the van he opened the door, reached inside and pulled out a paper sack. He tossed it to Dodd.

"There's your tapes, the reason you're not going to put a warrant out on me."

Dodd stuck the sack inside his slicker. "What good are they now? Both of them are dead."

"Merritt's still alive. And now you own him just like Sherill did. That means you've got the same power he had. You said you wanted to straighten things up. With him dead you've damn sure got the power to do it. Let's see if that's what you do, or if you end up being just like him."

"Now that I've got the tapes what makes you think I won't go ahead and issue a warrant for you?"

Glenn climbed in the van and started the engine. He rolled the window down.

"Because I made a copy of one of those tapes. It wasn't the one of Merritt either. Believe it."

CHAPTER
THIRTY

GLENN WALKED up the sidewalk to Darleen's house as if he still lived there. Nothing stirred along the street; it was midmorning and most of the neighbors were at work.

He inserted a tension bar in the lock of the front door and then the pick, tripping two tumblers. But he was tired, having driven straight from Belton, stopping at home only long enough for his set of picks, which caused him to allow the tension bar to slip, releasing the tumblers. He cursed and started over.

This time it wasn't easy at all. The first tumbler took a good three minutes. Sweat dripped from his nose before the last one fell. It had been over five years and he was out of practice.

It was hot inside the house, the air stuffy and musty. He turned the thermostat to sixty-five and heard the muted hum of the air conditioner kick on. He went back to the living room and sat down, trying to get a feel for the house again.

Five minutes later no ideas had come so he got up and started with the pictures, looking for a safe behind them. Next he walked from room to room, kicking the baseboards every few feet. They were all solid.

In the master bedroom clothes hangers were scattered

on the bed and on the floor between it and the closet. Clothes tossed aside carelessly showed the haste with which Darleen had packed.

It took two hours to give both the house and the garage a good going over. Nothing. All he found was two cabinets with false backs, one of them no surprise. He'd built it himself eight years ago.

He walked down the hall for the fifth or sixth time and stopped at the bathroom. No, she wouldn't use that. Darleen had more sense than to use a stash someone else knew about.

Just to cover all the bases he tapped the bottom half of the door, then tapped it again. The thumps didn't sound as hollow as they should. He took the door down and pulled the strip of wood from the bottom of it.

Sweet Jesus. It was packed with money, all hundreds, to the tune of sixty thousand dollars. A lot of it had Belton Commerce wrappers around it. It answered whether or not she would hold out on a fellow.

In the kitchen he found a paper sack and put the money in it. Still holding it, he leaned against the wall and slid down it until he was sitting on the floor. He lit a cigarette, exhaustion pulling the skin on his face tight. He smoked it down to the filter and got up, flipping the butt in the commode.

Back in the living room he spent a couple of minutes staring at a photograph of Darleen, then turned away and picked up the phone, punching her sister's number.

The sister answered and he was forced to make small talk before asking to talk to Darleen. She started the conversation by asking what was going on.

"It's over."

"By over do you mean I'm not going to have to worry about Sherill anymore?"

"He won't be a problem for you."

"Is he dead?"

"Yeah. Along with his son." Glenn hesitated, afraid his voice would break. "So is Tina."

"I'm sorry, Glenn. I'll leave right now. I can be at your place in three hours."

He noted her lack of curiosity. No wanting to know how, or why. Just worried about the goddamned money.

"Don't do that. I'll meet you tomorrow morning in the parking lot of the Forest Hills Shopping Center. It's right beside I-75 off the Woodlawn exit."

"Why tomorrow? And why not at your house? I'd rather divide it up today, Glenn."

"Because I'm not at home and I'm tired. It'll hold 'til tomorrow. I'll be there at ten."

She started to protest and he hung up, cutting her off in midsentence. He slipped off his loafers and stretched out on the couch, bunching a pillow beneath his head. Five minutes later he had escaped into sleep.

At ten the next morning he turned the van into the shopping center. Darleen was easy to spot, parked at the far end of the lot, away from any other cars. He swung in beside her.

"Get in," he called out the window.

She made no move to get out. "Why don't I just follow you?"

"It'll be easier this way. Come on, we're wasting time."

She got out, wearing a pale green silk pants suit with a yellow blouse, and a scowl. Before getting in the van she dusted off the seat, still arguing.

"I don't see why I can't follow you."

A bark came from the back of the van when she got in. She gave a startled jump and looked back at the fiberglass cage.

"Is that one of those pits back there?"

"Relax, it's in a cage."

"Well, why have you got it back there?"

"I've got to take it to the vet when we're through."

"I'm real glad all this is over. My sister's boy has just about drove me crazy."

The next few miles were spent with her complaining about this and that. He waited for her to ask about Tina, how she was killed or why, but it didn't come. He started to say something but bit it back. Better to just divide up the money and be rid of her for good.

She took no notice of where they were until he turned onto the road leading to his house. She looked at him.

"I thought you said you hid the money. We're heading toward where you live."

"Yeah, but we're not going to the house. We'll be there in a minute."

He turned in at the empty house and parked beside it. Before getting out he rolled his window down a few inches.

"Crack yours a little too," he told her. "I want to make sure the dog can get air."

He walked to the back of the van and opened the door. "Hold on a minute, Darleen. The cage door's slid against the wall. Let me move it away so the heat won't be so bad."

He turned the cage around, flipping the latch up. As he shut the door of the van he saw the dog's muzzle pushing open the cage door.

She stopped just inside the house, wrinkling her nose from the smell of animal droppings. Glenn walked over to the chimney, squatted down and reached up for the suitcase. After working it free he stood up and turned around.

Darleen stood in the classic shooter's stance, feet spread slightly apart, holding an automatic with both hands. Holding it steady, too.

He recognized it as the .380 he had bought her not long after they'd met. Not what you'd call a real powerful weapon but it carried more than enough punch to blow his brains out. And his brains were where she had it pointed.

"Put the suitcase down and back away from it."

He hesitated, long enough to search her eyes. What he saw convinced him to put the suitcase down.

"Now pull up your shirt and turn around."

"Come on, girl. You don't want to do this. Hasn't being greedy caused you enough trouble?"

"Just do like I told you."

He pulled his shirt up and began to turn. "I'm not carrying. Thought I was dealing with friendly forces and wouldn't need one."

He completed the circle and faced her again. "You planning on shooting me?"

"Not unless I have to. It all depends on you."

"That's a comfort. Why are you doing this, Darleen?"

"Because I want it all. It was my job. When I saw how much there was it became my fuck-you money. There's enough there to last me the rest of my life if I use it right."

"Is it enough to always be looking over your shoulder? Because that's what you'll be doing, girl, wondering how close I am."

"Don't threaten me, *boy*. The only reason I'm not going to shoot you is because I did love you once."

"Yeah, I can see that. Don't think the past will stop me from coming. Four people are dead behind this money, one of them totally innocent. If you stop it right here we'll go ahead and split it up."

"Another four could've died and I wouldn't care. And I'm not worried about you looking for me. It's a big world, too big for you to find me. Put the keys to the van on the suitcase."

He did as he was told. "Last chance, Darleen. Use good sense and put the gun away."

"Don't push your luck or I will shoot you. Back up."

He took a couple of steps back, keeping an eye on the pistol. She used it to motion him farther back.

"All the way to the corner."

The pistol never left him while she walked over and picked up the suitcase. "If you come out before I'm gone, I'll kill you, Glenn."

"You're making a mistake, one you'll never be able to fix if you go out that door."

She smiled. "You never learned when to quit, did you? Give it up. The game's over and you lost. At least I'm leaving you alive. That'll let you find a score of your own."

At the door she stopped long enough to say, "I mean it, Glenn. Don't come out until after I'm gone."

She hurried to the van, looking over her shoulder to make sure he wasn't behind her. She put the suitcase down, opened the door, and saw Mama Sue for the first time.

The dog was already in the air, lunging for Darleen's throat, as she would have done to anyone who dared open the door of the van without Glenn being present. Mama Sue's lips were curled back, mouth open, teeth gleaming whitely.

Darleen stumbled backward; she tried to bring the pistol up but there wasn't time. Her legs tripped over the suitcase just as Mama Sue hit her full in the chest and the combination sent her to the ground. The pistol flew from her hand, becoming lost in the high weeds.

Instinctively, she ducked her head against the dog's attack as she was falling. She heard Mama Sue's teeth snap shut on her ear and screamed, a wailing, high-pitched sound of fear mixed with pain.

Mama Sue jerked her head back, tearing off half of Darleen's ear. She slung her head to discard the chunk of flesh and came back for another try. Darleen managed to shove her off and get to her knees. Mama Sue was back before she could make it all the way up, knocking her down again.

At the sound of her scream Glenn ran out the door,

amazed such a sound could come from a human throat. He jumped off the porch and ran around the side of the van.

What he saw was Darleen on her back, the weeds flattened in a circle around her. She had her hands on each side of Mama Sue's head, trying to keep those teeth from her face. Even as he moved he knew it was a futile effort on her part. He was still a step away when Mama Sue ripped part of Darleen's cheek off.

Before she could bite again he was there, snatching her collar. For a moment he wasn't sure he would be able to hold the dog back. It took all the strength he had to wrestle the dog to the back of the van and into the cage. Mama Sue fought him all the way, intent on defending what she felt was an invasion of Glenn's property.

When he came back around to the front of the van Darleen was lying curled up on her side, moaning and holding both hands against the side of her face. Stepping across her he searched through the weeds until he found the pistol. He stuck it in his waistband, then picked up the suitcase and put it in the van. Then he knelt beside her to see how badly she was hurt.

He helped her into a sitting position and pulled her hands away from her face. Blood gushed from the two bites, soaking into her blouse and suit coat. The bite on her cheek bled the most. The skin flopped down loosely, a gash almost three inches long, exposing her molars. Surgery could fix that. Replacing the ear was going to be her real problem.

She looked at him, the terror still in her eyes, along with shock. Her words came out garbled because of all the blood flowing into her mouth.

"How . . . bad is it?"

He lifted the piece of flesh up and held it in place while he dug his handkerchief from a back pocket. After folding it twice he pressed it against the wound, then put her hand over it to hold it in place.

"You'll live. Even save some money on earrings from now on. Get in the van and I'll drop you off at a hospital."

She reached out with her free hand, silently asking him to help her up. Glenn looked down at her, then got in the van.

"You can make it on your own. There's nothing wrong with your legs. You weren't asking for any help when we were in the house."

The bleeding slowed to a trickle before they were halfway to town. Once she realized she wasn't mortally wounded, Darleen reacted in anger.

"You son of a bitch. You knew what that damned dog would do."

He kept his eyes on the road, said nothing. A few minutes later they were in sight of the hospital. He turned in at the emergency entrance and stopped in front of the double doors leading inside. He left the engine running, a sure sign he had no intention of going in with her.

She came at him from another angle, her tone sugary and contrite. "I'm sorry, Glenn, I really am. . . . The thought of all that money just went to my head. . . ."

She leaned over and put her hand on the inside of his thigh. "I know you're mad, you have every right. But it could be you and me again, like it used to be. I remember how we used to be, you haven't forgotten. . . ."

He turned his head and looked at her. "You really think we could have it the way it used to be?"

She seized on that. "Yes. Yes, we could, I'd make you love me like you used to. It can happen if you'll just forgive me. . . ."

He stared out the windshield. He had to admit they'd had some pretty good times. Besides, it was such a pretty sunny day, not a cloud in the sky. Too nice a day to hold grudges.

"Sure, girl, I forgive you. But your little stunt back there not only killed any chances of us getting back together, it also cost you your end. Believe it."

She stared at him, refusing to believe he could be serious. Before she had a chance to object he leaned across her and opened the door on her side.

"Hey, count yourself lucky, Darleen. I could've stayed in the house and let Mama Sue kill your sorry ass. After all, you told me twice not to come out until after you were gone."

AN ATTACHÉ case lay on the counter of the deeds-and-titles section of the courthouse. Ronnie Davis flipped the catches, then opened it, using the lid to keep the woman working behind the counter from seeing inside it. The layer of money that covered the bottom wasn't all that thick, but then it didn't take too many hundreds to make a nice sum.

He whistled softly as he closed it. "I really wasn't that interested in selling the place, but your offer was just too good to turn down."

He pulled out a pen and began to fill out a bill of sale, then stopped and looked at Glenn. "Too late now, but you could've got it cheaper."

Glenn shrugged. "I figured I could, just didn't want to waste time haggling. This way we're both happy. Put Frank's name down as being a co-owner."

Ronnie went back to filling out the bill of sale. "That's one way of looking at it, but damned if I wouldn't have tried to save a little."

"Frank'll probably get some of it back when he gets out. I'm going over to Dalton later today to buy a couple of dogs he said he wanted. You know he'll be wanting to match 'em against yours."

"Who you buying from?"

"Tommy Douglas. You know him?"

"Yeah, I know 'im. Good dog man. Just watch out for his

wife. If Sharon takes a shine to you she'll lock on you tighter'n any dog they got."

Glenn thought back to the night of his first and only dog-fight. The memory brought a smile.

"Yeah? Well, I just might see how hard the lady bites."